Sherlock Holmes
and the case of the
Hissing Shaft

Rex Harpham

First published in 2020 by
The Irregular Special Press
for Baker Street Studios Ltd
Endeavour House
170 Woodland Road, Sawston
Cambridge, CB22 3DX, UK

This is a work of fiction. Names, characters, businesses, places,
events and incidents are either the products of the author's
imagination or used in a fictitious manner. Any resemblance to
actual persons, living or dead, or actual events is purely coincidental.

ISBN: 1-901091-75-9 (10 digit)
ISBN: 978-1-901091-75-5 (13 digit)

Cover Concept: Antony J. Richards

Typeset in 8/11/20pt Palatino

Preface

It is to my enduring good fortune that the papers had ever come into my possession at all. It has long been a puzzle to me that Dr. Watson had written of only sixty cases involving the work of his friend, Mr. Sherlock Holmes. Over a career which is known to have lasted for at least twenty three years, (and I believe that it must have been for much longer than that), it indicates that he worked on less than three criminal cases each year. It is a surprisingly low number for one so talented. It may also be recalled that during some cases, such as the *Five Orange Pips*, the good doctor does talk of many other crimes upon which Mr. Holmes worked. He states that 1887 was a particularly busy year but although Watson spoke of retaining the records and went on to talk of giving us more details 'all these I may sketch out at a future date', regretfully he gave us no further information.

Allowing for this and the fact that there were also, albeit rare, occasions when Holmes had a dearth of work, there are clearly still large numbers of missing cases laying somewhere, undiscovered. These must number in the hundreds at least. It is impossible to believe that Watson did not write about them. It was not in his nature. He was known to keep very detailed records, so what happened to them? Where did they go?

It is a strange facet of life that without any seeming justification, the most unexpected events occur. Sometimes this leads to great opportunities and life changing directions. So it has been with me.

After my uncle died, my aunt confided that he had left, stored away in boxes, some important papers. When she had recovered from his death, she intended to search through them, locate those of value and dispose of the remainder. She never did this, which in view of events was probably just as well and several years later she herself died suddenly. It then became the duty of my brother and myself, as executors, to clear out the contents of her house and take all the necessary legal steps to dispose of the estate according to the requirements of her will.

No mention had subsequently been made to us concerning these papers, nor were they allocated in her will except by the general statement 'to take any items of interest for ourselves'. The boxes were therefore duly removed for us to inspect at our leisure. My brother had no interest in them so he gave them to me, to keep or destroy as I saw fit.

It was not until some time later that I was finally able to search through them. There were seven large rather battered boxes in all, heavily coated in dust. On opening, they revealed a vast wad of documents covered in faded and barely legible handwriting. Assuming these to be a detailed diary of some kind, which clearly covered a great deal of time, I set myself the task of deciphering these obscure scripts. I had felt it possible that the contents would reveal details which may be of interest to a museum or the local history society.

The papers were obviously old and on the bottom edges, frayed, as if eaten by insects. With care, however, and much help from a strong magnifying glass, I was able to bring them to life. What they revealed to my growing excitement was indeed a diary. It was though, not a diary, as one would expect, but stories of events from over one hundred years ago and penned by the hand of Dr. John H. Watson, M.D. concerning the detective work of Mr. Sherlock Holmes.

It can probably be guessed at the joy I experienced at this new discovery, and I took much time and trouble to ensure that is was indeed the hand of Dr. Watson concerning the famous sleuth, known to the world over for his outstanding abilities. I was also, of course, quite naturally intrigued as to how these most valuable manuscripts had come into the possession of my late uncle in the first place.

Thinking back on conversations I had enjoyed with them years earlier, I have recollections that in his early boyhood, his father had been killed in the Great War. After some time his mother had given up the unequal struggle to keep her home and had been forced to move in with relatives.

Many household effects were put into store and only retrieved after she herself had died. There was also talk of a distinguished family friend whom my uncle met on occasions. I never knew who he was but it appears that at some point he had left behind some 'very important papers' with the family for safekeeping. They had never been collected and it now seems certain that these papers were the very same as those left by my aunt and now in my possession.

The first story, for to date only one has been satisfactorily recovered, is set mostly in Scotland. Its origins however lie with events of long ago and in a far-away land. Watson has called it *The Case of the Hissing Shaft*. The full date is unfortunately missing. Its first two numbers though, look to be a one and an eight but the last two digits are indecipherable. The top of the third digit however was curved indicating that it was probably an eight or a nine. This would suggest a date of between 1880 and 1899. However, Holmes and Watson are known to have moved into 221b Baker Street in 1881, in order to share the cost of rooms and this first chapter shows clearly that they were there when this story began. Holmes was twenty-seven and already gaining a reputation for being so talented. Similarly, Holmes 'died' at the Reichenbach Falls in 1891 and did not return until 1894 in *The Adventure of the Empty House*. The likely date for this story therefore probably lies between 1881 and 1891, or 1894 and 1899. Beyond that I cannot go. You readers must decide.

Come with me now and leave behind the twenty-first century. Let the years recede to a time of gas lamps and hansom cabs, of running footsteps echoing through the grey swirling London mists and the cry of Holmes calling, "Come Watson, quickly! The game's afoot!"

Rex Harpham
Tavistock.

Chapter One

An Unexpected Telegram

"Ah, Watson, there you are at last. Tell me what you can make of this."

I had slept in late that morning and when I finally arrived in the study, saw that Holmes had already breakfasted. He was leaning over a small table, examining a large map closely. Barely glancing up as I came in and with just a brief gesture, he pointed to a telegram lying in the chair. I yawned, went over and picked it up. It read:

MR HOLMES STOP PLEASE DO NOT COME STOP VISIT UNNECESSARY STOP DAUGHTER WORRIES TOO MUCH STOP NO DANGER TO ME STOP SIR HUGH MCFARLANE STOP LAIRD OF INVERDAIGH HOUSE STOP

I sat down at the breakfast table, and rang the bell for Mrs. Hudson. Looking again at the telegram I re-read it through.

"Intriguing, Holmes. What does it mean?"

"That's what I intend to find out, old fellow," said Holmes, "But I had not realised that you were working on a case in Scotland, for a Sir Hugh McFarlane, or indeed his family. At least, Holmes, you never spoke of it to me."

"No you're right Watson, I'm not. Clearly, though, when this telegram was sent he thought that I was. It would seem his daughter had instigated our involvement before he knew of it."

Mrs. Hudson entered with my breakfast.

"It's a lovely day," she said, to neither of us in particular as she fussed over his dirty crockery. "I see that you found the telegram, Dr. Watson. It came late for Mr. Holmes last night when you were both out, so I left it for you when I laid out the breakfast table."

I recalled that the previous evening I had been out attending a patient. I called in briefly to my surgery before returning to Baker Street. Holmes had not returned by then either and I knew that he was working on an important case. I had lain half awake for some while before eventually falling asleep but some time in the early hours I had heard him return. He seemed quite unaffected by having only a few hours rest, indeed, I felt it likely that he hadn't slept at all having spent the remainder of the night mulling over his case.

"Thank you Mrs. Hudson," said Holmes, "it was most thoughtful of you. I found it when I came in this morning."

"It is a relief to see that you may have more work soon Mr. Holmes. A telegram is usually a good sign. Don't you think so Dr. Watson?"

I grunted an acknowledgement as she left the room to a clattering of plates and teacups.

"Well, Watson", said Holmes, "I am glad to see that your patient is now recovering."

"Yes of course", I replied, then stopped. "How do you know my patient is recovering?"

He looked across and smiled. "There's no secret," he said, "Just simple observation and deductions made from it. Last night I was out following a suspect in the Addison fraud case. By chance he took me down past your surgery. You nearly bumped into me as you came out."

I thought back. It had been late with few people about but all I could recall was nearly colliding with a coarse looking fellow, whom I took to be a labourer seeming the worse for drink. I remembered stepping out into the road to avoid him and nearly walked in front of a carriage. He grabbed at me pulling me back saying, "Be careful young sir, you must look where you are going now."

"Your breakfast is getting cold, Watson." I had stopped eating whilst remembering the previous night's events.

"Yes that was me," he chuckled, as if reading my mind, "The man you took for a poor drunk."

Holmes smiled again, his eyes glinting mischievously as he sat down in his armchair and awaited my reponse.

I looked up. "That surely could not have been you Holmes?" I said, incredulously. "If so, I confess I had no idea that it was, no idea at all, although I did think afterwards that he had very swift reactions." I started to feel irritated with myself that I had been so easily fooled, although I knew that it was a disguise he had used before. He was so good at it.

Holmes's smile broadened. "Of course not, my dear fellow. Why should you? After all you had not expected me to be there and your mind clearly was on other things." I could see that his successful disguise had pleased him greatly.

"Yes, Holmes, it was. But how do you know that my patient is recovering?" I asked again.

"Quite straight forward, Watson. You had already told me that you had to see a patient. Had your medical care not succeeded it is likely that you would have been at the hospital by then rather than your surgery. As you came out you had the air of a successful man, one who is pleased with himself. You weren't looking where you were going. That is why you nearly bumped into me when I pulled you away from the road. You murmured a cheerful thanks and walked on. Not the mark of a doctor who had just left a dying patient. You also slept in late this morning. Had you been concerned you would have been up at first light to visit. Not only that, but your bag and medical instruments were put away properly rather than just left on the table outside. Were you anticipating needing them again soon they would have been there ready for this morning. Finally, you walked home rather than taking a hansom. You will recall that it rained for a while after you left your surgery. There were no splash marks on your clothes when we met but there are now and on your shoes. You have not had time to clean them, also your coat is still damp. I have seen before that when your medical work has proved fruitful you will often walk back, even if it rains. It is as if you did not really notice. The walk seems to be the result of the energies you gain from your medical success!" Holmes looked across with an air of satisfied contentment. Here was a master lecturing to his students pleased to find that his lesson had gone well.

"Yes, you are quite right in all you say, Holmes, of course." I was still feeling irritated not to have recognised Holmes, and by his quick and accurate deductions arrived at from my behaviour.

"It goes to show," Holmes went on, just how little people notice when they expect not to. It is one of the differences between the trained, disciplined mind and that of an ordinary man." He leaned back looking at the ceiling, his hands linked behind his head.

"But I am a doctor," I replied, "It is also my job to notice things, otherwise how can I help my patients? How is it that I did not recognise you?"

"The reason," replied Holmes, still looking up at the ceiling, "Is that you are looking for different things and in a different way."

"Such as?" I said.

He sat up. "As a doctor, when you are called to visit a patient, you wish to cure them of their ailments. Concern for their wellbeing is the thought uppermost in your mind. When you meet them, you know that they are ill and your mind is already bent to their concerns. You will listen to them telling you of their symptoms and examine them before making a diagnosis, then offer the necessary treatment. If things go well and the patient can be cured you come away pleased that you have been instrumental in the patient's recovery, such as last night. If, on the other hand, your prognosis is poor, you must leave them, feeling a sense of failure. Your mood is likely to be depressed as if you had let your patient down. For me it is different. I realised long ago that as a consulting detective it was essential to be able to notice clues that to others were either not important, or indeed they had simply failed to observe them at all. In order to do this I have to approach a case with an open mind. I had to learn to be totally objective. I have to step back from the thought of failure or success, which would cloud my judgement and my mind would be closed to recognising other possibilities. I had to be alert, not only for clues at the crime scene itself but look wider and understand the importance of other elements which people such as Lestrade would deem trivial. Finally, I have to be able to recognise that which is relevant and that which is not. I have to formulate ideas based on the available facts and dismiss them if they prove to be wrong. What is left, however unlikely, must be the truth." He continued, clearly warming to his subject. "*The Case of the Serrated Tooth* is an example. The marks on the hull of the boat were clear to see, but Lestrade failed to notice them. His eyes may have seen them, but his mind did not."

"The problem is, of course, that whilst many people know this they do not really believe it. There is a big difference. It is as if they cannot trust their own logical deductions. Either they are afraid of them or else they do not like to. If they were ruthlessly logical perhaps they are fearful that it would make them cold and unfeeling. It need not be so of course, as I also consider it necessary to be able to cast out of one's mind any issue not directly relevant to the case. It is the precision of thought which makes the difference."

"I believe all of what you say, Holmes, but I also consider that most of these mental faculties are something with which one is born, an exceptional gift as it were." I could see that he warmed to my compliments.

"Why thank you, Doctor, but my brother Mycroft possesses these gifts to a greater degree than I."

"Perhaps," I replied, "but from what you have said he lacks the energy and purpose to apply it to solving crime. To him it is merely a game in which he is indifferent to any result, whilst to you solving the crime is the essential end result."

"Yes, I think that you may be right there. Possibly he and I should discuss it again," he mused.

"Quite so, Holmes, but what do you make of your telegram?" I said, trying now to change the subject. "It is the first time I recall you being asked not to investigate before actually being asked in the first place."

"Yes, interesting," said Holmes, "although it really does not tell us much beyond the obvious."

"Which is?" I queried, knowing that to Holmes the obvious was far from obvious to other people.

"That the Laird Sir Hugh McFarlane is likely to be a widower. That both he and his daughter have a close, loving relationship and she has a strong personality with her own mind; that she is probably an only child and hence heir to the estate. Finally, it is clear that we shall soon have a visit, probably from a senior family servant."

"Are you not jumping to conclusions prematurely? All the telegram says is for you not to come because the daughter is unduly concerned."

"Perhaps," said Holmes, "but like the scratches on the hull in the *Serrated Tooth*, we can draw some more information from it if we try."

"I would like to know Holmes exactly how you do so from such a brief message." I said, inviting yet more analysis.

"Very well, old friend; on the first point, if Sir Hugh McFarlane had a wife it is likely to be she who contacted us. If his wife was unconcerned, I doubt if the daughter alone would feel strongly enough to take action over her mother's head. Two women together being concerned would have forced a different response from him, requesting help instead of denying it, unless of course, he is mad which I am sure he is not.

"The second is clear, that if they did not have a good father and daughter relationship the daughter would have been less concerned about any danger she believes he is in. Indeed, it may be to her advantage not to. It also clearly shows that she is strong enough to take it upon herself to seek our help. When he found out, as he clearly has, he in turn sent us a telegram countering his daughter's request. It therefore suggests to me that he is a proud man with a stubborn streak in his nature.

"Thirdly, if she were not an only child, she would have discussed it with her siblings. If they had disagreed, no request is likely to have been made; if she had siblings the word daughter would have been replaced by daughters or children.

"Lastly, by sending a servant who would be reliable and hence have more seniority, she can be assured of our having more details upon which to act. It may have looked too suspicious if she had come herself. A large, Scottish town or city such as Glasgow would more likely be her normal place to visit. She may have needed a special reason to come to London. At short notice that may not have been possible."

That morning I had received a second lesson from the master.

"Yes, I see, Holmes. It fits in well with the telegram. So when do you expect this trusted senior servant to arrive?"

"Before you got up for breakfast, I examined *Bradshaws* to check the trains from Scotland to London. I think it likely that he arrived yesterday. It is probable that he would plan to stay for several nights in a small hotel. It would give him time to purchase some items for the family to help justify the visit. I am still sure that when their servant left for London, Sir Hugh McFarlane did not know of the real reason and that the telegram was not simply because he had changed his mind. The servant is probably staying in one of the hotels not too far away. He will go about his business this morning and come to see us this afternoon, I think."

He paused momentarily in thought, then said, "Yes, that seems about right to me, Doctor." As if confirming to himself his own deductions as well as to me.

"If you say so, Holmes. It's as good a time as any. But," I countered, "If we know, from the telegram, that we are not now required perhaps their servant is also aware and will not turn up."

"No, I don't agree. As the daughter wanted the real reason for his visit to London to be kept secret, at least until he had spoken to me, Sir Hugh McFarlane probably does not yet know where he is staying. As the laird now knows, however, that he is to come here, this is the obvious address to contact. It would then not matter whether we had already seen him or not. No, old friend, he will be here later today."

"It doesn't really matter, I suppose. I would like to know the reasons behind it though." I stood up and moved across to look at the map which Holmes had been examining earlier.

"But why are you bothering with this map, Holmes? We shall not be needing it. You have been asked not to get involved by Sir Hugh McFarlane."

Holmes came over. "Shall we say that it is just curiosity for the moment, Doctor. However, I am sure you will agree that it already shows some most interesting features." He had filled his pipe from the tobacco pouch in his slipper and lit it as he again peered intently at the map.

"This is where they must live," he said pointing with the stem of his pipe at part of the Scottish Highlands. "Just around this area, I believe. Yes, here it is, see Watson. What do you think?" said Holmes, indicating with his long fingers.

I peered down. The morning sun was now illuminating the room such that the details of the map could easily be seen. The part Holmes had pointed out clearly showed an area of the Highlands towards their more southern edge. The map showed a number of lochs and one in particular stood out because of its size. It was a very long and wide piece of water, which I estimated to be some miles in length and filled with many islands. The top arm of the loch reached up like a long, wide finger protruding into a region clearly depicted as being mountainous. The map showed that the whole area was rugged, with its peaks some of the most significant in the whole country. When not shrouded in mists they would doubtless offer the most wonderful views to anyone bold enough to make the climb. I could see from the close and twisted contours, the many precipitous cliffs and steep valleys down which I could imagine rushing streams must be flowing, hurling headlong into the loch.

The land around was also shown to have extensive wooded and forested areas. Some small roads or tracks and several villages clung to its shores, often situated near the foot of a glen. Crossing the loch a steamboat ferry service was shown linking the isolated habitations. Along the western side was shown a more substantial road, linking with towns further north.

"Wild and beautiful," I mused. "I assume that this is where they live?" I pointed to a spot marked as Inverdaigh House. The scale did not enable any more detail to be depicted but it was clearly an important place. No other building in that area had been given such prominence. "It looks very grand for that part of the country, Holmes. Do we know anything else about it?"

Holmes walked across to the bookshelf and removed *Who's Who*.

"Let's seek their guidance and find what they have to tell us. I am sure that the family will be listed."

He opened to the relevant page and passed it over to me. It read;

Sir Hugh McFarlane, Laird of Inverdaigh House, Scotland, youngest son, owner of large estate, Highlands, Interests – deer shooting, fishing, ornithology, geography, history and literature.

"A man of some wide ranging interests, eh? And some influence in the area too."

"Quite substantial by the look of it." Holmes returned the book to the shelf. "It gives us some background knowledge of the place which shaped our guest."

"Yes, and very different from London, Holmes. I would have thought that crime there was almost unknown."

Homes looked up. "Not so, Watson, not so. I am certain you will find that crime is as prevalent there as anywhere

15

else." He paused once more as if in deep thought, then said, "We shall have to see. Meanwhile, there's little more we can do for now, until our expected visitor arrives. We have all the information we can gather for the moment."

"I have to visit my surgery for a while so I shall lunch out. Do you wish to interview your guest alone, Holmes?"

"No, Watson, as usual I would value your presence. But do not concern yourself if you are late. I will give you all the relevant details, have no fear. Meanwhile, I have some work to do of my own."

Chapter Two

Our Visitor Arrives

I arrived back at Baker Street in the mid-afternoon to find that our expected visitor had not yet arrived. Holmes was sitting down smoking his favourite pipe; the room was full of tobacco smoke.

"I see that you have been working in your laboratory Holmes, even your pipe will not disguise the smell."

"Yes", he replied, "I am trying to find a way of identifying curare poison. I suspect that it, or something similar may have been used to murder a man found in the river yesterday. Gregson thinks that it was an accidental death but I am not convinced. The muscles were still too flaccid when he was found even though *rigor mortis* should have set in by then."

"Were there any other clues?" I enquired.

"When I was asked by Gregson to have a look at the body I made my usual thorough examination. On the sole of the foot I found by his toes a small, but significant mark which was, I believe, the site of poison insertion. Gregson wasn't there at the time but I left him a message about it. I also suggested that he compare the time a vessel from South America docked earlier, the state and run of the tide and where the body was found. With all those clues, one of Scotland Yard's best men should start to become suspicious," he said, sardonically.

I opened the window. The sound of London's busy streets came through and people were clearly taking advantage of the fine, early autumn afternoon.

"I had expected our visitor by now, Holmes," I said, without turning around. "Perhaps he has been recalled after all."

"Possibly", he replied, "We shall see. There is still time yet and there is tomorrow. However, if he does not arrive by this time tomorrow I am sure that he will not call and we shall never hear of the reasons behind our most unusual telegram."

He walked over and joined me by the window, looking down the street. "Ah!" He exclaimed, "I wonder, yes, I think that our expected visitor has just arrived, Doctor."

A hansom had just pulled up outside and a man wearing a tartan bonnet climbed out. Paying the driver he walked up to the door and rang the bell.

"An ex-military man by his bearing, but we shall soon see."

Downstairs we heard the landlady answer the doorbell and shortly after it was followed by a knock at our door. Mrs. Hudson entered.

"A visitor to see you gentlemen, a Mr. Duncan Cameron." She stood aside and into the room swept a tall, middle aged, sinewy man with sharp blue eyes, hooked nose and a strong but lined face, as one who has seen much of life's hardships. He had the air about him of an alert, confident but concerned man. He quickly glanced around the room, setting his eyes briefly on the large map Holmes had earlier laid out. Holmes smiled, strode across the room and introduced himself.

"Mr. Cameron, my name is Sherlock Holmes," he said shaking hands. He turned to me. May I also introduce my friend and colleague, Dr. John Watson, whose presence I greatly value on such occasions. Please sit yourself down, we have been expecting you," he said, ushering him to a chair, "Please tell us how we may help Miss McFarlane?"

Our visitor looked up for a moment, visibly surprised to find that not only was he expected but that we also knew his visit involved his employer's daughter. He sat down, looking distinctly uneasy. Holmes eased himself into a chair opposite and spoke.

"Please do not worry yourself, Mr. Cameron. I know how you must be feeling."

"Mr. Holmes," said our visitor, "I have heard of your exceptional skills ..."

Holmes raised his hand before he could go further.

"I assure you that you have no need to be concerned about us knowing that you would be coming and on whose behalf. I merely felt that in view of events it would be discourteous of me not to inform you as soon as you arrived. I had thought it possible that you may have been contacted by the lady herself since you have been in London, but clearly you have not. May I offer you a dram of whisky Mr. Cameron? I have a bottle of the finest single malt. It may help you to feel better from your shock and bring some Scottish cheer into your visit to London."

"Why, thank you," said Cameron "a wee dram of whisky will do very nicely." His voice was losing its edge of concern.

Holmes went across to the cupboard and poured a glass.

"I think that will help," he said, passing him the drink. Cameron sipped his whisky and visibly relaxed.

"Perhaps", he said, turning to us both, "You would kindly tell me of all you know. You clearly have the better of me in this matter. When I know of your position then I can give you the details of my story and why I was sent here."

"Of course," Holmes replied, "a most satisfactory way of proceeding". Holmes looked across to me. I nodded my agreement acknowledging his unspoken question.

"Yes, I think so, too. The sooner we all know the better. Although, from our position we have not a great deal to tell, eh, Holmes?"

"Dr. Watson is right. The truth is very simple Mr. Cameron and I assure you it is little to do with any skills which I may be fortunate enough to possess. Late last night a telegram arrived here. It was from Sir Hugh McFarlane, your employer, I believe?" Duncan Cameron nodded his agreement and took another sip of whisky.

"In essence", he went on, "it simply asked us not to come to Inverdaigh House and that he was in no danger. Perhaps, Watson you would kindly …"

Anticipating Holmes request I reached over and passed the telegram to our visitor. Cameron looked at it carefully.

"This puts me in a rather awkward position, gentlemen. I had been under strict instructions from Miss McFarlane that I was the only one to know the real reason for my visit to London. She wanted me to tell you of her concerns as she felt unable to come herself. It is her fear that something unpleasant is happening and that her father's life is at risk."

"He clearly disagrees, of course."

"He does indeed. I should not talk critically of my employer, Mr. Holmes, for he is a fine man. It is no secret, however, that he can also be very stubborn at times."

Holmes glanced across at me again and I remembered our conversation in the morning, on that very subject.

"Please do go on, Mr. Cameron," said Holmes, "give as much detail as possible. Only then can I make any judgement on the issue. Anything which you say to me or Dr. Watson will naturally be in the strictest of confidence."

Holmes sat back in his chair, his hands together, with his finger tips touching. His eyes were partly closed and somewhat languid looking to anyone who did not know him well. I knew, however, that he was keenly watching our guest as he spoke.

Cameron nodded his acknowledgement, took another sip of whisky and began.

"I am employed by the Laird Sir Hugh McFarlane who is the current owner of a large estate in the Highlands. It covers an area of mountain and glen which surrounds part of a very large loch. They live in an imposing house, he and Miss Caroline; I have known her since she was a wee girl, you see. They keep a number of staff and I am employed as his gillie. You may have heard the term, perhaps?" He looked quizzically at us both as if to ensure that we knew of it.

"I believe that it is something like that of a gamekeeper here in England," responded Holmes.

"Exactly, that is my understanding," answered our guest. "The Laird has given me, as part of my job, the responsibility for looking after his estate, the deer, wildlife and such like. Being very large it involves much walking or riding in the hills. I am sure you will realise."

"Indeed," said Holmes, "winter in particular must be a hard time for everyone."

"Yes, it is, but for those of us who have led most of our lives in the hills or have endured hardships, we inherit from our ancestors the love of the mountains and accept the difficulties as part of that."

"Hardships in military service as well I expect," said Holmes again, testing for Cameron's response.

"Oh, yes, Mr. Holmes, plenty of that as well, but it stood me in good stead in some of my India campaigns." Cameron looked up, "But how do you know about my military service Mr. Holmes?"

"Simple Mr. Cameron," Holmes replied, "your military bearing and general manner suggested it to me and you have just confirmed it. I note too that your bonnet is likely to be that of a Highland regiment. I know that several saw service in India including the Great Mutiny in '57. My good friend, Dr. Watson, saw service in India, is that not so?"

Cameron turned to me as if recognising an old comrade.

"It is," I replied, "as an army surgeon."

"Where did you go in your service Dr. Watson may I ask?"

"I finished up in the North West, took a jezail bullet in the shoulder and had to be invalided out."

Cameron nodded as if remembering his own experiences.

I continued, "The rugged terrain had, I feel, some resemblance of your own part of the country Mr. Cameron don't you think, rather hotter though, eh!"

He nodded again. "Indeed, it does Dr. Watson, indeed it does."

"Please go on now and tell us more of the reason for your visit Mr. Cameron," said Holmes, "and please continue to give us all the details."

He took another drink before continuing.

"The problems seemed to begin some time ago. I am sure that you can see from the map," he looked across and pointed to the one Holmes had laid out on our table, "that Inverdaigh House sits in a fairly remote area." He paused momentarily with a far away look in his eyes as if remembering his home. "From time-to-time the Laird and myself go out, usually on horseback, to have a look around the estate, particularly the more remote parts. On the day in question we had started early and were out riding to check on the deer in the hills. Naturally, we know the area very well, the best routes to ride, walk or climb, and those areas which are dangerous and best avoided. I am sure that you will realise that mountainous country such as the Highlands also have sudden steep drops over cliffs or boggy areas and such like."

Holmes and I nodded our understanding. I allowed my mind to drift back to the times when I too had traversed similar terrain in a far off land. Cameron continued, his voice bringing me back to Baker Street.

"We were taking a track around the side of a mountain that leads to a very steep gorge. The horses know it well. Down this gorge plunges a most dramatic waterfall. It is known in Gaelic as *Eas Na-Onghail* but locally as The Hissing Shaft because that is just what the waterfall is like. The sound of the water echoing around the sheer rock sides makes that noise, you see, like a white shaft plunging downwards with all the spray as well. It is a magnificent sight. It is no place to fall into, however, being steep, slippery and very dangerous. If you ever fell into it and survived, without help I doubt if you could climb out. There is talk that in the distant past people were thrown in, so it also has an air of menace. We don't do that now though, even to those from south of the border." He chuckled at his joke with us, pausing briefly for another sip of whisky. "Once in a while we check around there. Sometimes animals do fall in even though they're sure-footed. It is also a good spot for a picnic when the weather is clement. From there you can see miles with a good view across the loch to the far hills. That day, for I can remember it well, began clear, but as so often happens the mists had started to form over the mountains and threatened to close in over us. We gave it no thought however; we were clothed well and knew the area. We were passing around the very steepest section when without any warning the horses shied and a large rock crashed down landing on the track between the Laird and myself. The animals seemed to have sensed the danger and had moved just in time, otherwise one of us, most likely the Laird himself, would have been hit and killed. As it was he had been thrown from his horse and slid down the sheer drop alongside and lay some yards below against a narrow ledge. I could see that he was badly winded and bruised. I quickly dismounted to assist him and in so doing looked up quickly to make sure that no other rocks were coming down. As I did so I thought that I saw a movement, high up from where the rock must have fallen, as if someone or something was moving around."

"Could it have been an animal like a sheep or deer?" interjected Holmes.

"Well it could. It was impossible to tell, you see, as the mist was closing in."

"What happened next?"

"I went to help the Laird, of course," answered Cameron seeming slightly irritated that this would not be his obvious normal reaction to someone in trouble. "I managed to climb down with some difficulty and reach him. The fall from his horse had also stunned him so it was some time before I could help him back up on to the path again and remount his horse."

"Did anything else happen during that time?"

"No, nothing at all. When he was on his horse again we turned around and made our way back. It took us some while, as we had to stop frequently to let him rest a moment before carrying on again."

"And when you arrived at Inverdaigh House?" Holmes raised his eyebrows to finish his question.

"Miss Caroline was there. When she saw what had happened she was terribly upset. She had the servants help him to his room and one was sent for the local doctor.

Fortunately he had no serious injuries although the doctor suspected a couple of cracked ribs as well as much bruising."

"You told Miss Caroline what happened of course?" I interrupted. "It sounds suspicious to me. Don't you think so Holmes?" I said, turning to him.

"Well, perhaps it does, Watson, but we shall first have to consider several possibilities. Please go on, Mr. Cameron. What did she say when you told her?"

"She was very shocked and surprised. That area is well known to her as well as those of us who live around there. The rocks are solid and not prone to falling like that."

"But not unknown, surely?" said Holmes. "A simple accidental event seems to suggest itself." I felt that he was starting to probe Cameron for more details.

"There are parts, Mr. Holmes, where rocks do fall from time to time but we know where these are and avoid them if possible."

"Nevertheless it could happen," persisted Holmes, "perhaps dislodged by a deer or other animal?"

"Aye, it could, it's not impossible," concurred our guest.

"Let me refill your glass, Mr. Cameron. All this talking must be making you dry."

"Thank you. That is most appreciated," said Cameron.

"Now tell me," said Holmes on returning to his seat, "did Miss Caroline say or do anything else?"

"There was not a lot more she could do really, but she did ask me to go back as soon as I could to check out more carefully what had happened. She did not want anything like it to happen to anyone else."

"And did you?"

"Not immediately. The mists had come down by then and if I had gone back I doubt if I could have found out much in that weather."

"But did you go back eventually?"

"Yes, but I could not get there for nearly a week."

"Ah, a pity," responded Holmes, "but when you did return did you find anything?"

"Not really. The rock which had fallen and nearly hit us was nowhere to be seen. I believe that it must have plummeted on down."

"But I had gained the impression from you that the rock, having missed hitting you both, had landed on the track you were on."

"Yes," replied our guest slowly, "coming to think back over it I believe you are right Mr. Holmes. I believe that is what did happen. When I could find nothing I naturally assumed that is where it went. But if it did not, where can it be now?"

"Maybe an animal dislodged it, Holmes?" I suggested.

"Perhaps we shall never know after all this time," said Holmes. "Did you tell Miss McFarlane of your suspicions?"

"No, I did not. I did not want to worry her unnecessarily and I could not really be sure of what I actually saw up above us."

"Very reasonable, but she clearly seems unconvinced of it being accidental. Was there any other reason for this, Mr. Cameron, some other event perhaps? I am sure that Miss McFarlane did not send you all the way down to London for that incident alone."

"No she did not. You are correct. The young lassie has other reasons as well. Had the rock fall been all that had happened no more would have been said and I am sure the incident would have been forgotten."

"What were the other concerns?"

I could see that Holmes was listening intently as he prompted him for more information.

"Some time later, Mr. Holmes, a second incident occurred after Sir Hugh had recovered from the effects of his fall. One afternoon he decided to take a walk along a footpath through some woodlands. It was a glorious fine day without a breath of wind and he said that he felt in need of some exercise."

"And where were these woods exactly?" interrupted Holmes.

"About a mile away from the house, through woodlands which go around the loch. It's a well known pathway and local people often enjoy walking there. It is really on part of the estate but time and custom have allowed it to be used by others, too."

"I see," said Holmes, "please do go on", for our guest was now clearly relaxed and well into his subject.

"Some days before this second event occurred we had some very high winds. Quite a number of trees had been blown over, many in a wooded valley through which the footpath ran. Branches had been ripped off some of those still standing. As a result this pathway, which is normally kept clear by the foresters, was blocked in places so that people had either to climb over fallen trees or to crawl under them. Apparently, as he told me afterwards, when he was scrambling over a fallen tree there was a loud crack and a branch from a nearby tree fell upon him. By great good fortune the heavy part of the branch missed him and he was only hit by smaller pieces. After extricating himself he struggled back to the house. I was there when he arrived, covered in cuts, twigs and rather shaken. I sent for Miss Caroline who was not there at the time. After seeing that he was not badly hurt, he refused a doctor on this occasion. I recalled the falling rock incident so I then went straightway back to the place where he said the accident had happened. Sure enough the heavy branch had fallen on the tree trunk laying over the path. As there was no wind at the time I was puzzled as to why it had fallen now."

"Could it not have just snapped off and been left perched in the tree?" I suggested, "so that anyone moving around under it would have just been enough to send it crashing to the ground?"

"I considered that, Dr. Watson, and so because of more possible danger I moved slowly and looked very carefully as to where I was treading. If I had not done so I might have missed it."

"Missed what?" asked Holmes.

"I saw that the branch had indeed snapped but not cleanly, nor, I think, accidently."

"How so?" asked Holmes quickly with an edge to his voice. "Was the wood not split at all?"

"Yes, Mr. Holmes, but the piece holding it to the main trunk had been cut through where it had split in the high winds. It was just a clean cut on the remaining piece. The branch seemed to have been resting up in the tree, then cut through by someone and left hanging there."

"Well done indeed, Mr. Cameron," said Holmes, "but could not the local foresters have been at work starting to clear the path?"

"I did enquire," replied Cameron, "but they had not started work there by then."

"How high up was this branch?" I asked.

"It must have been about twenty-five feet, Dr. Watson. Whoever had cut it must have made a special effort to climb up and saw through it. The remaining piece, which was holding it in place, must have been finely balanced."

"But even if it was done deliberately just how did they get it to fall at the moment the Laird was walking underneath it?"

"Because it looked as if someone had tied some rope to it, Dr. Watson, so that it could be dislodged quite easily."

"How do you know?" asked Holmes quickly, his previous languid expression now vanished.

"As I was looking around the tree I saw it. It had recently been cut and had fallen to the ground. Some bark was still attached to it."

"Are you sure?"

"When I first saw it Mr. Holmes I did not know why it was there. It seemed strange to find such a thing just lying there. As I stood looking at it, I suddenly realised that it could have been used to pull the branch down. Normally I would have not even seen or considered it, but under the circumstances I was becoming very suspicious."

"That was very sharp eyed of you," said Holmes.

"Well," Cameron replied, "in my military service it became necessary to look out carefully for danger. I was good at it, and well, I have never lost the habit."

"Excellent!" said Holmes. "Mr. Cameron, I congratulate you. There seems to be little doubt about it this time. We'll make a detective of you yet!"

"Thank you," replied Cameron, clearly swelling with pride at the compliments of the great detective.

"What did you do next?"

"I returned to the house."

"Why did you not look around further to see if you could find the place from where it was pulled? It must have been quite close by," said Holmes, reprovingly.

Our guest looked abashed. "I am afraid I did not," he said, rather embarrassed. "I went back to the house to see if Miss Caroline had arrived. She had and when I saw her I told of what I had found. I'm sorry, Mr. Holmes, but my concern for them was uppermost in my mind at the time."

"No matter," he replied, "you did well nevertheless."

Cameron regained his composure.

"And what did Miss Caroline say?" asked Holmes.

"She went very quiet, almost as if she was expecting something to happen."

"I see. Thank you," replied Holmes, "but tell me Mr. Cameron, one thing I have not asked you is just how frequently did the Laird make that walk through the woods?"

"Well, not very often. He had recovered from the rock fall incident but naturally he had the running of the estate to attend to and that kept him busy."

"I understand that he was an amateur ornithologist," I interrupted.

"Aye, Dr. Watson, but his special interest was in golden eagles you see. You probably know that they nest high up in the mountain crags mostly."

"So there are no golden eagle nests in the woodland itself?"

"None to my knowledge. I believe that they have been known to nest high up in a taller tree but he never mentioned there being one in the woodlands to me."

"Is there anyone who would have known that he was going through the woodland at that time?" asked Holmes again.

"None to my knowledge."

"Then perhaps it was just coincidence, after all, just another unfortunate accident?" queried Holmes.

I looked across at Holmes, who had now seemingly raised doubts. "Looking at it like that I suppose so but I find it hard to believe and so does his daughter. I have to say Mr. Holmes that around that time a change did come over her as if she had some concern on her mind."

"You have no idea as to what it could be?"

"I have not, although I believe some of the servants have heard them discussing matters and having some disagreement."

"Was that unusual?"

"Very, in fact, it was almost unknown. As she is his only child, you see, he dotes on her, especially as her mother died many years ago."

Holmes remained in thought for a few moments whilst our guest finished the remainder of his drink.

"Were these the only two incidents, Mr. Cameron?" he said at last. "I can understand the lady's concern but, apart from the piece of rope and cut branch, on that alone a jury would never convict. Both can be attributed to genuine accidents or natural events. There would seem to be no certain proof of any malign intention. Why would anyone wish to harm him? Is he known to have any enemies?"

"Mr. Holmes," protested our guest, "as I said before, the Laird is known throughout the area to be a fine upstanding man. I'll no' have it said otherwise. I am sure that he has no enemies at all."

"But even fine upstanding people have a past Mr. Cameron and sometimes pasts which they would rather no-one knew about, even their families ..." He paused momentarily. Then said, looking directly at Cameron, "or loyal servants perhaps?"

I could sense that Holmes was goading him for his reaction.

Duncan Cameron looked across. I saw that he was beginning to feel angry, as he had quickly realised the intended slur.

"If this is the best you can do, Mr. Holmes, I can see that I have come to the wrong place. I'll no' have him or me insulted. If you'll excuse me I'll be on my way. Perhaps Scotland Yard would better serve us after all."

Cameron started to rise as if to leave.

"Mr. Cameron, please calm yourself," said Holmes whilst extending his hand to Cameron's shoulder, "I can see that you are indeed a good and loyal man who diligently carries out the instructions given to him by his employers. But please try to understand that it is essential for me to examine every aspect of this case, which you have put before me, as objectively as I can. I need to be sure that I know as much as possible about all the people concerned, including of course, your good self. I need to be clear where people's real loyalties lie and whether or not they are misplaced. There are, of course, the other servants as well." He paused briefly to let the idea sink in before continuing. "For me not to do so would be a disservice to your employer and his daughter. I am sure that if you think about it you will realise the truth of what I say even if it is sometimes painful. Of course, if you are not happy with this consultation you are naturally free to leave and seek the services of Scotland Yard. I think you will find that Lestrade or Gregson are likely to be the best that they can offer," he said disparagingly. As he said this he waved his hand as if dismissing an inferior.

Cameron paused, half-standing, then slowly sat down again and settled himself into his seat. He sat quietly, thinking for a moment, then said, "I apologise for my outburst, Mr. Holmes. I can understand your purpose when I think about it. Miss Caroline said that you have an unsurpassed reputation and now I can believe it."

I sensed Holmes relax and enjoy the accolade our guest had just given him. He smiled broadly and said, "That is most kind of you Mr. Cameron. All of my talents are naturally at the disposal of your employer's family."

Cameron acknowledged Holmes's comments with a nod of acceptance and spoke, "What then do you intend to do now, Mr. Holmes? I have given you all the facts as far as I know them. I have no knowledge of any other incidents as things are at the moment. Miss Caroline herself may be aware of other things but if so she has not told me. For that you will have to ask her yourself."

I could sense the frustration in Cameron's voice as he spoke.

"I think, Mr. Cameron, that we are all in a difficult position as matters stand. I share your frustration and feeling of helplessness at the position in which you find yourself. Like Miss Caroline and yourself I believe that there is every reason to be concerned for Sir Hugh McFarlane's welfare but until I am asked to investigate further there is little more I can do. What do you think, Doctor?" said Holmes, turning to me.

"I agree, Holmes, the telegram certainly stops us investigating the matter any further for the moment. You have been very frank and told us all you know in great detail, Mr. Cameron."

"What will you have me do now?"

"My advice for the moment," said Holmes, "is to return home as soon as it is convenient for you to do so. Once there you can discuss the matter with your employer and his daughter. Please say to them that I believe his life may be in danger and that further investigation is warranted. Before I can do anything further, however, I need him to realise this for himself and to request me to come and investigate."

Cameron paused.

"Gentlemen, I understand your position. When I first came to see you and before I knew of the telegram I had fully expected you to make haste and return with me to Scotland, but I can see now that it is not possible. What Miss Caroline will make of it though I really do not know."

"She is a strong minded woman," replied Holmes. I feel sure that before long we will soon be hearing more from her or her father."

"Thank you, Mr. Holmes, Dr. Watson, for your time. I'll bid you good afternoon." He shook hands with us both and turned to leave.

"Just one other thing, does anyone else know of your visit to London to see us?" asked Holmes.

"I don't believe so, but these things have a habit of becoming known more quickly than one would think. Why do you ask?" replied Cameron.

"Oh, it is probably not important, but please tell Sir Hugh to be careful and for that matter I would do so yourself. If the criminal knows that you have been to see me he may well regard you as a threat to his plans and act accordingly."

After Cameron had gone, Holmes stood for a while in deep thought.

"I am sure something is happening in Scotland, Watson and that Sir Hugh McFarlane also knows more than he is saying. It would not shock me to hear from them again. I think it likely that some other incident will occur soon and that we shall be summoned."

"What of the piece of rope attached to the tree, Holmes?"

"Yes, that is the factor that makes a suspicious accident into a possible attempted murder.

I can only hope we will hear in time for us to avert a tragedy," he replied.

"You really have no doubts?"

"No, I have not, but I am sure that there is more to come. We have no choice in the matter, for now at least. We must just wait, trying though it is! In the meantime there is a Brahms violin concerto playing at Wigmore Hall this evening – I feel like some light entertainment. I have two tickets, Doctor. Shall we go?"

Chapter Three

Scotland

After Cameron left us we heard nothing more from him or Inverdaigh House, for some while. Holmes in the meantime was busy with other cases. The body found in the Thames led to the arrest of two sailors for murder, and it was Gregson whose name appeared in the papers as the detective who solved the crime. Holmes had been right all along. He had correctly deduced that the man had been incapacitated by means of curare poison then drowned after being thrown into the river.

One afternoon, several weeks later, I was sitting in the study making notes on some of Holmes's more recent cases, when there was a knock at our door.

"A telegram for Mr. Holmes, Dr. Watson," said Mrs. Hudson. It was another communication from Inverdaigh House but this time from the daughter, Caroline McFarlane. It read, 'MR. HOLMES STOP PLEASE COME AS SOON AS POSSIBLE STOP BOAT ACCIDENT OCCURRED STOP'.

I stood looking at the telegram in my hand, with the growing realisation that there was surely no accident this time, even if there had been any doubt about the others. I recalled Holmes's parting words for them both to be careful. Little did I realise how prophetic that warning would be. I re-read the telegram. It provided no other details save that there had been a boat accident, and that this time they wanted Holmes to help them. My mind raced as I wondered how and where this accident had occurred.

"Will there be a reply, Dr. Watson?"

Mrs. Hudson's question interrupted my thoughts and returned me to Baker Street.

"Er, yes Mrs. Hudson, there will. Please say that Holmes and I will be coming immediately. I know that Mr. Holmes is not here yet but he should be soon and I am quite sure that he will agree."

When she had left the room I sat down and tried to gather my thoughts. After Cameron had returned home from his visit to us Holmes had mentioned the case on only a few occasions and then not at length. I knew, though, that he was mulling over possibilities as one day he was sitting in the chair by the window smoking his pipe, he quizzed me on my knowledge of Scottish clan history. I had to admit that I knew very little save that of the Jacobite rebellion and the subsequent 'clearances'. I knew, however, of the long standing bitterness it had caused. I had resolved to read up on the matter in case it proved to be relevant for what seemed to be a developing case. As yet, however, I had not got around to doing so.

Before long I went into my room to pack my things. I had just finished when Holmes returned.

Mrs. Hudson had already told him of the urgent telegram and his face answered my unspoken question.

"Well, old fellow, it looks as if the criminal has struck again."

"I suppose you are sure, Holmes that this is not an accident. We have no other details yet."

"Yes, Watson, whoever the criminal is, he goes to much length to make it look as though whatever happens was just that. Until we have more knowledge upon which to base deductions, we can do no more. At least it is clear that Sir Hugh McFarlane has changed his mind. Something serious must have happened to make him do that. If we hurry we might just be in time to catch the night train."

The journey north to Scotland proved uneventful but on the way I had managed to obtain a copy of a book giving a little of the troubled history of that beautiful country, although I have to confess fell asleep whilst reading it.

Early the following morning saw us in Scotland and well before midday we found ourselves on a small steamboat travelling along the large loch we saw displayed on our map.

The weather was fine but a Northerly breeze had put a chill in the air, reminding me that Autumn comes earlier in these parts. Out on the loch, white caps were forming as the wind pushed up waves which would hit our bow, sending spray high up over the boat. Shivering a little, I moved over by the vessel's engine, enjoying its warmth and finding the steady pulsating rhythm to be strangely comforting. In the cabin I saw Holmes close the windows and went in to join him.

"Bracing, Watson, is it not?"

"It is Holmes, very different from London."

From the steamboat we could look out across the Loch at the shoreline on either side. At the water's edge the land rose up steeply into mountains with massive rocky outcrops thrusting upwards as if asserting their grandeur. Thin wisps of white, cotton like trails showed where the water was plunging from the heights, falling headlong downwards into the loch. Movement on the mountains, just discernable as tiny dots, showed through my glass to be herds of deer making their way across to seek out luscious pastures. The sun threw dark shadows into relief within the glens, cleft deep between the heights. I recalled my thoughts of this place whilst looking out of the map in Baker Street several weeks previously.

"I think our arrival is anticipated," said Holmes, pointing to a small carriage waiting by a wooden jetty to which the steamboat was now fast approaching.

As we landed the driver came over to us, "Mr. Holmes and Dr. Watson, I believe. I am the Laird's coachman. My name is MacGavern. I have been sent by Sir Hugh and his daughter to collect you when you arrived. They have been hoping that you would arrive today."

He took our luggage and placed it in the coach as we climbed on board before setting off along the road. The route took us by the shore, then gradually wound its way through woods until it came to a private carriageway. Very soon we came in sight of a large and splendid residence.

"Inverdaigh House," said our coachman confirming our thoughts. As we drove over the gravel, the building revealed itself to be of mock Gothic style with wings on each side of a large entrance. Standing in this entrance was a slim, beautiful, dark haired young woman of medium height and with an air of poised calm and self-possession. As we alighted she stepped forward and introduced herself, smiling as she held out her hand.

"Mr. Holmes and Dr. Watson, my name is Caroline McFarlane. Welcome to Inverdaigh House. I am so delighted that you may be able to help and am indebted for you coming so promptly."

She spoke in a firm but gentle voice and in a way which made it clear that she carried authority.

"Why thank you, Miss McFarlane," replied Holmes. Dr. Watson and I had been looking forward to meeting you after receiving your urgent telegram. I am sorry that you have been troubled so much recently, but we came at once."

She smiled again and turning, ushered us through the entrance and into a long, imposing corridor.

Hanging on the walls were magnificent oil paintings, mostly landscapes but also imposing figures in traditional costume. Claymores, broadswords, targes and armour were displayed on stands, creating an atmosphere of violent and turbulent history. At the far end a large stairway led up to the next floor. Alongside, fitted into a glass case was a large, golden eagle and all around were cases exhibiting other birds. I was minded to recall the Laird's listed interest of ornithology.

"I hope that you had a pleasant journey, gentlemen," she said to us both as we walked beside her, "my Father is in here and is looking forward to meeting you."

She opened a solid wooden door and led us though into a large but comfortably furnished room with blazing logs burning in the grate of a stone fireplace.

"Gentlemen, I am Hugh McFarlane. May I welcome you both to my home."

Sir Hugh arose from his chair alongside the fire. He was a man of about fifty years, an inch or two shorter than Holmes and of medium build. I could not help noticing his intense, warm blue eyes set in a face pale as if subject to a recent shock. His manner reflected a gentle nature but I felt also hinted at a Gaelic stubbornness.

"It is a great pleasure meeting you, Mr. Holmes," he said, smiling as they shook hands. "I have heard so much about you."

"That is most kind of you, Sir Hugh," replied Holmes. "You, of course, know of my colleague, Dr. Watson," he said, turning to me.

"Indeed I have," said Sir Hugh as he introduced himself. "I believe that we all have good reason to thank Dr. Watson for taking the trouble to write of your exploits, Mr. Holmes. Without his efforts many of us would be none the wiser as to your great accomplishments."

Hugh McFarlane's compliments were not lost on Holmes and I recalled his analysis from the telegram of the laird being a polite and kindly man.

"Please sit yourselves down, gentlemen and make yourselves comfortable. You have had a long journey; I trust that it was pleasant?"

"Yes, thank you, Sir Hugh, it was. After we received the latest telegram, we naturally came straight away on the night train from London."

"Caroline and I are most grateful to you both for coming without delay" said Sir Hugh. He rang the bell and a servant appeared with refreshments.

"I have had your luggage brought in and taken to your rooms. As we were expecting you I had an early luncheon prepared. You must both be hungry. Perhaps afterwards we can talk at length on the matter."

We ate a fine meal and afterwards Holmes and I returned with our hosts to the comfortable sitting room. The fire had been stoked with more logs and gave out a warmth such that it was hard to imagine anything unpleasant happening to our host. The solid walls of the building made me feel that they could resist any onslaught of evil design. The afternoon light shone in through the lattice windows, which faced out on to the entrance carriageway cut through the trees. From the room the loch could not be seen, only the mountains on the far shore which were beginning to be wrapped in the thin cloud wraiths of departing summer.

"Sir Hugh" said Holmes, breaking the silence, "you have said little of your family history, I would find it most helpful a case such as yours. The antecedents of events may hold a key part in finding a solution to what is happening here."

"I do not believe that there is much to tell Mr. Holmes," replied Sir Hugh. "The family has been settled here for some generations. My parents were well regarded and respectable members of the community, as were my grandparents and their parents before them. I did have an older brother though, he went to India, you see."

"His was a rather wild and adventurous spirit, who found life around here rather too dull, and thought that he would make a mark for himself in one of our colonies. Apparently he became caught up in the great mutiny, he just disappeared and it was obvious that he had been killed. The family had all the usual searches done but all we could find out was that he had gone off with an armed troop to fight their way through to a relieving force of sepoys, they were ambushed and annihilated but his body was never found. I was very young at the time. Later on, after my father died, the estate passed to me."

"Did you have no ambition to travel yourself?"

"No, I did consider it but I got married and Caroline was then born. I felt it was my duty to stay here and run the estate, especially after my wife died some years ago. Since then Caroline has looked after me and I have been content with my own interests."

"Tell us more about your older brother, Sir Hugh," said Holmes, "do you have any knowledge as to what he did in India, before the mutiny. You seem to hint at some difficulties whilst he was here, could you elaborate?" he asked, his eyebrows raised in a questioning manner.

Sir Hugh looked uncomfortable and paused as if considering how best to reply to Holmes's probing questions. Before he could do so, Holmes, seeing his discomfort, spoke again.

"I do not wish to cause you any embarrassment Sir Hugh, as I can see that it is something that is causing you difficulty. As I said earlier, I merely ask as it is possible that it may throw some light on what is happening to you now. After all it may affect Caroline as well," said Holmes, indicating to her with his hand.

Sir Hugh and Caroline looked across at one another and I could see that, despite Holmes's languid expression, he was watching them closely.

For a few moments Sir Hugh and Caroline said nothing, then as if a decision had been made, Sir Hugh spoke.

"Yes, you are quite right, gentlemen, there were some considerable problems concerning my brother. I said just now that he was a wild and adventurous spirit, the truth is that he was always getting into difficulties; got into bad company and we were constantly having to bail him out from some scrape. It was either women, drinking or money. Sometimes he became involved in gambling of one sort or another, and he shot a man once. My father despaired of him. You see he was really a very talented man but seemed unable to use his abilities well. He also had the peculiar way of inspiring others to support him. In short, Mr. Holmes, he formed around himself a group of men who were always in trouble. They seemed to follow him in whatever venture appealed to him at the time. They would do anything for him. His going to India was a relief, and we all thought that the challenge would sober him up. When we heard that he had been killed there was both shock and relief."

"There can be no doubt that he was killed then in India … during the mutiny."

"None at all Mr. Holmes, none at all. We would have heard something had he survived. No, my brother died long ago. What do you say Caroline?" he said turning to his daughter.

"Father is right, Mr. Holmes, I was not born then of course, but naturally I have heard much of events when my uncle was alive. But that was many years ago."

"I am sure that you see how we feel about the matter Mr. Holmes," said Sir Hugh.

Holmes nodded his acquiescence, recognising Sir Hugh's sensitivity on the matter. He said no more and the room went silent for a while, the only sound being the fire crackling in the grate.

Holmes lit his pipe and moved over to the lattice window.

Caroline moved across to stand by him.

"Do you like the view, Mr. Holmes?" she asked.

"Yes, it is splendid," Holmes replied, "I am sure that Dr. Watson will approve of us getting away from London and into the fresh Highland air."

"Indeed, Holmes. It will do us both a great deal of good." I replied. "The lochs and mountains are very inspiring to those of us who live in the city."

"Even so," Holmes continued, "we have to face up to the fact that there is a criminal who is trying to harm you Sir Hugh, we must keep our attention on that."

Holmes paused for a moment in deep thought, then, as if he had come to a decision, turned around and faced our hosts.

"Perhaps you would now tell us of your most recent boating incident, Sir Hugh. I think that the sooner we now know all the details, the better."

"Yes, of course, Mr. Holmes." He turned to his daughter, "I believe that Duncan Cameron should be back by now. As he was also involved I think that we should include him in this conversation."

Miss McFarlane left the room and a few minutes later returned accompanied by the estate's gillie.

"Mr. Holmes and Dr. Watson," he said as he came in, "it is so good to see you here at last."

We all shook hands.

"Duncan here, is, as you already know, our trusted servant and it is thanks to him that I am still alive today and not in the bottom of the loch. Duncan, sit yourself down and have a drink. We are to tell Mr. Holmes of my most recent accident and it may be that he will have some questions to ask you too."

Duncan Cameron poured a glass and sat down.

"That was no accident, Father, you know that," interrupted Caroline McFarlane, looking anxiously across at him. "It is the third time in recent months that something has happened which threatened your life. It cannot be allowed to continue. I believe that whoever wishes to harm you will eventually succeed unless he is caught soon. You have been lucky so far; it will not last forever. What do you think, Mr. Holmes?" I could sense the fear in her voice as she spoke.

"I share your daughter's view, Sir Hugh. But tell me why is it that you delayed and did not call me earlier, say, after the second incident when the tree fell upon you?"

Our host paused as if considering his reply. I sensed that he was feeling slightly embarrassed. He looked up as he replied. "Pride I suppose, Mr. Holmes. Pride and a natural stubbornness. You will probably have realised that I have a certain standing in this part of the Highlands. I feel that it is my duty not to be intimidated."

"Who else knows of these events, Sir Hugh?"

"Probably everyone by now. Here in the hills we are really only a small community, compared to, say, London. It is surprising just how soon news such as this can get around."

"Can you think of why anyone would wish to harm you? What would they have to gain?"

"That is what I would like to know," interrupted Caroline, "he has done nothing and no one would seek to harm him who knew him well."

"Somebody does and for their own reasons. That is what Watson and I intend to find out. Have you no idea at all as to a possible suspect or any reason, no matter how implausible?"

"I can think of nothing Mr. Holmes, nothing at all," replied Sir Hugh.

"Tell me, Sir Hugh," I asked, "you have a large estate here. Do you not suffer from poaching?"

"Duncan," said Sir Hugh looking over to his gillie, "you can perhaps enlighten Dr. Watson on this point."

"Yes, I can. We do have problems from time-to-time and there is a particular family who live on the far side of the loch. They are very poor and I have caught them once or twice. McCall is their name. Brodney McCall is the father and head of the family."

"What is he like?"

"A quiet and rather sullen man, devious, too, in small ways. He has a wife and five bairns to feed though. The family ancestry goes back a long way, back to the clan cattle rustling times, I believe."

"We have indeed caught them for fish poaching," said Sir Hugh, "but the truth is I feel rather sorry for them and I let them off with a warning each time. I suspect that he still tries his hand once in a while, when food is short and I'll no' blame him for that as long as he doesn't catch too many."

"Most generous of you, Sir Hugh," said Holmes, "Do I take it that you feel he is not the kind of man to do this sort of thing?"

"I find it hard to believe, Mr. Holmes. I just cannot see him trying to harm anyone."

This is the first time I had heard Sir Hugh admit to the full implication of the attacks he had sustained. Miss McFarlane sighed, as if both relieved that her Father had, at last, fully acknowledged the seriousness of the threat to his life, but was dismayed that it existed at all.

"Very well," said Holmes, "but you have to realise that it is surprising what people will do if they have motive enough."

Holmes went silent for a moment and I knew that he was thinking of this latest revelation and how it would fit into the information he already had.

"Please now tell me about yesterday," said Holmes, "Leave out no detail, however insignificant it may appear to be."

"Well, yesterday morning the weather was fine and as I had recovered from the tree falling down upon me and was in good spirits again, decided to go on a day's fishing in the loch. In truth, as time went on, I had begun to dismiss the idea of an attack upon me and thought that the fresh air would brush away the sullen cobwebs of doubt which had ensnared me. Caroline was not too happy with the idea at first but realised, of course, that I could not shut myself in the house for long."

"I should have thought it an excellent idea, Sir Hugh," I said, "very healthy, in fact. Don't you agree Holmes?"

"So it would seem, at first anyway. Presumably you have your own boat, Sir Hugh?" asked Holmes.

"I do."

"What sort of boat?"

"I have two boats Mr. Holmes, just simple rowing boats, but quite sturdy as the loch can blow quite rough at times."

"Yes, I can well imagine," I replied.

"Please go on," said Holmes.

"Fortunately it was a fine morning and so after I collected together my fishing equipment, Duncan here took it down to the boat. We also had sent down a large basket with food and drink plus a large waterproof canvas cover. This was purely in case it rained when I could cover myself and the food. It was just as well I did. Duncan pushed me off from the shore and I set off, rowing whilst he returned to the house. I had no' gone out very far onto the loch, not far from the islands out there, when I noticed some water in the bottom of the boat. It was not much at first and I thought that it was just some rainwater, or that one of the seams had opened a little and that it would soon swell up and seal again, so I ignored it. Not for long, however, as within a short time it was obvious that it was coming in fast and that the boat was sinking. Naturally my first thought was to row for the shore but I realised it was too late for that. I had time to grab my canvas cover and managed to trap air in it to make a float. It was done just as the boat went down under me and left me struggling in the cold depths. You see the water was very cold and even though I can swim, with the cold and my sodden clothes I was in real difficulty." Sir Hugh turned again to Duncan

Cameron, "Duncan, would you care to tell what happened next?"

"Of course, Sir Hugh. After I saw the Laird rowing away I began walking back to the house. There is part of the pathway where you can see through a gap in the trees and obtain a good view of part of the loch. By chance I looked back. I had expected to see Sir Hugh way out on the loch by then, maybe already fishing. To my horror, instead, all I could see was the boat barely afloat and what appeared to be Sir Hugh struggling in the water. I raced back down to shore but our other boat, the one I usually had, was away for repairs. All I could find was a large log pulled up on to the beach. I managed to roll it down to the water, and holding onto it as a float, I gradually paddled myself to Sir Hugh."

"And none too soon, I can tell you, Mr. Holmes," interjected Sir Hugh, "I was getting cramp and the canvas sheet I had was by no means airtight. A minute more and I would have been done."

Duncan Cameron continued. "I had just managed to reach Sir Hugh and for him to grab the log but by then he could barely hold on. With great difficulty we paddled back to the shore. There was no-one else around and so after getting our breath back we made our way to the house."

"Mr. Holmes, what with the cold water and the effort of getting to the shore I was completely exhausted. Without Duncan here I doubt that I would have managed it."

All this time Caroline McFarlane had said nothing and just sat listening. I could see, however, by the paleness and distress on her face the effect that this was having on her.

"You said that there was a large log on the shore, Mr. Cameron. That was fortuitous. Was it there for a reason?"

"Yes, Mr. Holmes. It was originally from an old tree which had been blown down in the recent high winds. It had been partly cut up and was due to be made into planks with which to repair our boat house."

"Which boathouse is this?"

"It is where both of Sir Hugh's boats are normally kept."

"I see. And why did it need to be repaired?" asked Holmes again.

"Some large wooden planks on the side had been broken."

"When did it become damaged?"

"We believe in the same storm which brought down the tree. It was also how the other boat which I use was damaged. Part of the hull planks were wrenched apart."

"So the tree damaged both."

"It did."

"I take it that this boat house is nearby? We did not see it as we came in on the steamer."

"Yes, it is just around a small headland which goes out into the loch. It is partly concealed behind some trees. You would not see it from the jetty where you landed."

Holmes re-lit his pipe. "Sir Hugh, do you know where your boat is now? Did you have it recovered?"

"No, it is at the bottom of the loch, Mr. Holmes. I doubt if we shall see it again."

"A pity. I should have liked to examine it, but no matter."

"Sir Hugh", interrupted Duncan Cameron. "It may yet be possible to recover it."

"How so, Mr. Cameron?" I asked.

"Well Dr. Watson, it may be that it has not gone right to the bottom of the loch. It is just possible that it is floating a wee way beneath the surface, being held down by the things in it. But even if it is on the bottom we know whereabouts it went down. It may be possible to drag a large hook along and catch it. I have seen it done before. As long as it is not too deep I believe it is worth a try. At least we would have located it exactly and can then work out how best to bring it back up to the surface."

"A most resourceful idea, Cameron, but we will need another boat for that."

"Aye, we will, Mr. Holmes, but in a day or so we should have the other one back and when we do we can try then."

"Please do," said Holmes, "I am sure that Sir Hugh would like his boat back and it should show us exactly what caused it to sink. I assume that the boat was previously in good condition."

"Yes it was Mr. Holmes," said Cameron, "I make sure of that."

"Could it not have been damaged by the tree as well, without you realising it?"

"No, I checked the boat most thoroughly, I have no doubt that the tree did not damage it. I would have noticed, and I am sure that Sir Hugh would have done so as well."

Sir Hugh nodded his agreement.

"But were you not expecting a problem, Sir Hugh, or you, Mr. Cameron?"

"Not with a boat. Whatever caused it to sink can only have been by chance surely. Perhaps the wood in the hull had dried out and we had not noticed it." Sir Hugh's manner, however, and tone of voice, indicated that he was doubtful even of his own interpretation of events and merely wanted to reassure himself. Holmes looked at him. "Very well," he replied, unconvinced.

"In the meantime I will use this opportunity to take a look at this boat house. I assume that you would rather stay here, Sir Hugh?"

"Yes I will Mr. Holmes if you do not mind. Caroline insists on keeping me here for a while yet.

Duncan will be pleased to take you and show you what happened."

"What are you going to do about investigating the other incidents which happened to Sir Hugh, Holmes?"

"I shall have to look at those later, Doctor," he replied. "As the boat sinking only happened yesterday there is a good chance that many useful clues can be found and I want to take every opportunity to find them before they are destroyed. Later on we will be able to go and look at what happened in the woodlands and where the rock fell. With luck we might still find some useful clues although it was several weeks ago. Meanwhile, Cameron, would you kindly show us the way?"

Chapter Four

The Boathouse

On leaving Inverdaigh House we made our way through a woodland path leading down towards the loch. It was clear that some while ago a heavy storm had done much damage as many trees now leaned over at exaggerated angles. We passed through a gap and found that we had emerged beside the boathouse itself. Some yards away to our left, near the water's edge, lay a large log. It had clearly been part of a very substantial tree but was now partly sawn up and other pieces were lying nearby, higher up on the beach.

Holmes walked over to it. "I take it this was the log you used to rescue Sir Hugh, Mr Cameron."

"Aye, it is Mr. Holmes. We decided that we could use it to repair the boathouse later on."

Even though it had been sawn and separated from the other pieces it was still a substantial piece of wood, showing where it had been torn away from its base in the recent storms. The drag mark was very clear.

Holmes went across and looked over it carefully, saying nothing but peering down and examining it through his magnifying glass. Then reaching out and holding a piece of broken branch, he rolled it over onto its other side and examined it again. Going over to one end he then grasped the main trunk, lifted it clear of the ground, and with a twist of his body he flipped it back over to its original position. Cameron, standing alongside me gasped.

"That was some feat of strength Dr. Watson," he said. "Under normal circumstances I would struggle to do that even though in my younger days I could throw the caber with the best of them. I am sure that the laird's desperate situation gave me the extra energy I needed though."

"Yes, as a doctor I can say that your body will indeed give you much extra strength in a situation like that. It still helps to be fit though and I am sure that your work helps."

"I believe that you are right Dr. Watson."

Holmes, now brushing his hands clean, came over to us. "It was fortunate that you had that log nearby Mr. Cameron. It is not too large to move into the water but big enough to hold on to in an emergency and stay afloat. An exhausted man could, with help, roll up and lay on top of it until he got to shore. Sir Hugh was very fortunate that you were there, eh, Watson?"

"Yes, indeed he was, Holmes. What do you wish to do now?"

"Let's take a look at the boat house and the surroundings."

The very substantial shed, for that was its structure, was sited a short way along the beach and lay close against the woodland. Its front consisted of two large doors hinged at each end. Both closed against a central strut. In front of the doors, and going down to the water, lay a number of wooden pieces which were clearly used as runners, enabling boats to be slid across them for launching and recovery. Holmes walked over, first looking at them and the ground between, then, looking up at the boathouse and woodlands beyond it.

"What are you looking for Holmes? I can see very little except sand."

"You know my methods, Doctor I believe this boathouse was probably a factor in yesterday's events. It is crucial for me to understand what has been happening here, and I need to open my mind to any clues the scene may give. I am trying to put myself in the mind of the criminal Watson. As he was certainly around within the last day or so, there may be some useful information we can recover. I am particularly interested in the ground around here at the moment."

"Can you see anything useful?"

"Possibly, there is nothing on the wooden runners but there are many interesting footprints."

"Yes. I can see quite a few myself but which ones are the most important. They all look very much alike."

"Ha!" Holmes exclaimed, "to the untrained eye Doctor, they do of course. But by careful study subtle differences can be seen. Look closely just here," he said, now kneeling down on the sandy beach.

"You may recall that some time ago, during one of my cases, I had cause to study the art of tracking. Some Indian tribes excel at this and claim to be able to follow a fugitive or animal over the most difficult ground, where most people could not see even a trace of any sign at all. To them even the position of a leaf or a stone can mean a great deal. It can, for example, say in what direction the quarry is moving, how fast, whether or not it is injured, or how heavy they are. I confess I am not up to that standard, but I believe I can hold my own against many. Footprints tell their own story. It is important to notice the way in which people walk. Some, as their foot leaves the ground, may twist it a little. In soft sand or mud this will distort the shape of the footprint, leaving a small ridge on one side. The other foot may not show this as we do not always walk evenly on each side. Let me show you, Doctor. Look, see here."

Holmes's long fingers were pointing at two footprints in the hard sand.

"What can you tell me about these, eh? Look carefully now."

"I can see the distinct tracks of two people Holmes. One footprint is partly on top of the other slightly to one side. I cannot see much else though."

"Look again" said Holmes. "The marks made by the shoe on top have not only partly obliterated the other one but also pressed deeper into the sand, which fortunately is firm around here. The shoe on top is slightly larger, as you can see by the heels. It indicates, does it not, that the man whose shoe mark is underneath was lighter than the second and is probably smaller. He was obviously here first, see, his tracks go over there," he said pointing, "and disappear into the woodlands."

"But they could have been made by anyone, Holmes. There have been a number of people around here, surely."

"Well think about it old friend. Within the last day or so I doubt that not more than ten people at most have been to this spot. Some such as Cameron here have left very clear tracks, others would have been made by people who work around here and can easily be found and, if necessary, eliminated as the boots they wear are quite distinctive. Others, however, cannot be ruled out of our investigations and these we must take note of."

"Yes Holmes, but they could still have been made by a number of people, none of whom was the criminal," I protested.

"You may be quite right Watson; in themselves all they tell us is that some unknown person was here. If, however, in the course of our investigations the same, or very similar, shoe pattern is found, then we can be suspicious at the very least. If these also link in with other clues, it increasingly narrows down our possible suspects. Let us now follow these smaller footsteps where they go into the trees."

Holmes now stood up, and asking Cameron to stay by the boathouse, we made our way into the woodlands behind it. Holmes kept peering around at the ground then at some of the broken trees, all of the time keeping his own counsel. Finally, after circling around we returned to the path near where it came out by the beach.

"Did you find anything useful, Holmes?" I asked.

"Yes, although the undergrowth was very thick, people had obviously been through. There were also signs on the ground of soil removal. I found a shallow depression, as if small amounts had been removed."

Cameron, who had been standing back watching, came over to join us.

"What would you like to do now Mr. Holmes?" he asked.

"I would like to examine the boat house. I am certain that it will yield information if we look closely enough. Let us start with the side which was damaged by the tree falling over upon it. I take it that this is it here," he said, pointing to the side of the building which showed signs of recent damage and repair.

"Yes, you can see where we have made some rough repairs. When we have time later on we will have to renew some of the planks and struts inside."

Holmes moved over to it and again using his magnifying glass, looked carefully at the damaged section and the subsequent repairs.

Several times he stopped, looked upwards again towards where the tree had stood, prior to falling over.

"Are all the pieces of this tree lying around here?" he asked Cameron.

"Yes, all of them. The tree which caused most damage was the large piece you moved by the water, Mr. Holmes."

"Which is the piece of branch which struck the boathouse?"

"Over here," replied Cameron, pointing to a pile of branches laying nearby. "This is the actual piece. You can well see how it caused damage to the shed and boat inside."

Holmes grunted an acknowledgement. "Yes, possibly," he replied.

"Would you like to go and look inside now? I have the keys."

"In a moment, perhaps," replied Holmes "there is more to examine outside first."

"As you wish," said Cameron, standing back and looking at me as if so doing would give him the illumination he sought for Holmes's motives.

Holmes, saying no more, went around to the front of the boatshed and using his glass examined carefully all around the doors. It was like watching a terrier on the scent of its prey as he probed and searched, finally finishing at the hinges.

"Who uses this boathouse besides yourself, Mr. Cameron?" Holmes asked, almost as if absentmindedly.

"Some of the staff at the house occasionally come here, but none lately, I believe. Sir Hugh as well, of course."

"Who puts oil on the door clasp and hinges?"

"Why, I do sometimes."

"Recently?"

"No, not for quite a while."

Holmes returned to examining the door hinges, looking particularly at those on the same side as the damaged planks. He then ran his finger over the metal and around the top and bottom of the hinge pins, feeling carefully. Finally he put his nose closely to the metal and smelt carefully. During all this time he said nothing as I watched engrossed in curiosity, occasionally exchanging glances with Duncan Cameron. "You can undo the door now, Mr. Cameron," he said.

The boathouse was now empty save for two small hand winches at the back of the sloped earthen floor, which were used to lower the boats into and back up out of the water. In front of each winch, ran two grooves showing where the keel of each boat had rested. Holmes looked around for a few moments, then moving across to the right hand side started to examine the inside of the wall planks where the boat had been hit by the falling tree. He reached into the damage and I saw him retrieve a wood splinter, again checking it carefully. Kneeling now onto the floor he examined it and after rejecting several tiny pieces found one to his satisfaction.

"Ah, look, Watson," he announced, "another piece."

"So it is, Holmes, so it is. What now?" I retorted, completely baffled by his innocuous find.

"It is a piece from where the branch impacted and burst through damaging the boat, can you not see?"

"Yes, Holmes but we know that already, Cameron here has already shown us."

"Yes, indeed he has Doctor, but let us keep looking a while longer". Saying no more, he resumed his searching on the floor by the damaged area. Finally he stood up. "No there is nothing here Doctor, nothing further to help us. Let us go and see what we can find over here."

Holmes moved across to the left hand side looking at the marks, which showed where the boat had been resting. He again paused, using his lens, moving methodically from side to side, gradually covering the area where the boat's hull had been sitting. After he had searched the whole of that part of the floor, he went over it a second time. Finally, he knelt upright. On his face was an expression of puzzlement and annoyance.

"This side is where Sir Hugh's boat was, I suppose, Mr. Cameron, after the storm."

"No, Mr. Holmes, it was on the right hand side. After the storm when the tree had damaged the boat house and the boat in it we changed them around as we felt that there was a possibility of other trees falling on to the other side. We did not want to have both boats damaged at the same time."

"Ah," said Holmes, looking up excitedly, "that probably explains it. There are several trees leaning over dangerously. Unless they are soon removed I can well see why you were concerned Mr. Cameron." Saying no more he sprang back across to the right hand side to where Sir Hugh's other boat had been moved, sank to the floor and again started to carefully examine it. He had only just begun when he exclaimed, "Yes, I was right! Look Watson, this is how it was done." He was now jubilant.

Still puzzled as to what he meant, I joined him, kneeling down on the floor, with his long finger pointing to what appeared to be some specks of dull, white dust alongside the left of the groove made by the keel and some tiny split wood chippings nearby. Passing me the magnifying glass I could make out through its lens grains of wood sawdust in a small, scattered pile. "There should be more, yes, here it is, and yet more here, and here," he said as he ranged over the floor, peering intently at each as he found them in turn.

Altogether there were eight separate groups. Some of them had clearly been disturbed by being trodden on as people moved around. When, I wondered?

Holmes read my mind. "The small piles of sawdust were scattered after the boats were changed around, and the remaining one loaded and moved down to the water. You can see what happened."

"Not entirely, Holmes."

"It shows how the criminal managed to sabotage the boat so that it sank when it was out on the loch. It is all very clear now."

"I am not clear either, Mr. Holmes," said Duncan Cameron. "Are you saying that the boat was deliberately damaged here rather than on the shore? If so, how did he get into the boathouse without us knowing, or seeing the damage he had done? After all, we took the boat out yesterday morning on to the water and around to the beach when the Laird decided to go fishing. It was perfectly all right then. I thought that something must have happened to it between those times, although it was difficult to see how. There was such limited time and any damage done would have been so obvious. That is why I could not understand why the boat had sunk out on the loch and so quickly, too."

"It has been done by a very clever and resourceful criminal," said Holmes. "A man who is very determined that one way or another he will eventually succeed. This is his third unsuccessful attempt and it is only by Sir Hugh's good fortune that the criminal has failed so far. There is no doubt that he will try again, but certainly use another method next time. He must know, however, that we are here and on his track, so now he will be extra careful. There is no telling what form another attempt will take. We all must be on our guard."

"But I still do not know how the boat was made to sink yesterday morning just when he was out in it on the loch. Please explain, Holmes."

"Of course, my dear fellow. We have to remember that the first two attempts on Sir Hugh were made on land. Naturally, as you have just said, it would be difficult to see how any harm could come to him if he were far from shore in a sturdy boat. Any damage done to it causing it to sink would be obvious to see beforehand. Therefore both he and yourself, Mr. Cameron, were not expecting any problem to arise."

"But I did my normal checks over the boat, Mr. Holmes, and could see nothing wrong," said Cameron, anxious to emphasise that he had not been negligent.

"Yes, that part was very clever. The criminal naturally realised that you would both be on your guard so he had to go to great pains to cover his tracks."

"He did very well then, Holmes, considering he had so little time," I said, "especially when the tree was blown down damaging the boathouse and one of the boats inside."

"As it turned out, Watson that worked to his advantage. It is clear to me that after he had failed twice he would seek another opportunity and by using a different method. I believe it likely that he already had in mind a way of sabotaging one of the boats. He had to be careful, though, as it had to be done in such a way that he left no clues. As there were two boats in use he had to find a way of putting one out of action so that he could be sure it was the other one which would be used."

"But it could have been me in that boat, Mr. Holmes," interrupted Cameron, "how could he have known it would be used by the Laird?"

"He could not," replied Holmes, "but it was a risk which he had to take. As Sir Hugh is known to love fishing there was a good chance that it would be him using it at the time, which as it happened is exactly as it turned out. Had it been you then at the very least he would have likely removed a loyal and able servant such as yourself, Mr. Cameron."

Holmes's compliments were again not lost on Cameron. "I do my best, Mr. Holmes," he said, "I can do no more."

"Just so, Mr. Cameron, you do very well. You must remember that on the first occasion when the rock came down and Sir Hugh fell from his horse and went down the cliff it was probably you who saved his life."

"How so, Mr. Holmes? He could probably have climbed back up himself and on to his horse, although I admit with some difficulty."

"But you were there to help him, Mr. Cameron. Had you not been there to protect Sir Hugh who knows what would

55

have happened; the criminal would have him at his mercy as Sir Hugh tried to get back up the cliff. He would almost certainly have succeeded by means of dropping another rock onto him or simply pushing him over. After all he was injured and there would have been no witnesses to what had happened. It would just have been regarded as being an unfortunate accident and no more. No, had it been you in the boat, your demise would have at least for him had the satisfaction of removing someone who had prevented his evil plan from succeeding earlier. By removing you, would also make it easier for him in the future. Either way he could not lose."

"I suppose if you put it that way, Mr. Holmes," replied Cameron.

"In my mind there is no doubt," he said.

"But you still have not told us how the boat was damaged so as to sink in the way it did, Holmes," I asked yet again.

"It was like this, Doctor. After the tree damaged the boat house, the criminal discovered it and immediately conceived of a plan so that he could turn it to his advantage. He needed to be able to obtain access to the boats without leaving any trace. First, he carefully oiled the hinges so that the pins could be removed easily. This would allow him to open the doors at the hinges so that he did not need to obtain a key. He did it most carefully so that to a casual observer the oil did not show. I could, however, smell the fresh oil. After he was able to get inside he did two more things. The falling tree had damaged the boat on the right hand side all right, but not so as to make it impossible to use. He therefore had to make it worse than the tree impact had done. There were some small pieces of wood on the floor by the hole in the boathouse wall. They could not have been created by the impact of the tree alone. The small piece I found clearly did not come from the wall as a result of the falling tree. No, it came from where he did further damage to the hull in order to make it look like damage from the tree. He had obviously used a metal tool of sorts to open up the seams. On the other boat, the one Sir Hugh was to use, he needed to make it sink, but slowly, so as not to cause alarm. The only way he could have done this was by making a number of small holes in the hull. These were likely drilled in places where they would not easily be seen, probably against the keel and at an angle through the garboard plank. The small piles of wood dust on the boathouse floor clearly show this. However, at first I could not understand why there were no signs of boat damage on the floor on the left hand side, where Sir Hugh's other undamaged boat had been. After Cameron had told me of the boats being moved around, it was obvious what had happened."

"Not to me, Holmes."

"Or to me," retorted Cameron.

"When the criminal had come back into the boat shed to further damage the first boat he obviously needed to damage Sir Hugh's other boat as well. It is likely that he was either disturbed or needed more tools so he went away but on returning found that the boats had been changed around. To him it did not matter as he went ahead anyway just as he had planned originally. Not knowing they had been moved, I had looked at where that boat had been placed initially which is why, on finding no clues, I asked Cameron here to confirm where they had been. On learning he had moved them around I looked at the floor on the other side only to find my suspicions confirmed.

"You see, Doctor, the criminal also had to make holes underneath the boat on the side away from the damaged wall. It gave him more room to work. It is why I did not see the wood dust from the holes when I first looked. Not knowing that the boats had been moved I naturally looked on the left hand side. I can also make out traces of where he had been lying underneath it in order to do his vile work. They had not all been erased when the boat was moved down to the loch. If you look carefully you can see the marks", he said, pointing them out to us both. "You see, Watson, even small differences in the position of clues can make a big difference, and tell the investigator a great deal when seen as part of the overall scene of crime. The wood dust is the key of course. Its existence and position confirms it. Without it, my deductions would be invalid and I would have to rethink as to why, and how, Sir Hugh's boat sank in the way it did."

"Yes, I see what you mean, Holmes".

He went on, "he must also have filled the holes with clay or something similar. He probably obtained it from the depression I found in the woods behind the boathouse. He needed to ensure that it would dissolve slowly not allowing in water at first until the boat had been taken further out on the loch. As it dissolved, water would pour in and the boat would sink rapidly. That, of course, is exactly what happened. I could see no traces of any unusual material on the wooden boat runners which led down to the water, and it was therefore reasonable to conclude that the material filling the holes under the hull was firmly in place, before the boat entered the water."

"But the plan failed, Holmes, the boat sank very quickly quite close to shore. The holes opened up too early."

"Yes, Watson, because what he did not foresee was that the boat would be taken out from the boathouse first and moved to the beach nearby before being loaded with Sir Hugh's fishing equipment. By doing that, water must have already started eating away at the material filling the holes and weakened it. The result was that even as Sir Hugh was rowing out on the loch some water was already starting to dribble in. Fortunately, before he had gone out too far the remainder had dissolved and the water surged in. The rest you know."

"Amazing Holmes, and elementary really when you think of it though."

"Yes, Watson, these things often are; when you think of it. Shall we go back to Inverdaigh House? It's late afternoon and it looks as if we shall have rain before nightfall."

Chapter Five

The Woodlands

After a sound night's sleep, Inverdaigh House awoke to a fine morning. I arrived at breakfast to find that Holmes had already eaten and was preparing to sample the morning air.

"Good morning, Watson, I trust that you slept well?"

"I did, Holmes. I see that you have, too. Have you any special plans for today?"

"I thought that we would walk along the woodlands to where the second incident occurred. But there is no hurry, Doctor. Your breakfast is ready for you now. We can go as soon as you have finished. Meanwhile I will find Mr. Cameron and discuss his finding the sunken boat."

After eating I returned to my room and now dressed in sturdy boots and clothing, went downstairs again where I met Sir Hugh.

"Good morning, Dr. Watson, I trust that you had a restful night."

"I did indeed, Sir Hugh, most comfortable. The quietness takes some getting used to after London but I find it to be most refreshing. How are you feeling now, yourself, Sir Hugh. Fully recovered from your swim in the loch, I hope?"

Sir Hugh chuckled. "Yes, thank you, Dr. Watson, I am that. I see that Mr. Holmes is discussing the possibility of Duncan finding my boat and raising it from the bottom of the loch. I think that he has a few ideas of his own. Do you think it can be done, Doctor?" queried Sir Hugh. "He seems to think so. It will be a difficult operation but he believes that they can succeed. It is probably worth a try."

"I hope he is right, Sir Hugh. If the boat can be recovered then we can find out for certain whether or not Holmes was correct yesterday."

"Yes, Doctor, if so it will be the first time that we can be absolutely sure that it was deliberate. It should confirm all Caroline's views on the matter all along."

"Is she in this morning; I haven't seen her yet?" I asked Sir Hugh.

"No, she had to go out early on some errand of her own. No doubt she will be back later."

Just then Holmes entered. "Ah, Doctor, there you are. Sir Hugh, I understand that your damaged boat is being returned later today. Apparently the arrangement is to have it taken directly to the loch by the boathouse. Mr. Cameron will meet it there with some helpers. With any luck we could have your other boat located before the day is out?"

"I hope so, Mr. Holmes. Dr. Watson and I have just been discussing that very same thing. If we can get the boat out it may be that I can recover some of my fishing equipment, too. What do you and Dr. Watson propose to do until they have everything ready?"

"I intend this morning, Sir Hugh, to go into the woodlands and find the place where the tree fell upon you. If I understand correctly the pathway itself has been cleared but nothing else."

"That is so, Mr. Holmes, the foresters have been too busy to do anything other than initial clearance work for the moment. In any case, I do not want anything removed or cut down unless it is absolutely necessary."

"That could not be better," Holmes replied.

"But Holmes," I interrupted, "the incident with the tree happened a while ago. Surely there will be no clues left by now."

"Possibly, Watson, we shall see. Under normal circumstances you are probably correct. Any clues would have been destroyed some time ago but these are not usual circumstances. We are not in London where vehicles and people are moving around all the time. The very remoteness and relative isolation of the site leaves a distinct possibility that something of value to us may remain. If it is there, I intend to find it. You never know what may have been missed? I know exactly where it is located. In any case I have some ideas of my own that I wish to test. By the time we return, Cameron should have the boat back and everything prepared. If you're ready to leave, Doctor, it's a fine morning."

With that Holmes shouldered a small canvas sack I had not seen before and we set off. We walked briskly through the grounds of Inverdaigh House and soon passed into some most attractive deciduous woodlands. The trees were now starting to show their colours of early autumn and the air had a clear freshness that spoke of untamed nature and the hint of coming winter.

As we passed along the pathway, wild flowers still exuded their fragrance, as if determined to hold on to the last of the summer and defy the change of seasons. After about a mile the pathway climbed a little and through the heights of the trees the mountainside could be seen rising above, the morning sun glinting on the rocks. I looked up. Wheeling around in the sky far above, I could see a large bird.

"Is that a golden eagle I can see, Holmes?" I said pointing upwards. He stopped and joined my excited gaze.

"Probably. Apparently Sir Hugh is hoping that some nesting pairs may breed."

"Yes, he is quite unusual in that. Most estate owners try to be rid of them. They blame them for losses of fawns or lambs."

"That may be true, but Sir Hugh is clearly happy to tolerate it. He is a great ornithologist. He has arranged for a gathering soon at his house; for local ornithologists from all around the area."

"That should be interesting. I should like to go myself and see what they have to say. Will you go, Holmes?"

"Yes, to my mind, it may help to throw some light on recent events."

Our conversation died away and as we walked on I noticed that the character of the woodlands had now changed. The deciduous trees were slowly giving way to pine and fir. The pathway dropped and after a short distance opened out into a lovely sunlit glade.

"This is it", said Holmes. "At the end here is where the tree fell on to Sir Hugh if I am right."

We walked along to the far side. Lying across the footpath in front of us were several large trees, which had clearly taken the brunt of the storm. Their roots had been ripped out of the ground and branches had been split away from their main trunks. In the way of such events, however, other trees nearby had been left standing, seemingly untouched as if the wind's wrath had left them, unselected. The fallen giants now lay jumbled amongst them, in unhindered silence, as if awaiting final execution at the hands of local foresters.

Earlier, in order to reopen the footpath, someone had cut away smaller branches, pushing these over to one side. We eased our way through, Holmes leading. He stopped and taking out a small telescope, started looking up into the higher parts of the trees.

"What are you looking for, Holmes?"

"I am looking to see if I can find the tree from which the branch was cut so that it would fall on Sir Hugh as he passed underneath. Several look as if they have been cut back, but I think I can see which one it was. Here, Watson, see what you think."

Adjusting the small telescope to my eye, I pointed it at the tree Holmes had selected. Looking carefully, I was able to pick out the large branch obviously snapped off in high winds but at the broken end it was seemingly too clean a break to be completely natural. It looked as if part of it had been sawn through.

"Yes, I can see what you mean there. But if that is the tree, what more can it tell us?"

"I am interested to find how it was that the criminal was so able to hold the branch securely in position and yet so easily release it at just the right moment without being seen."

He bent down and started looking around the woodland floor, much as he had done back at the boathouse the previous afternoon. Holmes disappeared into some bushes, and I then glimpsed him some way off by some large trees. He disappeared again. I was left standing around for a while wondering what he was doing when suddenly I heard a voice above my head.

"Just up here, Doctor, if you please." He chuckled at seeing my surprise. I looked up and saw Holmes just above me. He had in some way managed to climb the tree near to where the broken branch had been cut. In each of his hands he was holding a pronged hook, which I could see he was using as if they were a pair of claws. Around his shoes there was a leather strap which appeared to be holding a small metal frame against the sole of each shoe. The whole effect, with his wearing the deerstalker hat, made him seem to be like a giant squirrel. I threw back my head and burst out laughing.

"I say, Holmes, that looks good, have you found any nuts yet? What are you doing cavorting around in the trees?" He smiled in response.

"No nuts, old fellow, but I have found something even better." So saying, he threw down to me a wooden object which fell at my feet. I picked it up and looked at it closely. It was a triangular piece of wood, around twelve inches long and about three inches wide. At the broad end was a small hole through which ran a long weather-worn thong of leather. It had obviously been made from the branch of a tree, cut and shaped to form into a large wedge.

"What was this used for, Holmes? Do foresters have these type of wedges, I have not seen one before?"

"Yes, they do, Doctor, but not this particular piece. What do you think of it?" Holmes sat down, his legs on either side of the trunk.

I could see that it was roughly hewn with what appeared to be some pressure indentations impressed into it, as if it had held a heavy load.

"I supposed just to split wood," I suggested. "I believe that carpenters use small pieces for that purpose."

"Yes they do, but not that one I think," he replied, pointing to the wedge I held in my hand. "No, it was used for something else. It was clearly the key part of a very clever linkage, which held in place a large branch above the trunk. From what I can see it was used as a loosening device. It was finely balanced but held securely until needed. When moved, it displaced a second branch which was braced in turn, so as to hold back the large tree itself," he said patting its trunk. "This is the one which then fell and nearly hit Sir Hugh. Up here, back in the wood, I can see where a notch has been cut into which the wedge must have been fitted. A most skilful and cunning device. In all my years as a consulting detective I have never seen anything quite like it before."

"Wouldn't that have been a major task, Holmes, in order to fit the branches together?"

"Yes, it would I am sure, but possible for a strong man who knew what he was doing. To form such an arrangement of mutually supporting levers he would have needed a block and tackle. The piece of rope found by Duncan Cameron was obviously part of it. I think, also some judicious cutting. If you look carefully you can see where some trimming has been done, higher up ... see?" he said pointing up at several places where branches had been interlaced.

"Yes, I can see what you mean. Surely though Holmes, all that work, he must have been seen or heard by someone?"

"Maybe, old friend, but you have to remember that because of the storm with paths being blocked and the possibility of more trees falling over, people kept away from here. Until it was cleared sufficiently well he was able to take advantage of all the confusion of overlaying trees. Remember, much clearance work was taking place all over the area and if he had been seen it would merely look as if it had been part of that task and raised no suspicions. Even so, I wonder ..."

Holmes's voice tailed off and I could see that he had retreated into that deep thought with which I was so familiar at times in Baker Street when he was working on a problem.

I interrupted "How did he release the wedge at the right moment, you have not said?"

"Yes, you are right, Doctor. Come over this way. I want to show you something else."

I pushed my way through bushes and around large trees whilst above me I could see that he was making his way along branches and trees leaning over at various angles. In all this time he never once came down to the ground. At last, after going some way into the woodland and out of sight of the pathway he climbed down and joined me on the forest floor. He sat on a piece of fallen log and took off the metal frames from his shoes. I could see them more closely now and he handed one to me. The metal frame, which was made to fit under the sole of each shoe, had seven metal spikes firmly fixed into it. Each of these spikes was curved backwards, very slightly. When held firmly to his shoes by the leather strap, it was as if each foot had taken the form of a claw similar to that of a large cat. The hooks he held in each hand were much more simple with just two metal prongs each, more like those of a butcher's hook used for moving around carcasses in an abattoir. The main difference was that they also had leather straps, which held them firmly to his wrist, so that if necessary he was able to free one hand from the need to hold onto the hook itself. It was clear to see that by using the combination of shoe spikes and hand hooks he was able to climb trees and branches with relative ease. He replaced them into his small canvas shoulder sack.

"I have not seen those before, Holmes. Where did you get them from?"

"When I heard Cameron telling us about the tree incident I thought it possible that some tree climbing may become necessary. I recalled that in forested areas, lumberjacks sometimes use special equipment as an essential part of their work. I therefore went down to one of our local blacksmiths and had him make, to my own designs, these devices. They work well do they not?"

"Yes, I can see that without them it would be very difficult to move around safely high in the trees. So what else have you to show me, Holmes, besides these most ingenious devices?" I said.

"Look carefully along here," he said, pointing up at several branches. On the top of each a groove had been cut across. On two of them I could detect fine threads of string caught on the bark. And see here again," he said, kneeling down and looking closely at the ground.

I could make out a faint trace of a man's shoe in the firm earth. "This is how it was done, Watson, can you see now?"

"I think so, Holmes, but please explain it. Is it the same shoe mark as the one we saw yesterday? Holmes, it seemed to be very unclear to me?"

"Yes, unfortunately it is, Doctor, time and weather has obscured it too much. However, it is possible to make out just where the criminal was waiting and why. The undergrowth shows signs of someone being around here for a while as parts of it have not yet fully recovered when you compare it to some only a short distance away. He had devised a most ingenious way of releasing that wedge you have in your hand, from over here," he said, pointing at the ground.

"Those grooves in the wood were used as a guide for a length of string which was clearly tied to it. They also had to be made very smooth so that the string ran easily across them. If you look carefully you can just see that he even went to the trouble of using beeswax to reduce friction." As he said this he handed me his magnifying glass. I reached up. Some small droplets of water were on the grooves but the wax had acted as a waterproof lubricant. "He could not risk the string slipping off or snagging just at the instant he needed to pull."

"And what was the piece of leather for?" I said, holding up the piece fitted through the hole in the wooden wedge.

"In order to have the wedge work properly, it had to be held at exactly the correct angle to the small branch it was to support. Otherwise it would either jam or come loose. The leather thong was needed to secure it at just that angle. He could not risk using string as it may have broken if under tension for too long. He used leather as it was stronger. String, however, would be good enough just to give a quick pull at the right moment. All it had to do was move the wedge so that it could release the weight of the branch it held."

"Where is the string now, Holmes?"

"He obviously took that away with him. I could find none of it. The wooden wedge I believe, he dropped and lost, as I found it in one of the bushes under the trees. He probably was not over concerned as in the unlikely event anyone finding it would not realize what it had been used for. The smaller branch it had been holding has gone too, probably deposited elsewhere in the wood. It does not matter now, however. If you crouch down here under the bushes you can just see anyone walking along the path."

As he said this we both crouched down so as to see along a tunnel formed by the bushes.

"All he had to do was watch for Sir Hugh to come along then simply pull the string just before he walked under it. The clever assailant would not be seen unless the victim knew where to look. He would have needed to crouch down as well, so the criminal was quite safe from view."

"Very intricate indeed, Holmes, and quite ruthless. Quite remarkable in fact."

My statement could not hide the sneaking admiration I had formed for our adversary even though I knew that Holmes and I were there to bring him to justice.

"Yes, but another question we have to consider, Watson, is just how did the criminal know that Sir Hugh would be walking along at that time?"

"Perhaps he did not, Holmes, could he have set it as a spring trap? During my time in India I found out that some of the native tribes, who lived in the jungles, developed some very ingenious traps, which they used against tigers and other wild animals."

"I did consider that possibility, Doctor, but was forced to dismiss it as being improbable."

67

"Why?"

"Well, think about it, old friend. This path is used from time to time by people other than Sir Hugh as well as the deer and other animals which roam around these parts. The criminal could not risk someone else setting off the trap in error. And suppose that they had, whether they survived or not, all that careful work with the tree branches would have been for nothing and it must have taken him quite a while to prepare. It would, of course, also have warned Sir Hugh again that his life was in danger and that he must be careful."

"Which is what did happen."

"Yes, but it was again to Sir Hugh's good fortune, not the lack of a well made man trap. One cannot rely on good fortune like that for ever, as his daughter has pointed out before. It is part of the puzzle I still have to solve."

"What shall we do now, Holmes?"

"A quick luncheon at Inverdaigh House I think, then back down to the loch to see how Duncan Cameron is progressing."

We turned on our heels and started walking back to Inverdaigh House. We had not gone far when Holmes suddenly held out his arm for us to stop.

"Did you see that?" he whispered.

"All I saw was a bird flying off, startled."

"Yes, but someone frightened it and it was not us. I thought that I saw a movement further back in the trees, above where we are standing; up towards the tree line."

"Probably a fox, Holmes. There must be dozens of them around here."

"I don't think so, at least if it was, it was one which stood upright on two legs. We are being stalked!"

"Shall we try and find who it is?"

"Good old Watson, that's what I like to hear. Perhaps you would work your way quietly up there to the left and I will drop back a little and go up from the other side. One of us should catch him."

Over the years one of the many things I had learnt about Holmes was just how quickly and quietly he could move when the occasion demanded. For the second time that morning I saw him quietly disappear into the undergrowth and I knew that he would already be working his way towards his quarry.

As we had agreed, I struck out around to the left and made my way up through the woodland. Try as I might, I felt unable to stop myself sounding like an express train. I seemed to catch every twig, branch or bramble that came my way. As the ground rose ever steeper it was not long before my breath came in increasingly heavy gasps. At last I came to the edge of the wood and a stone wall. I looked over and away to my right. I could see Holmes, running. As I watched he stopped, looking at something in the far distance through his telescope, which I could not see. Then he turned around and came walking back. It took him several minutes before he joined me, sitting on a rock recovering my breath.

"No luck then, Holmes?"

"No, he had the heels of me. I think he soon realised that we had seen him and had too long a start on us. All I saw was his back from a distance."

"Would you recognise him again?"

"Yes, I might although he was far off."

"Do you think he saw us by the glade, where the trap was laid for Sir Hugh?"

"Possibly, but whether he did or not, what was he doing here, I wonder?"

He sat pondering for a while, then looking around he pointed. "If our fugitive continued in the direction he was going I think that we may be able to cut him off. I have an idea of where he may be heading. I believe that it is worth a try. We may have our quarry yet. It means going back down through the woodlands again and following the path around the top of the loch. He may think that we have given up the chase and now be taking his time. Are you still game, Watson?"

"Yes, I am, Holmes," although I have to confess that I tried to sound more enthusiastic than I felt.

Holmes clearly sensed my fatigue and pulled out a small flask of brandy.

"Some of that will help I think," he said as I took a quick swig and after a short while we were again making our way downward back to the footpath. We came out further along the path than where the tree trap had been set for Sir Hugh, and with barely a backward glance passed along as quickly as we could.

Holmes set a fast pace and before long had gone some way ahead of me. After some while I saw that the pathway was becoming muddier and was being crossed by small rivulets. I saw that we were nearing the top end of the loch. I soon arrived at the river, which fed into the loch from the one above and on crossing over could see marks in the mud left by Holmes's shoes. A short distance on a thicket marked the edge of the woodland and it was here that I came upon Holmes. He heard me coming and raised his hand for me to keep hidden. I crept up until I joined him, crouching down by a fallen log.

"See there, Watson," he said, pointing to a figure in the distance, "I was right. He has made his way around thinking that he had thrown off the pursuit. Can you see him now?" So saying, Holmes handed me his small telescope. Through it I could easily see a tartan clad man making his way jauntily down the steep mountainside across to our right front. From his demeanour he showed no sign that he was in a hurry, on the contrary he was the picture of a man enjoying the day. I returned the telescope to Holmes.

"He seems to be very contented with himself, Holmes," I said. "Are you certain it is the same man you saw earlier?"

"Without a doubt. It's him all right. I recognise his clothing. If I am not mistaken he is heading home, without a care in the world."

"Where is his home then? There are precious few habitations around here."

"Further down the loch there are some cottages dotted about here and there. There is a wide spur of water further along. I expect he has a boat hidden away somewhere to get across."

"If we can follow him home we stand a good chance of catching him still."

"Yes, but let him get over that next outcrop of rock first, then we'll move. I don't want to catch him though. It would be better if we can just follow him for the moment and learn where he was coming from."

The moment the receding figure had passed out of sight, Holmes and I broke cover from our thicket and moved quickly along in his tracks. We had now turned the tables on our pursuer. The ground rose steeply on our left as we now jumped over rock and tussock until we arrived at the spot from where he was lost to view. Peering over carefully at first we could see nothing except the long rock covered hill going down towards a long sheet of water that led from the side of the loch and into the hills. My sudden fear was that he had seen us coming and taken evasive measures so that we would lose him and any valuable information we could gain. My concerns were unfounded, however, as Holmes leaned over to me and whispered, "Look Watson, there he is. He is moving faster downhill now but I am sure that he has not seen us."

Again he took out his telescope and stayed a while focusing on the man below us. Holmes passed the telescope back over to me once again.

"Take a good look, Watson, so that we may both recognise him when we see him again."

Although he was still far off, the magnifying lens enabled me to determine that he was a young man, probably in his early twenties, and by the way he was leaping over the rough terrain was obviously very fit. As I watched he made his way down into an area of reeds and scrub alongside the loch and disappeared. I moved the telescope to and fro trying to locate him to see where he would emerge. After a fruitless search with the telescope I again started to suspect that he had seen us after all and had given us the slip by crawling away, under cover. I turned to Holmes and said, "He's vanished, he's nowhere to be seen."

"Not for long, Doctor. Here he comes now. Keep your head down, or he will see us."

As Holmes spoke our quarry emerged from the reeds in a small rowing boat and with powerful strokes moved swiftly across the spur of water.

"Just as I said, Watson, he had a boat hidden. As he rows away, he faces the way he came and can spot any pursuer."

"Can we not get around this inlet?" I asked.

"We can," Holmes replied, but it's at least a mile of very rough ground and he will be long gone by then. At least we know where he is heading and something about him. He moved back behind the rocks and sat down to think. Then after a while said, "We can do no more here for the while, Watson, but it has served our purpose for the moment. I am sure that we will meet him again very soon."

"Shall we return to Inverdaigh House now, Holmes?"

"Yes," he replied, standing up. "I am ready for my luncheon. I am sure that you are too Doctor. I wonder how Cameron is getting on with his preparations?"

Chapter Six

The Sunken Boat

Early afternoon saw Holmes and I back beside of the loch. It was a fine calm day with the surrounding hills bathed in sunshine. On the far horizon, however, dark clouds were forming, telling us of rain arriving later. Gazing out over the surface of the sun-clad loch I tried to imagine the recent drama of the sinking boat and how the silent waters now hid the evidence within its dark and looming depths.

Holmes interrupted my thoughts. "Those islands over there look to be interesting Watson." As he spoke he pointed across at two tree covered islands some way out in the loch.

"Perhaps they are used for picnics, Holmes. On a summer's day I could imagine nothing more pleasant."

"I am sure that local people use them for that," he replied, "but for other things too I shouldn't wonder."

We walked over and sat down on the tree trunk which had recently been the means of saving Sir Hugh from a watery grave. Nearby lay a pile of freshly sawn logs together with a hammer and box of large nails.

"I see that someone has been busy Holmes," I said stating the obvious.

"Yes," he replied, "Cameron and the foresters have been working hard getting materials together."

"What for?" I asked.

"You will recall, old friend, that Cameron spoke to us earlier about locating Sir Hugh's boat."

"When I talked to him again he spoke to me of a method he had seen used before for raising a sunken boat."

"What method is that? I assumed that some sort of crane would be necessary. Quite a difficult job without one I would think."

"Getting a crane in will be difficult and expensive, Doctor, but as we do not have one we had to look at an alternative."

"Sounds interesting, Holmes" I replied "What have you in mind?"

"It is an intriguing idea, Doctor. Apparently his plan is to build a raft of logs then insert under it floatation chambers, which are filled with air so as to lift it higher out of the water. If before inserting these air filled containers the boat can be located underwater and fastened with ropes, as the air chambers lift the raft, the boat comes up, too."

"But only by a few inches surely, not enough to bring it to the surface," I said incredulously.

"Yes, Watson, you are right. But you have to remember that part of the problem is breaking the suction of the mud if it is indeed lying on the bottom. Once that has been achieved it should be possible to loop more ropes under the sunken boat and lift it higher up each time. All one then has to do is drag it to shallower water."

"It sounds rather hit and miss to me, Holmes, if you don't mind me saying so. You not only have to locate Sir Hugh's boat but fasten on to it securely as well. Just how does one do that?"

"When Cameron was in military service, he told me that he had seen a method used by the Corps of Engineers of raising items that were under water. By skilful application of a winch it's surprising what can be achieved; that and human muscle."

"I do have to confess, Doctor, that I have not seen the idea used before but Cameron seems to know what he is doing. I believe that it is worth a try. I even mentioned to him some ideas of my own."

As Holmes said this I thought I could see a gleam in his eye and I suspected that he was secretly relishing Cameron's as yet undisclosed idea and the unusual challenge it would evidently present.

"Besides," he went on, "I cannot help but wondering if our friend Duncan Cameron has something else in mind as well. We shall soon find out as he will want our help of course."

I was about to ask Holmes to explain this further, when a rowing boat appeared rounding the nearby headland. At the oars was Duncan Cameron. He drew up on to the beach. Cameron jumped out and spoke to us.

"As you see gentlemen the boat is now repaired. Whilst the foresters started preparing materials for a raft this morning, I had the local blacksmith help me with these."

At this Cameron turned, reached into the boat and pulled out two long struts of wood. At each end of these was attached a length of rope and at the end of each of these four ropes was tied a four pronged grappling hook.

"I have also had a few other hooks made, gentlemen, in case extra are needed. I hope they meet with your approval, Mr. Holmes."

Holmes picked up one of the hooks and examined it. The general shape of the hook closely resembled those which Holmes had used on his tree climbing activities that very morning.

"Excellent," said Holmes, "I see that you have plenty of spare rope as well. We may need that, too."

I could see in the boat Cameron had stacked several long coils and a piece of netting.

"What is the plan now?" I asked.

Cameron replied "What we are now going to do, Dr. Watson, is to row out to the area where I judge Sir Hugh's boat to be and by using these hooks locate his boat lying on the bottom. We will row to and fro, dragging them along until we find it. I think also that the piece of netting between the two will be useful, rather like a fishing trawl. Just a different type of catch though."

"I see, but when you have found it you still have to secure it to the raft before bringing it ashore."

"First things first, Watson," said Holmes, "we believe that by using these hooks and the wooden struts holding them we can not only find the boat, but hook on to it firmly enough to either lift it or drag it free. The net will be ideal to help us."

"Will the raft really be able to lift it?" I said, still sounding doubtful about the whole thing.

"Yes, if we can locate it and get a firm hold with the hooks. But it will take time and some luck, too," replied Holmes.

"Building the raft will not take too long, Dr. Watson," interrupted Cameron, clearly heading off any further objections which I might raise. "We have all the materials available that we require. For the moment we just need some patience."

Cameron spoke with an optimism which, try as I might, I still felt unable to share.

Holmes turned to Cameron and a quiet serious note crept into his voice as he said, "You have instructed the foresters to say nothing about our plan I assume, Mr. Cameron. The fewer people who know about this the better. There is no point in the whole countryside being aware."

"I have, you may be sure of that," he replied. "They will find out soon enough though."

Holmes grunted an acknowledgement as he and I climbed into the boat and with a firm push, Cameron launched it back into the water and leapt aboard. Fitting in a set of oars, he started to row out into the loch, whilst Holmes and I made ourselves as comfortable as the clutter in the small boat would allow.

"Do you know how deep it is out where Sir Hugh's boat is, Mr. Cameron?" I asked.

"About thirty feet I believe, Dr. Watson. Unfortunately it is too deep and cold for someone to dive in and fit a rope to it. I am still confident though that we can get it out. Have no fear, Dr. Watson." Cameron clearly sensed my continued misgivings on his boat recovery plan. We rowed on in silence for several minutes whilst the only sound I could hear was the creaking of the oars and splash of the blades as they dug in to the resisting black waters. Looking around over my shoulder

I could see in the distance the steam of a train as it climbed its way north through the hills. Further around I could make out a river as it cascaded over rocks and down into the loch. My mind drifted as I imagined generations of fishermen eagerly seeking to wrench out their lurking trout.

I was awakened from my reverie by the voice of Cameron. "I think that we are about there now gentlemen. It was around here that it sank. Dr. Watson, perhaps you would be kind enough to get ready two of the hooks now."

I reached over pulling the hooks with their attached net and wooden strut from the bottom of the boat. Passing the strut to Cameron he made it fast to one of the longer ropes.

"Mr. Holmes," he said, "can you now take the hooks and drop them overboard whilst Dr. Watson does the same with the wooden strut." We watched as they descended rapidly into the depths.

After a few moments the line went slack.

"Right gentlemen," said Cameron, "I'll start rowing to and fro now and with luck we shall catch our fish this afternoon. Perhaps you will keep an eye on the island to help me stay on course Dr. Watson?"

For the next few hours our small craft was rowed back and forth across the area of loch where Cameron thought Sir Hugh's sunken boat lay. At his request I took the end of a piece of spare rope and fastened it to a marker buoy he had brought along to drop over the sunken boat when it was found. During the course of the afternoon Holmes and I took our turns over rowing, in order to give Cameron a rest. For much of the remainder of the time, Holmes sat quietly saying very little, obviously in deep thought. Had we been in Baker Street I have no doubt that by now he would be sitting in his chair with his pipe, consuming several ounces of tobacco. From time to time he would look up and gaze around the loch and at the mountains all around us, as if their very presence had been responsible for some new insight into his thoughts before again returning to his own solitude.

Occasionally we had a false alarm when the grappling hook caught on a large stone and once on an old sunken log.

Wildlife seemed to abound and we took particular delight as a heron flew around our boat.

"He is hoping for an easy meal," noted Cameron.

"Perhaps he has seen Sir Hugh fishing," I replied.

"Aye, no doubt, Dr. Watson, although the laird also enjoys a spot of ornithology, too."

"From a boat?" I queried.

"Yes," he retorted. "You see those small metal loops fitted around the gunwales," we nodded as Holmes and I had seen these earlier and I was curious as to their use. "The laird had them fitted in order that they could hold in place a number of metal hoops which could go over the boat. He would then pull over it a large canvas sheet so that it would then act as a floating hide as well as a cover for when it rained."

"Just like they have on the river Thames, Holmes," I said.

"Yes, but then it's usually to keep off the sun I think." Then turning to Cameron he asked, "Was it one of these canvas covers that Sir Hugh used to help stay afloat, Mr. Cameron?"

"It was, and a good job it was that I had put it in the boat beforehand. Sir Hugh did not normally use it when he was out fishing. He said that he needed a clear space in which to cast his hook, but as I thought it may rain later I put it in anyway."

"Good thing, as well," I replied.

"Very fortunate," confirmed Holmes. "Tell me, Mr. Cameron," asked Holmes looking across the loch, "those islands over there, they appear to have once been inhabited. I can see traces of stonework amongst the trees by the beach." As he said this he pointed to two islands in the loch. They were both covered in trees and thick undergrowth. The larger island was closest and we were floating between it and the shore.

"They were once, Mr. Holmes," Cameron replied, "at least a hundred years and more ago."

"By whom?"

"The clans who lived around here."

"What did they use them for?"

"They fortified them. In those days there was much clan warfare going on, that and cattle raiding. So they built houses on the islands and put up walls in places, usually against the beaches, so they could prevent their enemies from landing. If the island was big enough they would keep their cattle on them so that they could not easily be stolen. If they also went raiding they could leave their families there, too, knowing they would be safe."

"Are they used for anything now. Smuggling perhaps?" he suggested.

"No, not really. Their old buildings are in ruins. Perhaps a local fisherman may use them occasionally but people around here believe that they are haunted and most will not go near them."

"What makes them believe that?" I asked. "I thought all of that nonsense stopped years ago."

"You have to remember, gentlemen," replied Cameron "that this is a very remote area and beliefs linger on. Many people who live around here have clan links going back a long way, well before the uprising in '45."

"Uprising?"

"Aye, the last Jacobite uprising which ended at Culloden in 1746."

"That was a long time ago, Mr. Cameron" I said.

"Indeed it was, Dr. Watson, but people have long memories. Much blood was spilt and vile deeds committed. Later on, of course, came the clearances when many poor, hard working folk lost their lands to English landlords who wanted them for sheep."

"I see, Mr. Cameron, but how do these islands fit in to this?"

"Oh, it's just talk, what with all the fighting that took place. People around here sometimes say that on some nights, usually when it's dark and the wind is blowing down the glens and across the loch, that lights can be seen over there." He said, looking across at the nearest tree-clad island, "these stories get exaggerated of course but it feeds the minds of the ignorant to be sure."

"You don't believe it then?"

"No, I do not. But when I was a wee bairn my grandmother used to tell me tales. And if it were a stormy night I would snuggle down and fall asleep listening to her stories of life here in the Highlands when she was a young girl."

"Do people still hold on to their clan allegiances?" I asked. "I know that tribal peoples all around the world needed to bond together for safety, the gathering of food and so on. I would have thought it now unnecessary, in these modern times."

"You would have thought so, Dr. Watson," Cameron replied, "but up here at least old ways die hard and there is still much pride in the old clan system. Often old slights between clans are well remembered."

It went silent for a while, as if we were all remembering the times of long ago when the clans gathered and raiding parties would venture forth into the night.

The afternoon was now passing into early evening and the light was starting to fade. An easterly breeze had sprung up, sending ripples across the loch. We stayed sitting silently in the boat, resting from the exertions of the afternoon. Suddenly Holmes looked up. "Are we moving?" he said, "I am sure that the island is still where it was some minutes ago. We should have drifted nearer to the shore by now."

I looked down at the rope. It was pulling, gently taut, as it held the boat against the breeze whilst the hook was clearly lodged against an object on the bed of the loch. Holmes and I both reached out and pulled hard on the rope. The grappling hook remained firm as our boat was slowly pulled up into the face of a sudden cold breeze.

"I think we may have it, Watson," exclaimed Holmes as Duncan Cameron quickly came forward. "It could be," he said, "I am sure that it must be around here somewhere." He peered down into the water as if by so doing his eyes could penetrate the murky depths and locate the elusive vessel. We pulled again, this time with the combined effort of all three of us. The boat again pulled up into the increasing wind. Waves were now forming, growing in size as the wind gathered in strength. The rope became vertical in the water as our boat was pulled down by our efforts.

"You're right, Mr. Homes, we have it for certain. The hook has located it and is held firmly. We are right over it now," shouted Cameron.

"Can we at least loosen the boat from the bottom by tonight do you think?" I asked. He looked around him. "If we are quick, Dr. Watson, we may even succeed in bringing it up to the surface but we do not have long. There is much to do yet."

"Let's see if we are able to raise it off the bottom at least," Holmes called out. "If we know we can do that then we may not need to finish building the raft." As he spoke a large wave hit the side of our own small boat and sent water cascading over us. The three of us again stood up in the boat and heaved on the now taut line.

"I think I can feel it moving," I said, more in hope than anything. Again another wave hit the boat covering us in spray.

"It is getting too rough to stay here," shouted Cameron above the sound of the increasing wind.

"I will drop the buoy down here to mark where it is and make for the shore now. If we don't soon we will join Sir Hugh's boat on the bottom of the loch."

At that, he picked up the rope holding the buoy and after tying it securely to the rope, which was now fast to the sunken boat, threw it over the side. Without waiting any longer he threw himself at the oars and sped us back across to the shore.

We leaped onto the beach.

"None too soon," observed Holmes, looking back and seeing the size of the waves through which we had just passed.

"Aye, the wind can rise very quickly here at times and you have to keep a close eye on the weather." As he spoke, Holmes and I helped him pull the boat higher on to the shingle. It started to rain heavily and we ran for the shelter of the boathouse.

"It'll not last long, gentlemen. Tonight there should be a full moon and in my experience the weather should have cleared again by then." Even as he spoke the sudden squall was starting to ease. We passed through the open door. Stepping inside I looked around at the interior Holmes had examined so carefully the day before. Cameron had been busy. A number of containers were now stacked around the floor. Duncan Cameron joined us.

"I had these brought down this morning," he said, pointing. "They should fit well underneath the raft and give us all the buoyancy we will need."

"Yes," replied Holmes stepping over to them. "I am sure that they will prove to be adequate. We can always add more if required."

"I can fit one of the small winches if necessary, gentlemen, but we'll try to lift Sir Hugh's boat without them if we can."

We all nodded in agreement as our discussion subsided. We stood quietly, looking out across the loch, listening to the wind.

"Hello, is anyone in there?" A man appeared at the door. "I was nearby and saw you take shelter here. I was walking by the loch, and was caught in the squall as well. May I come in?"

"Of course you may," replied Cameron.

Our new visitor stepped inside. Before Cameron could say more our visitor spoke. "My name is Harrison by the way." He shook hands with us both as we introduced ourselves. He was a slim man in his early fifties and of small stature. His skin colour made me think of tropical climates and of the Europeans I had met whilst in India.

"Mr. Harrison is one of the laird's group of ornithologists, Mr. Holmes," volunteered Cameron.

"Indeed, I am," enthused Harrison. "Birds of prey are my speciality, particularly *Aquila chrysaetos.*"

"*Aquila* what?"

"Golden eagle, Doctor," Holmes confided.

"Ah, I see that you are a fellow enthusiast Mister, er ... did I hear your name was Holmes?"

"Yes, it is Sherlock Holmes, and this is my friend and colleague, Dr. Watson."

"Not the famous detective from London? This is indeed a privilege. May I enquire if you are on holiday?"

"Just for a few days. We felt that the Highland air would brush away some of the cobwebs of London."

"Yes, I can understand that. Are you ... er ... on a case as well at all?" Harrison looked around him, seeing the containers. "I say how interesting, are you building a raft? I saw some logs out on the beach as well. What fun. Are you going to do a spot of fishing? A raft will be very stable I should think."

"We would prefer a boat, Mr. Harrison, but as you may have seen we have had some problems"

"Oh, dear," replied Harrison, "yes, I heard that there were some difficulties, perhaps Mr. Holmes and Dr. Watson can help."

"I doubt it. Mr. Holmes and Dr. Watson are staying with Sir Hugh, Mr. Harrison," said Cameron.

"They are our guests for just a few days, just to relax for a while, away from the hustle and bustle of a large city."

"How wonderful," responded Harrison, changing the subject, "I do envy you, staying with Sir Hugh ... such a lovely house. How is Miss McFarlane by the way, I haven't seen her recently?"

"She is well enough, thank you, Mr. Harrison," said Cameron.

"Splendid, please give her my kind regards when you see her."

"Will you be coming to the ornithologists meeting, Mr. Harrison?" asked Cameron. "I believe Sir Hugh has one arranged shortly."

"Yes, I shall be giving a talk on my favourite subject," he replied looking outside. "I see it has stopped raining already and the wind eased, so I shall be on my way. Please excuse me. I hope to meet you all again there. It's been a pleasure. Goodbye."

"Goodbye, Mr. Harrison." He turned out through the boatyard door, walked along the beach passed the boat without looking and vanished into the trees.

"I assume that Mr. Harrison is a local man, Mr. Cameron," queried Holmes, waiting until Harrison had gone out of earshot.

"Yes, he lives on the far side of the village just a few miles away," he replied.

"I feel sure that he has spent some time abroad, in the tropics," went on Holmes, "the colour of his skin suggests that to me. I am sure that you noticed, too, Watson."

"Yes, I did Holmes. He had that look about him. It has that effect on the European skin after some time."

"Yes, Dr. Watson," replied Cameron, "rumour has it that he was out in India somewhere, working as some sort of colonial officer, paper official or similar. Not a very robust fellow. I believe that his health was affected and he came back here to recover."

"Has he been here long?"

"Only a couple of years or so. Seems to spend much of his time researching the various birds in this part of the Highlands, he has quite a reputation for his extensive knowledge. Has written a few papers on the subject I believe."

"Does he do anything else?"

"No, I do not think so. Seems to manage on what he has."

Holmes peered out of the door and turned to Cameron, "The squall has passed I see. Shall we start work? Can the raft be completed by tonight do you think?"

"No, but we can get most of it ready now, and I will work on it later this evening. If necessary it can be finished off in the morning. Perhaps Mr. Holmes, you and Dr. Watson would kindly assist me. We can start by bringing over here the two largest logs. We will build it at the water's edge but it should be safe enough here tonight."

It was getting dark when we decided to finish for the night. We had worked hard and the framework was completed, needing only a few more logs to form a decking under which would be fitted the buoyancy containers.

"We can do no more now gentlemen. It will soon be too dark to see properly. But it will only take an hour or so to complete it."

"Are you returning with us to Inverdaigh Hall, Mr. Cameron?" I enquired.

"No, Dr. Watson "I'll stay here a while and tidy up before coming back. Later on the moon will give any light I may need to carry on with the work. The weather should be clear by then so I'll bid you both goodnight."

Chapter Seven

Cameron Goes Missing

I was awoken in the early morning by the sound of someone knocking hard on a door further down the corridor and a male voice calling urgently for Mr. Sherlock Holmes.

After a few moments I heard a door open followed by a brief animated conversation. I rose quickly and started to dress, aware by now from the general hubbub that something was clearly amiss. Moments later my friend knocked on my door.

"Watson, are you awake?"

"How can I stay asleep with all the noise going on, Holmes, of course I am. What's happened?"

"Come downstairs as soon as you can, old fellow," he replied, without giving further details. His voice was sounding anxious and strained. I hurriedly finished dressing and quickly made my way down. As I entered the large study I was confronted by a group of people engaged in earnest conversation.

"Ah, Doctor, there you are," said Holmes, turning to me. "I am glad you're here, we may be in need of your services soon." The concern I heard earlier in his voice was now clearly reflected in his face.

"What has happened?" said I, addressing the group as a whole. Caroline McFarlane answered.

"It is Duncan," she said, "he has gone missing. No-one has seen him since last night Dr. Watson, and we are very concerned as to what might have happened to him."

"Who saw him last?"

"I think that it may have been me, sir," said the footman, stepping forward. "I was just telling Sir Hugh and Mr. Holmes that I saw him about an hour after you both returned from being at the loch."

"It seems, Holmes, that Cameron came back as he said to us that he would, after finishing his work on the raft. He collected his own fishing tackle and then apparently made his way back."

"He did not say to us that he would be going fishing," replied Holmes, looking questioningly at me.

He turned to the footman. "Did he say why he was going fishing at that time?"

"No, sir, but he seemed to have just the usual equipment fishermen have." He looked around as if seeking confirmation that he had done no wrong. "But he was wearing that old coat and hat of Sir Hugh's, the ones you gave him a while back," he said as an after thought turning to the Laird. I saw Holmes's eyebrows rise.

"Don't concern yourself," Sir Hugh said to his servant, "you've done well." He turned to Holmes, "What do you wish us to do now, Mr. Holmes?"

"I think, Sir Hugh, that we must go down to the loch immediately and find out whether he did actually go fishing. When we know that we can decide further."

As the group broke up and prepared to make their way along to the loch, Holmes turned to me and said in almost a whisper, "This is a bad business, Watson. I fear the worst for Cameron. If harm has come to him I shall blame myself."

"You mustn't do that, Holmes. We warned him to be careful; one cannot do more than that. In any case we do not know that he has come to any harm yet," I said unconvincingly.

Holmes put his hand on my shoulder. "Good old Watson, always a friend and supporter."

As he said this there was a noise outside in the hall. A servant lad came running into the house. "Sir Hugh, someone has just told me that a boat has been seen out on the loch. No-one can be seen in it from over here." We all exchanged anxious glances.

"I have instructed the pony and trap to be made ready gentlemen," said Sir Hugh speaking to us both.

He turned to his daughter, "Caroline, would you stay here and organise a search of the grounds, just in case ..." He left the remainder of the sentence unfinished as if not wanting to express his fears for the safety of his trusted gillie.

Some minutes later, after a fast trot down to the loch side, we arrived at the spot where we had left Duncan Cameron the previous evening.

"By Jove, Holmes, there's a boat right over on the far side of the loch," I exclaimed as I pointed out in the distance. "It looks like it may be your other boat, Sir Hugh. The one we were using only yesterday."

Holmes put his glass to his eye. "Yes it has drifted right across. It seems to be against some rocks. Sir Hugh, have we another boat available?"

"The early steam ferry should be along soon. I'll speak to the captain and have it commandeered when it gets here. He and Cameron knew one another well so he will not object I am sure. It should not take long."

The three of us immediately set off and followed the footpath, which wound through the undergrowth and trees. On arriving at the landing stage we could see the ferry approaching and as it drew up alongside Sir Hugh stepped aboard. He spoke briefly to the captain and we were soon making our way across the loch with all the steam the stoker could raise. Within minutes we were fast approaching the small boat and could see that something was obviously wrong. Over the bow a rope hung loosely and as we closed with it any lingering doubts we may have entertained as to its ownership were dispelled, as it was clear that it was, indeed, the boat we were using the previous day. The last we had seen of Duncan Cameron was him standing by it after finishing our work on the raft as we returned to Inverdaigh House.

The boat's oars were now hanging loose in their rowlocks as if the oarsman had suddenly given up rowing and left his seat without bothering to bring them back into the boat. The hull was gently moving with the motion of the waves, constantly being nudged against some rocks forming the base of a steep cliff at the edge of the loch.

The steamer stopped a few yards away, its propeller churning as it was brought to a halt.

"It is too shallow to get closer, Sir Hugh," stated the captain. "We will try and get a line to it," as a deckhand moved up to the steamer's bow and threw a 'Turk's head'. At his second attempt he succeeded in catching it around the front thwart of the small craft and, after pulling it over, secured it against us as the steamer slowly backed away. We could see no sign of anyone aboard.

"We need to have a look at it on the beach where it is kept, Sir Hugh. We cannot examine it properly here. There are too many eyes!"

"Very well, Mr. Holmes. The ferry captain will take us back across and then he can resume his normal route."

No one spoke very much during the short sad return journey across the loch, as it was clear that something sinister had befallen Duncan Cameron during the night.

On arriving back at the beach we jumped off down into the shallow water, unfastened the small craft from the steamer and pulled it ashore. The steamer backed away, spun around and with just a brief toot from the captain, resumed its journey down the loch. The three of us then turned to examine the beached craft.

"What do you think happened, Holmes? The rope with the hooks attached has been cut."

"Yes, and with a sharp knife."

"Did Cameron normally carry one, Sir Hugh?"

"Yes, probably, most of us do so when out fishing."

Holmes leaned over and looked into the boat, "And did he normally carry one of these as well?"

As he spoke, he reached inside and pulled out what looked like a long fishing spear. "What do you make of that,

Watson?" said Holmes, showing it to me. I could see that it was a long wooden spear, constructed with a number of barbs, probably used by a primitive tribe. It was clearly well made and, well wielded close up, could prove to be a most formidable weapon.

"Where exactly was it, Holmes?" I asked.

"Just lying in the bottom of the boat," he replied. "There seemed to be no attempt to hide it underneath anything. It was just readily available to hand if needed."

Holmes took out his large magnifying glass, examined it closely, smelt it, then turning to Sir Hugh, passed the weapon across to him. "Have you seen this before, Sir Hugh?"

"Yes," he replied, surprised, "but not recently. It is from my own collection, a fishing spear from the Solomon Islands."

"Why would he need that?" I queried.

"I do not know," replied Sir Hugh. "We do have some big fish hereabouts; I suppose he thought that it would be helpful to bring them in. Duncan must have looked it out specially. It was kept locked away in a cabinet."

"I do not think that it was for any fish in these waters, gentlemen," replied Holmes. There is a gaff hook lying in the boat as well. Perhaps he had in mind a bigger type of fish, eh." As Holmes said this he stepped over the gunnels of the small boat, climbed inside and peered around.

I leaned over into the boat and could see that a box of fishing flies was overturned and the contents left floating around. Strewn about were a number of fishing hooks of various sizes, some still attached to their fishing lines. Holmes was now closely examining the inside of the boat.

"The water has washed over much of the equipment," he said, as much to himself as anyone. "See here though, Watson, look, despite the water, there is clearly some blood splashed around."

Holmes pointed to some dark stains around the hull and on the centre thwart. "That often happens, Mr. Holmes," replied Sir Hugh, looking over Holmes's shoulder. "It could be from any fish Duncan may have caught last night, as he

91

clearly intended to do. Look at all the fish scales lying around in the boat and in the water. Does that not prove it?"

"Yes," conceded Holmes, "but we need to keep an open mind. We do not know for certain where this blood is from."

"Perhaps he may have had an accident, Holmes," I suggested. "After all, we know that he had a sharp fishing knife. Could he not have just cut his hand?"

"Where is the knife then?" returned Holmes, "and who was it who cut the rope to the grappling hooks?"

"Well he may have been making some adjustment to the line," suggested Sir Hugh hopefully, "and in the process cut himself and the knife slipped overboard."

"Was he then the same person who also released our marker buoy, Sir Hugh?" said Holmes.

We all looked up and across the loch to where the marker buoy had been placed yesterday. It was gone.

"Our grappling hooks and net are probably still attached to your boat, Sir Hugh, and, along with most of their rope, are lying on the bottom. To bring your boat up to the surface we shall have to start over again. Even the extra ones have gone. They had been left here in the boat." Holmes turned to me and said, "Someone objects to our work here, wouldn't you say so, Watson?"

"Indeed I would, Holmes," I said nodding my agreement. "But why harm Cameron, he was by himself and it is Sir Hugh who we believe is the intended victim."

"I believe that he had suspicions of his own which he was unwisely pursuing and before he had time to tell us, the criminal struck."

"Do you think that he is dead then?" asked Sir Hugh, with a tone of voice that said he could not, or indeed would not, believe it unless seen with his own eyes.

Holmes paused before answering him directly, and then said, "I regret, Sir Hugh, that I believe it to be most likely. Something clearly happened out here on the loch last night, and I fear that Cameron may have come off the worse." Sir Hugh looked distraught and his shoulders sank as if wearied by a burden he could no longer carry. He went on, "Duncan

Cameron has been with our family for many years Mr. Holmes, and I will do all I can to find out his murderer if that is indeed what has happened." He then fell silent.

"This mystery continues to deepen, Sir Hugh, and we must prepare ourselves for more dangers yet before it is over. You may of course continue to rely on myself, and Dr. Watson, to assist all we can. We have known Cameron only a short while but can understand the great respect and admiration your family held for him. Now, with your permission, I wish to continue with my investigations." He turned and went on, "Let us have a look at the raft whilst we are here. We may yet find some use for it. It is nearly completed I see."

We all walked across to where it lay floating by the water's edge. The buoyancy containers were lying nearby, clearly having been moved there by Cameron the previous evening.

"It seems not to have been touched. What do you think, Doctor?"

"Yes, it seems perfectly all right to me, Holmes, exactly as we left it in fact." He was looking carefully over the raft as we spoke. Pausing for a moment he stood up, then turned and looked back over at the buoyancy containers.

"Yes, it does, Doctor, but let us look at these as well, although from here they seem to have been untouched." Splashing back out of the water he walked across.

"Not so; we are wrong, look here." He had taken out his magnifying glass and, after looking at the edges of the containers, passed it to me. "Look carefully just along here." He pointed to the rim on the cap on the first of them. It had been damaged just enough to ensure that it would not be airtight. "And all the others I suspect," he said. After a brief examination I passed the magnifying glass to Sir Hugh. He examined them each in turn and looked up. "They have all been damaged," he said.

"Just enough to make it difficult, if not impossible, for us to make use of them," said Holmes.

"Without those the raft would not work in the way intended. They were needed to give it the extra buoyancy to lift your boat, Sir Hugh."

"Yes, Mr. Holmes, whoever has done this he has clearly put a stop to any work on raising my boat, at least for a while." He paused in thought, then went on, "In view of what has happened gentlemen, I am sure you will understand that I must now call in the police. They will need to instigate a full search and official enquiry. In cases such as this they will also have to inform the procurator fiscal, its procedure you know."

"Naturally," Holmes replied. "We will need a properly organised search for him. We cannot do it by ourselves."

"When you return to Inverdaigh House would you kindly arrange for that, Sir Hugh? Meanwhile I would like to take a look at yonder island. We cannot use this boat here," said Holmes, pointing to the recovered boat, although it has given us all the clues it can yield, the police will no doubt wish to examine it as well. I would not wish to deny them the chance to draw their own conclusions, eh, Watson."

As Holmes said this he gave me a glance as if to say that he had little confidence in their investigatory methods here in Scotland any more than those in London.

"Is there no other boat available, Sir Hugh?"

"Well, Mr. Holmes, the only boat we have nearby is a canoe, old but serviceable. It is usually kept around the corner, tucked away in the trees, moored alongside a houseboat we use in better weather. Would you like to see it?"

"It sounds ideal, Sir Hugh, are you ready for a paddle, Doctor?"

"If you insist, Holmes, but they can be very unstable you know. I used one as a boy."

Sir Hugh chuckled despite himself. "I should not worry Dr. Watson, I feel sure that you will regain your skills. No one has overturned it yet. Caroline used it as a young girl."

As we were talking, Sir Hugh led us along the beach and across a small tree covered headland.

Pushing our way through we soon emerged by the side of a tiny sheltered inlet upon which a houseboat floated. Lying against it almost on the beach was the canoe. I breathed a sigh of relief on seeing it as it was clear that although of open design it was for a canoe quite broad of beam, making it more stable than most.

"I think that will meet your needs for the moment," said Sir Hugh.

"Thank you," replied Holmes, "this will be excellent."

"Splendid," retorted Sir Hugh. "In that case, I will leave you to your little voyage. I will be away now to Inverdaigh House to help organise the police search. Perhaps I will see you both later on, after you've seen over the island?"

"Yes, but I think that for the moment it will be prudent to say nothing of our visit to the island, at least not yet. Please leave that to me. The police can look over it later if they so wish."

"As you say, Mr. Holmes, I will tell them nothing of it. I will leave it to you to inform them when you are ready."

With that Sir Hugh turned on his heels and disappeared away through the trees.

"Well, Watson," said Holmes turning to me, "will it suffice do you think?"

"Yes, Holmes, I am sure it will, better than I had hoped for," I said.

With that Holmes pulled the canoe further up the beach and looked inside. It was empty save for several paddles and a bow rope.

"These are all we will need," he said, standing up and looking around him.

"Almost a secret place I think, and very sheltered. There is hardly a breath of wind," he went on. The only sound came from a small stream trickling down on the far side. I looked around me. We were almost totally surrounded by trees, the only gap being where the inlet emerged into the loch. The island itself could not be seen as the trees by the entrance obscured the view.

"Shall we go now, Doctor?" said Holmes, interrupting my thoughts.

"Of course, Holmes," I replied as we climbed into our craft and pushed away from the beach. Easing our way through the trees at the entrance, we moved out onto the open loch, the canoe sliding easily through the water as we paddled on, saying nothing. The loch had a dull, lifeless, leaden look, our wake quickly dispersing into flatness. A short distance away a fish leapt out making barely a sound, just leaving a slowly expanding ripple. We paddled on saying nothing, each engrossed in his own thoughts.

"Let's just wait here a moment please, Watson." We stopped paddling and drifted to a halt.

Holmes looked around, first at the island and then back across the loch.

It was me who broke the silence. "What is it, Holmes. Do you think that Cameron came to the island last night?" Holmes nodded.

"Yes, I suspect that he may have done, or at least was planning to. You remember what the young footman said to us this morning, that when he saw Cameron last night he had on Sir Hugh's old coat and hat and that he took along with him his fishing equipment. I believe that he had his suspicions and had taken it upon himself to follow them up. I also believe that he may have deliberately tried to impersonate Sir Hugh in the hope of luring out the criminal."

"If that is where the criminal was hiding out last night, Holmes? Can you be certain?"

"No, I am not yet, but we must also recall that Cameron spoke of people seeing lights over here. It surely has a tale to tell. Look over there, I can see a small gap in the trees, we'll go in there, it is just room enough."

A few powerful strokes enabled us to propel the canoe forward with sufficient way to drive us up onto a small gravel beach. Holmes jumped out and pulling the canoe up higher, tied the bow rope to a low overhanging branch. I followed to join him, splashing through the shallow water. Standing in the silence we looked around us. I felt a drop of water fall onto the back of my head and roll slowly down against my collar. A small bird called, then flew off as it became aware that strangers were close by and should be avoided. From under the gravel, water seeped up to form small puddles beneath our shoes.

"Rather spooky, Holmes," I spoke into the stillness.

"Yes, some would see it that way of course, but to me, old fellow, it is just a puzzle to solve. We need to ask where does it fit into the whole picture of events around here." Holmes looked around. Behind us against the edge of the shelving beach we could see the remains of a low wall, now crumbling as vegetation eroded its structure. Climbing on to it he made his way around some large trees, then nearly disappeared as he went down on all fours. Emerging on the far side he stood up looking carefully at their trunks as he went from one to another. From time to time he stopped and peered out across the loch.

"Can you find any signs that Cameron was here last night, Holmes? He may have been following up on that rumour of lights."

"Yes possibly, Doctor, but I can see nothing here to indicate that he actually came onto the island last night, although there are signs that people have been here, but, of course, that is just to be expected."

"What sort of signs, Holmes?"

"Just fishing, there are some used flies around, and bits of line and bent hooks. Nothing beyond that at the moment. Any marks on the beach would have long faded. Even ours are fast disappearing. I would like to look over the island though. All around here seems to be part of the defences of long ago, of times when the local clans used the islands to protect themselves," he said pointing to walls nearby. "See how the trees and undergrowth have grown through."

Holmes suddenly stood still and started to sniff the air. "Watson, can you smell anything?"

"What sort of smell, all I can detect is the fresh smell of plants and trees?"

"Are you sure, try again?"

Like two carnivores trying to locate their prey, we stood by that small beach under the trees smelling the air.

"Well, Holmes, for what its worth I think I can just make out a slight smell of fish, fish and wood smoke."

"That's just what I mean Doctor. Someone has been here very recently and lit a small fire. The smoke aroma can linger for days under the right circumstances. If you remember, once the squall we were caught in last evening had passed, the weather was very calm so almost certainly it was lit then."

"Perhaps Cameron did come here last night, caught some fish and lit a fire with which to cook them," I suggested.

"But why do that when he could have gone back to Inverdaigh House and had them cooked for him, say for breakfast?"

"Perhaps he enjoyed the taste of fish being cooked outside on an open fire."

"Is that why he took along that dangerous fish spear then Doctor, to hold the fish over the fire? No," he chuckled, "he didn't need to go to that length when a simple twig would do. It is quite obvious that he was anticipating trouble and that he took it along for self-defence."

"If so, Holmes, then it did not help him much it would seem. It was still in the boat."

Holmes gave no answer, then said, "Let's each of us go around the island from opposite directions, Doctor, and see what we can find. Once we meet up on the far side we can then examine anything else in the centre. The place is so overgrown. Anything can be hidden there so I would mind your step, old friend," he warned.

As with the previous morning in the woodland, Holmes and I set off in opposite directions. Within seconds I was engulfed in undergrowth of plants, bushes and lush leaves. This time, however, fast movement was out of the question as nearly every time I stepped forward, I came upon the remains of the past. Several times after placing my foot down carefully, I felt the ground under it give way as a piece of stone, once forming part of an old building, rolled over on its soft bed of moss, in which it was covered. I passed alongside walls of undergrowth, which I found to be hiding the remains of what once had obviously been a house. I was obliged to crawl around trees, and once leapt over a gap seemingly designed to break the legs of the unwary. Once I nearly fell into a large hole, the bottom of which I could not see. Eventually, bathed in sweat and out of breath, I reached the far side of the island. Here I found Holmes already waiting for me, as I swung down from an overhanging branch to join him. After gathering my breath, I outlined briefly what I had found.

"Well done, Watson, now come over and look at this." He led me around a large tree and along a barely discernable track, which ran through undergrowth around the edge of the island. He stopped, "See over there, Watson," he indicated to the remains of a low wall, which opened out into a wide gully full of water like a small quay. "This is where a boat could be brought in directly from the loch. We are now, of course, on the opposite side from where we landed. When in here the overhanging trees would completely hide it from anyone passing the island. And see over here," he pointed over to where steps had been cut into the rock.

"Let me show you, old friend," said Holmes, "but be careful, the steps are very slippery." Climbing cautiously, Holmes made his way up. I followed on, several times nearly slipping back before arriving at the top. In front of us was a flat open area, well surrounded by trees and yet more ruined walls. What, however, held our attention were lines of fish skewered by poles. Under them were the remains of several small fires.

"There's our answer, Doctor and I see that some are still warm," he said, as he moved embers with his feet and felt around with his hands.

"Poachers, Holmes, surely."

"So it would seem," he said, "he must have been very busy last night." As we talked, Holmes walked over looking carefully at the lines of hanging fish. Over to one side stood a large metal pot. He went over, peered in and using a large twig he found nearby, stirred around the glutinous mass inside.

"Planning on some cookery, Holmes," I laughed.

Holmes chuckled. "Not with this I think, look over here as well."

I went over to a large flat rock upon which were lying piles of fish skins. "A poacher's hoard it looks like to me. Probably enough to see them through the winter. Who can blame them with many mouths to feed?"

"Yes, Doctor," replied Holmes, "I am sure that you are right. I think though that for the moment we will say nothing about this."

"Do you not consider it relevant then?"

"Yes it is, but possibly not in the way it may at first appear, anyway I want to show you something else I have found. Come and look at this."

Saying no more Holmes turned around, walked across to the steps we had just ascended and with great care made his way back down. With some difficulty I followed him and we were soon standing back by the water filled gully. Holmes led the way but we had gone only a few paces when we were immediately forced to stop against the base of a high wall which looked as if it was once the side of a substantial building. Growing over it was a mass of ivy. I turned to the side with a view to making my way around this obstacle. Realising it could not be done I turned back. Holmes had vanished.

"Where are you, Holmes?" I called. "In here, Doctor," he replied, as at that moment he reappeared directly out of the wall of ivy in front of me; I gasped and almost fell backwards in the gully of water.

"How did you get in there, Holmes?" I asked astonished.

"Because the original inhabitants thoughtfully built a tunnel Watson. It starts here where they could bring in a boat and if I am right it will lead us directly under a fortified house built in the centre of the island. I have no light with me so I cannot follow it far. There must have been a strong door fitted here at one time but now it is totally overgrown. See how the wall was built to subtly follow around the contours of this ledge of rock. The entrance is brilliantly concealed and whilst it's in ruins now the wall would undoubtedly have been an ideal platform for the defenders if attacked."

"I wonder," said Holmes, half muttering to himself, "it may just be ..." He left the sentence incomplete as I saw him reaching around in the ivy overhanging the entrance to our newly discovered tunnel. "If I had been in his place, Watson, it is what I would have done."

"What exactly are you trying to find, Holmes?"

"A lantern of sorts, Doctor, our criminal is certainly a man who takes much trouble over details. I doubt if he would have overlooked this, just a little patience should find it," he said as he continued.

Suddenly he gave a whoop of triumph and stepped back brandishing aloft a lantern. "Just as I said, Watson, he left it there last night. See the fresh soot. He has also left plenty of oil inside by the sound of it," shaking the lantern as he spoke. He had opened the front and was adjusting the wick cleaning from it the excess soot that it had accumulated.

"Do you have a match, Doctor? We will need light to explore this tunnel."

"No, I am afraid I don't, Holmes. In my hurry earlier I left them behind."

"So did I. Never mind, we will have to manage. If we are careful we may find out where it leads to."

So saying Holmes stepped forward into the tunnel and in a moment had disappeared through the wall of ivy and into the blackness beyond. With some trepidation I pushed the ivy aside and followed. Inside was pitch black. The climbing plant had so successfully covered the entrance that even from inside, almost no light could be seen through it.

"Are you there, Holmes?" I called. "Can't see a thing here." There was no reply. All I could hear was a faint scraping sound and a slow steady drip of water. The air had the scent of moist vegetation.

I moved forward very slowly, carefully placing one foot down at a time on the uneven floor. I seemed to have gone only a few yards when, suddenly, in my ear, Holmes spoke. "Stay exactly as you are, Watson," his voice echoing down the tunnel. "Good, now reach up here." At the sound of Holmes's voice so close I jumped, then following his instruction I reached up with my hand. A short way above my head my fingers came into contact with the roof of the tunnel. The surface was smooth and damp.

"If you feel around you should find a large hole." I did as Holmes bid, then after a few moments located the edge of what seemed to be a wide vertical shaft leading down from above.

"Yes, I have it, Holmes," I said.

"What do you believe it was for?"

"I am not sure," he replied, "some sort of defensive work or just possibly a way of carrying items up to the house above. It was surely linked to one and meant that things could be moved around inside. Particularly useful in bad weather don't you think. In winter the snow and rain must have made life very difficult."

"Yes, it certainly would, but how do you think the criminal may be using it?"

"It looks like he may have it as some sort of store. We cannot tell though unless we have some better light."

"Shall we return and collect a lantern from Inverdaigh House," I suggested.

"Yes, Doctor, but the police will be there soon, I am sure and I do not want them trampling around ruining any other clues which may be around. We can decide what to do when we find out who is there, and what actions they intend to take."

Saying no more we returned to the canoe and a brisk paddle saw us back at the inlet. It was with some relief that I climbed out and after pulling it from the water, we made our way back to Inverdaigh House.

"I see that the police have arrived already, Watson."

In front of the house now stood a carriage with the word POLICE printed on the side in large letters.

"It will be interesting, Watson, to find what inspiration the Highland Constabulary has to offer the good people around here. No doubt we will soon be acquainted with their best officer," said Holmes as we walked through into the main hall.

Chapter Eight

Inspector Lennox

"Mr. Holmes, it is indeed a privilege to meet you." A large bear of a man stepped forward and introduced himself. "I am Inspector Lennox of the Glasgow police." He held out a 'paw' and shook hands vigorously with Holmes. "I have heard so much about you from some of my London colleagues. I recognised you immediately. I believe that you have met with Inspectors Gregson and Lestrade," he said.

"Indeed I have. Inspector Lennox," replied Holmes. "I am well acquainted with them both. We have worked together from time-to-time. May I also introduce you to my good friend and colleague, Dr. Watson," he said turning to me.

It was my turn to be shaken by the hand and subjected to Inspector Lennox's effusive greeting. "Of course, I should have known," he said, "the famous Dr. Watson, the chronicler of Mr. Holmes's cases. We are all most grateful for your meticulous work Dr. Watson, without which we would all be none-the-wiser about many of the terrible crimes Mr. Holmes has helped to solve over the years." He smiled genially at us both as he spoke. "Why thank you, Inspector," I replied, feeling slightly embarrassed at his enthusiastic compliments.

"Not at all, Dr Watson, not at all, both my London colleagues have told me about the occasional help Mr. Holmes has been able to give. I understand that his slight re-alignment of their thoughts has enabled them to make a breakthrough in some of their more difficult and complex cases. I am most impressed."

I winced in spite of myself at hearing Inspector Lennox's comments on Holmes's 'occasional help' and of his slight realignment in their more difficult and complex cases. I immediately began musing over the many times they had approached my friend for help in cases where they were completely baffled. His skilled deductions had brought clarity to a murk of facts and motives, illuminated the hidden facets and finally led to the criminal's arrest. In one case at least, he saved an innocent man from the gallows.

Inspector Lennox interrupted my thoughts as he turned to the Laird and said, "Sir Hugh has been telling me about why he invited you here, gentlemen. A bad business don't you think. And now to make matters worse Sir Hugh's most trusted servant and key witness has disappeared in a most unfortunate accident and is most likely now dead. What do you make of it Mr. Holmes, Dr. Watson?" he said looking at us both.

I was about to reply when I saw Holmes shoot me a glance that required my silence. "Inspector Lennox," said Holmes smiling, "I am sure that Gregson and Lestrade have told you of my methods, that I require facts before making any deductions, especially in the more difficult and complex cases." His words, echoing those of Inspector Lennox just moments before, were not lost on him. The Inspector coughed quietly to himself in response. "To which 'accident' are you referring, Inspector?" Inspector Lennox paused for a moment, realising that he and Holmes were not necessarily interpreting the reason for Cameron's disappearance in the same way.

He went on in his Glaswegian accent, "Do you not believe that Mr. Cameron has met with a fatal accident, Mr. Holmes?"

"What, in your opinion, do the facts tell us, Inspector?"

Inspector Lennox, now beginning to look uncomfortable, evaded answering Holmes's direct question. To the Inspector it was clear as to what had happened, and he was surprised that anyone should question his views on that.

"Surely the facts are clear for us all to see," he replied with a hint of puzzlement in his voice. "From what Sir Hugh has told me we have enough evidence to conclude that Duncan

Cameron had died in an accident, last night, whilst fishing in the loch. Is it not obvious?" He looked at Sir Hugh as if to confirm him as a supporter to this view.

Holmes gazed at him steadily and Inspector Lennox looked even more uncomfortable, something to which he was clearly unaccustomed. Nevertheless he would not be put off and continued to emphasise his point.

"The facts show us that the boat Duncan Cameron went out in last night has been found, and that you brought it ashore and examined it for yourself. I understand, Mr. Holmes, that inside you found his fishing equipment in some disarray together with a spear from Sir Hugh's collection of weapons. There was also a small amount of blood in the boat. Sir Hugh has told me of it. To my mind all of this clearly points to a fishing accident, and that after injuring himself Duncan Cameron almost certainly fell out of the boat and was drowned."

"And the spear, Inspector?"

"What of it, Mr. Holmes?"

"Why did he take it?"

"Well, yes, but I believe that he likely took it along in lieu of needing it if he caught a big pike, say. They grow very large up here, Mr. Holmes." He grinned as he again turned to Sir Hugh as if to confirm his knowledge of local fisheries. "Anyway," he said, turning back to Holmes, "what else would he need it for out on a boat, on the loch, during the night?"

"That is not yet clear Inspector, but that Duncan Cameron is probably now dead and in the loch I would not argue. But what happened to him and why is, I believe, still open to question." Holmes looked at him and continued, "As the boat is available now do you wish to examine it yourself Inspector? Perhaps you may reach a differing conclusion, even throwing more light on the mystery. Any helpful observation of yours would I am sure be most welcome to us all. Don't you agree, Doctor?"

"Yes, I should think so Holmes, after all Inspector Lennox is a man of much experience in criminal matters," I responded, first looking at Holmes then across at the Inspector.

The Inspector paused as if not quite sure as to the motive behind my compliment. He was clearly uneasy about making any further statements that might not stand up to Holmes's detailed scrutiny.

"All in good time, Mr. Holmes, all in good time," he replied. "As you yourself have examined it there seems to be little point in me doing so right now. Perhaps later on, eh."

"As you wish, Inspector. We are of course at your disposal. It may be," he went on, "that any other clues we may subsequently find could well conflict with those we already have ... without realising it." Holmes's questioning tone over these last few words made it seem as if the whole matter was still, in his view, open to interpretation.

"I am sure that you have a point," said Inspector Lennox. From his manner and rather puzzled look however, I sensed that he was not entirely clear as to how this may affect his current investigations. Inspector Lennox was nothing if not persistent, and continued with his argument.

"Whilst I am sure that you have reasons for saying that, Mr. Holmes, I really cannot see how one man, alone in a sturdy boat, out in the loch, can be harmed by any malign action, even if there was a criminal who wished ill of him. It is just impossible to reconcile with anything else. After all Duncan Cameron was a tough, strong man who knew how to protect himself. He had served many years in the army and seen plenty of action in his time."

He paused again and looked around at us all as if seeking confirmation that he had now finally persuaded us to his views. He stood back and looked at us. I felt that he was like a predator looking at prey about to be devoured. Holmes just stood still, saying nothing.

The Inspector, realising that Holmes was still unconvinced decided to try another approach. He stepped forward and like a friendly overweight bear placed his hands upon our shoulders.

"Mr. Holmes and Dr Watson," he said, "we are men of the world, are we not? We have seen much of life's unpleasant side, and in our line of work it is so easy to see crime everywhere and in every unfortunate event. Don't you agree?" He again looked at us both, allowing us time to reflect yet more on the wisdom of his words and their implications for this case.

"Of course," he continued, "we shall naturally drag the loch and search for the body, in fact I have already arranged for this to be started today. But when we locate it I have no doubt that any clues we may find will still point to it being merely a fishing accident, that and no more." He smiled at us again with his seeming bonhomie, as if it summarised all the recent events and would bring about its own inevitable, though tragic conclusions.

"But what of the matter of Sir Hugh's boat sinking, Inspector. Surely that alone has some implications?" Inspector Lennox once again avoided Holmes's direct question.

"To be true, Mr. Holmes," he replied, "I do believe that Sir Hugh's life is in danger, and I am taking all necessary steps to have him protected."

"And they are?" Holmes asked again.

"I intend to have a constable stay at the house for a while, and another to call regularly and search the grounds. I shall, of course, pursue my own enquiries in the meantime. I have some ideas of my own about the problem, you see."

"Which you do not wish to share with us?"

"For the moment shall we say that it would be prudent to keep my own counsel on the matter. I am, however, confident that within the next few days I will lay my hands on the culprit and the case will be solved. Then you will both be free to return to London."

Holmes looked up and smiled. "In that case, Inspector," he said, "we will have had a pleasant change of air and scenery and no doubt be better for it. Don't you agree, Doctor," Holmes said, turning to me.

"Well yes, if you say so, Holmes. There would be no reason for us to stay any longer, as long as you believe that Sir Hugh would indeed then be safe." These last words of mine discreetly reflected the doubts I already harboured as to the accuracy of Inspector Lennox's deductions.

"Agreed then," said the Inspector, who by now, from his manner, had already in his mind, found the criminal, seen us away from his domain and out of his hair. He rubbed his hands together in an ill disguised sense of relief. "I did wonder," went on Inspector Lennox, "that after your visit to the loch this morning, whether, er, you may have found anything that may, er, be of some extra interest in this case. Apart from the boat that is. I would naturally still like to hear of any, shall we say, developments." He now spoke in a gentle questioning manner clearly seeking information and probing our own investigations. It seemed clear that despite his confident and genial manner of moments ago, that he still entertained doubts. Even at this stage he felt unable to completely hide them.

"Nothing of any significance," Holmes replied diffidently, "although those islands look to be most interesting. I am sure they have been used by local fishermen for centuries. I even wondered about trying a little fishing for myself, before we return to London that is."

"Yes, of course, Mr. Holmes," said the Inspector, realising that we may now be staying on with Sir Hugh for a while longer, and despite his hopes will not yet be out of his realm.

"Well now, I shall have to go and supervise the dragging of the loch for poor Duncan Cameron and look at his boat. I will keep you informed, Sir Hugh. Perhaps you gentlemen will excuse me." So saying, Inspector Lennox departed.

"What do you wish to do, Holmes?" I said, not believing for one moment his intentions to stay for some fishing.

Holmes turned to Sir Hugh. "I am not satisfied that the Inspector has reached anywhere close to solving the case. I believe that your life will still be in danger despite the Inspector's best efforts. I therefore intend to continue with my investigations, unless you object that is."

"No, of course not, I will be most happy for you to do so, and I know that Caroline will be, too."

"Yes, that is right." A woman's firm voice made us all turn around to find that Caroline had stepped into the room behind us. "I am afraid that I was listening at the door," she said, "and heard your discussions with the Inspector. I agree with Mr. Holmes. I want you both to stay until the real culprit is found, Mr. Holmes and Dr Watson," she smiled and nodded to us her confirmation. "In the meantime, gentlemen, luncheon is ready."

A chilly breeze had sprung up as Holmes and I returned to the loch, and I pulled my coat tighter around myself in response. Holmes pulled his hat down tighter, and as we gazed across the loch he lifted a 'glass' to his eye.

"I see that Inspector Lennox has been as good as his word, Watson. Look over there," he said, pointing to across the water. In the distance we could make out a fleet of small boats strung out in a long line and clearly linked together by ropes. Netting was being pulled in and out of the water between them. The Inspector had drafted in two of the local steamboats to assist and on the nearer we could make him out, directing operations. After a short while it was clear that one of his men had noticed our arrival and spoken to him. He turned to see us, and within a few minutes had called a boat alongside, clambered down into it and was being rowed rapidly over towards us.

Holmes and I made our way across to where we had left Duncan Cameron's boat that morning and reached it just as the Inspector's boat ground onto the beach alongside. He sprung out and waded through the shallow water.

"Well, gentlemen," he said walking up to us. "Here it is," now turning to Sir Hugh's boat beached alongside of him. "I have made a close examination as I said I would and found only what I expected to find," he said looking at us both. "Fishing items and some blood. But what else do you expect if he had been fishing and caught some fish, yes", he said, as if confirming the obvious to us all. As he spoke he looked inside the boat and pointed to all the fishing rods and equipment Cameron had been using. He reached in and pulled out Sir

Hugh's Solomon Islands fishing spear, which Holmes had left when we found it that morning.

"Unusual I admit," he said, "but it is a fishing spear, perhaps he wanted to try out a new technique. A big pike could be settled by using this," he went on, making a stabbing motion with it before returning it to the boat. "Could not the blood be his?" queried Holmes.

"Yes," replied the Inspector, "but if so doesn't that just point to an accident as I said earlier? He cut himself then fell overboard into the cold water and drowned. After all, how can any other harm have come to him out here alone in a small boat? Inspector Lennox's voice now carried an edge of exasperation as he so obviously felt that Holmes was taking over the investigation, and in the wrong direction as well.

Holmes smiled, "Very well, Inspector, perhaps you are right after all. A simple fishing accident explains it, what else?"

The Inspector visibly relaxed. "Splendid, what else, indeed? Then we all seem to agree that it can only have been a most tragic accident, to one of Sir Hugh's most loyal and valuable servants. It has clearly been a great blow to him. I do not know what he will do now. Cameron will not be replaced easily." He paused looking at us as if to join with him in mutual understanding of what had happened, but that he must now move on. Inspector Lennox looked across at us, "As far as you and Dr Watson are concerned, Mr. Holmes, do I recall you saying that you would like to visit one of our islands, possibly for some fishing yourself. Like to give it a try perhaps, a wonderful sport you know."

"Yes, I would, but I will of course need access to a boat." Inspector Lennox's mood had now changed, and he seemed to be of the view that it was in his best interest to help us in any way he could.

"That will be no problem, I will get my constable here to clear Cameron's boat, then you can use that." I almost sensed that he was humming to himself, as if he had a huge burden lifted from him and life was sweet again.

It did not take long for the boat to be cleared of all of Cameron's fishing equipment and placed neatly in a pile on the beach.

"I will have them collected later and taken to Inverdaigh House," went on the Inspector, "but won't you need some fishing rods for yourselves?" he queried.

"Yes, of course," replied Holmes, "but as beginners I think we would be better to take a look for possible places first. After all there are many trees there and I can see that it would be easy to get a line caught. Perhaps afterwards we can come back and collect some equipment. What do you say, Doctor?" asked Holmes turning to me.

"Good idea," I replied, "we can also bring a picnic basket with us."

"Yes," returned the Inspector slightly hesitantly, "I see your point, gentlemen. Stake out the land first, eh." He smiled as if now being convinced of our motive for going to the island was just for finding a fishing site, and would be the first part of us leaving any further investigations solely to him. In this he was to be disappointed. His face fell as Holmes then said, "You will, of course, let me know when you do find poor Duncan Cameron, Inspector. I would like to find out how he died. We had come to know and admire him, and would naturally like to pay our respects. I am sure that you understand."

"Why, yes, of course, Mr. Holmes, I will see to it personally, have no fear. Sir Hugh will of course need to arrange things with relatives and friends. In the meantime I really must return to my work on dragging the loch. Perhaps you will both excuse me again."

With that Inspector Lennox climbed into his boat and made his way back across the loch to his awaiting steamer.

I turned to Holmes, "You did not really mean for us to look for a fishing site on the island. After all we were only over there this morning. I also find it hard to believe that you will now leave everything to the Inspector."

Holmes laughed, "Of course not, old friend, but I want to look more closely at that tunnel. I suspect it has more to tell us, and we can examine it at leisure whilst Inspector Lennox is organising the search for poor Cameron. Later on I believe that he will come over himself to look it over. In fact, I will encourage him to do so."

"Won't he find the fish skins as we did?"

"Of course, Doctor. It will be interesting to find what he makes of it all. I do not want the police to go trampling around there just yet, until we have finished that is. There may be other possibilities which can be considered."

"If you say so, Holmes. I am sure that you will tell me when you are ready. Do you wish to go over there now?"

"Yes, the sooner we go back and explore that tunnel the better. It has been a challenging day, with more yet to come I am sure."

Chapter Nine

The Hidden Tunnel

It took only a few minutes for me to row us back across to the island.

"Let us find the hidden quay, Watson, it will save us climbing around the ruins and take us right outside of the tunnel entrance."

I did as Holmes suggested and as we swung around the back of the island, I could see across the loch and in the distance, a string of boats looking for Duncan Cameron.

"Over to our left should do it, Doctor," said Holmes, as he guided our boat through into the small quay cut into the rocks by hands of long ago. We bumped against it, and I leaned over to hold us steady as Holmes stepped out and tied us to a protruding rock. Moments later I joined him as he took out of his coat a small folding lamp. Walking up to the wall of ivy he reached in and found the lantern still in place where we had found it earlier that day. "I think a light each will do, Watson, don't you," he said as he struck a Lucifer. Moments later, with both oil lamps lit, we pushed our way through the ivy and entered the tunnel.

"This is much better, Holmes," I said as we moved along the tunnel and within a short distance found the vertical shaft above our heads which a short while ago we had located with only our hands. Holding up our oil lamps we could see that the tunnel was hewn out of solid rock but in places had also been lined with bricks. The floor was uneven and we walked along slowly, placing our feet carefully, mindful of a twisted ankle. In places, small parts of the tunnel roof had fallen onto the floor. Water seeped down through the walls.

After walking a short distance we emerged into an underground room. Holding up our flickering lamps we looked around us. The room was around twenty feet square and presumably had once been used as a storeroom. Against one of the side walls stood a ladder which reached up against the ceiling. On the opposite side, we could see an entrance to another tunnel which led away into the darkness. In the centre of the room, however, stood a solid wooden table. Holmes walked over to it.

"Why is that here, Holmes?" I asked. "I cannot see much use for it in this situation."

"That is not clear yet old friend unless you do not want to be seen using it," he replied.

"But what is it for, Holmes? There is no food stored here. I can see no sign of anything although you will remember the fish we found outside only this morning?" I asked, answering my own question.

"No, you're right, but I do not believe that the recent user had food in mind. Look over here."

Holmes had moved over to one of the walls and looked at them carefully. "Can you see these," he said, pointing out to me a number of round recesses. "What do you make of them?"

I joined him and with the help of my lamp placed my own fingers into the holes.

"They are not very deep, only a few inches at most. Some seem to run into one another."

"Yes, Watson, but why, there must be at least a dozen."

"It looks as though someone was starting to enlarge the room, either that or make another tunnel, Holmes. My view is that someone wanted to make a recess of sorts and he has only just started on the work."

"Yes, perhaps. Lets see what else we can find."

Holmes looked around him. Even though the light was very poor, we could both make out on the opposite wall, three small metal rings which were hanging loose. He walked over and reaching out lifted them up one by one. Then with the help of his oil lamp he peered closely at their fixings on the wall.

"What do you make of these?" he asked again.

I went over and on close examination I could see that they were held by strong metal pins which had been driven deeply into the wall. I lifted up one of the rings and pulled on it as hard as I could. It was fixed so well that even with all my effort it would not move an inch.

"Well, whoever put them there intended them to stay in place."

I looked up. "It seems to me that they were linked to some sort of hoist, probably up to a door in the ceiling. They could then raise or lower items as they required. It would make it a lot easier than constantly carrying them up ladders."

"Well done, Watson, but what would they need to carry up and why? If they brought in food or anything else it would need to come by boat. Such items could then be transported by the steps outside. Whoever it was, they needed them to be held firmly enough so that even with a heavy load they would not come loose. Let's have a look at the floor now, although it is so hard I doubt if we will find it has much to tell us."

As with the previous day at the boathouse, and with the reluctant help of his flickering oil lamp, Holmes carefully worked his way around the floor. Even with our poor light it was clear that he was still able to find items of interest. Several times he reached down, picked up something and placed it in his pocket. After some minutes of careful scrutiny he stood up.

"Let's now examine the table, Watson," he said, as he walked over to it. "It's very solid," he went on, musing to himself.

The table was wooden and clearly of very strong construction with metal reinforcing pieces at the corners. Suddenly and without any warning he leapt up upon it and started jumping up and down. I looked up at him in amazement. "I say, Holmes, is this a new form of exercise? I might come up and join you," I laughed.

"Please do so, Doctor, there is just room for us both, but I don't think that it will make any difference."

"What difference do you mean?"

"That this table, like the rings in the wall is made to take a lot of weight and sudden impacts. See, it has not moved an inch. Not many tables of this size will stand that for long."

He leapt down and looked around at its top.

"There is not much of any interest, Doctor, except these holes, the pressure marks on the edges, the grooves around the top and the sides that is." As he said this, Holmes pointed out to me the various parts he had identified. .

"Where, Holmes, I cannot see them?"

"You can be forgiven for that, old friend, as we are not in daylight, but a careful look will show you. See here." I looked more closely.

"Try this, Doctor," Holmes passed me his magnifying glass. I was just able to make out a number of small circles on the table top.

"They have been filled in Holmes," I said, "to make it smoother to work on I suppose."

"Yes, it is clear that he had finished with their use and found a better way of working. Now look here," he said pointing at some others. "Some of the tops of these holes have become distorted. Whatever he was using them for was damaging the surrounding wood, it was not strong enough so he had to find a different way of using it. The load on the edges was too great, which is why he did this."

As he spoke he ran his hands along the sides of the top and invited me to do the same. Moving my own fingers along I was able to just discern the edges of a slight indentation.

"And here, too," he said, pointing out another set. Again I felt with my fingers to confirm his observations.

"Could they not have been made before the table came here, Holmes?" I asked, questioning his views.

"Possibly, Doctor, but it is unlikely. It is very clear that this is a workshop that has been especially set up. The criminal wanted to work unhindered and unobserved. There are also some cut marks probably made with a hand tool. The colouring of the wood is too even. No, this has all been fitted and used around here. Hello, what is this?" As he moved around the table Holmes had been scuffing with his shoe in some loose soil around the table legs. He lent down and carefully pulled up a piece of string-like material several inches long.

"Well now, look at this," he said peering closely at it. "Here is something else to add to our collection." Depositing the short length of string on to the table, he took out of his pocket the items he had found on the floor earlier and put them alongside. There were three more in all. One was a small metal pin-like object, slightly bent, the second a short piece of shaped hard material and the third what I took to be a broken piece of a cutting tool.

"Not much to go on there, Holmes," I commented. "It just looks like cast offs or rubbish you will find in any workshop."

"Exactly, Watson, that is precisely what they are. But you have to remember that by looking at cast offs or rubbish anywhere it can tell you a great deal about the work undertaken by those who disposed of it. Once you know that, it will illuminate more facts, which will help to build up a picture of the crime scene. These will form a background as it were, rather like that of a picture and that in turn will lead on to solving the crime. You know my methods by now, old friend."

"Indeed I do, Holmes, but when we discuss it you are able to clarify things so much more. Most people would either ignore them or dismiss them as being of no value. It demonstrates a precision of thought to those of us not so well endowed with your talents."

As on previous occasions Holmes said nothing in reply but I could see nevertheless, that my compliments were not lost on him. He smiled in acknowledgement.

"What do you believe they are then?"

"Well," I said, picking up the small bent pin-like object, and with it the short piece of broken string.

"To my mind, Holmes they are clearly pieces from fishing equipment which have been damaged in use. It must happen from time to time. A large fish and a hard fight to bring it on board or to the bank, perhaps catching it on a tree or part of the boat. It gives way and needs replacing. The damaged parts are simply discarded and replaced."

"Yes, that does seem to be a plausible explanation. I am sure that Inspector Lennox would agree with you."

"And what of the third item, Doctor?" I picked it up and twirled it around in my fingers.

"I don't know, Holmes, difficult to tell, probably a broken piece of rod or fishing hook which has splintered off, although it looks to be more like a piece of bone."

"And the fourth item?"

"Just a piece of broken blade, nothing of special note."

"Thank you, Doctor, well done."

"So what do you wish to do with them, Holmes?"

"Would you please look after them, for the time being. When we are able to examine them in better light, no doubt I will form a clearer view as to their use, and why they came to be here."

"You do not seem convinced by my explanation then?"

"Let's just say for now, that when you see some fishing equipment have a good look at it, especially at the line and reel and tell me what you think. Now let us examine this ladder."

I returned the four items to my pocket.

Placing his hands on the sides of the ladder he pushed and gave it a slight shake. A small piece of soil came down. "It looks to be firm enough, it was clearly made here but it will do. I am sure that the criminal will not have one which is unsafe for him, otherwise why go to all of this trouble," he said pointing back across at the table again.

I could see that the two side struts were indeed made from substantial pieces of rough cut timber. The actual cross pieces forming the rungs were laid across but held in place by a small triangle of wood beneath them at both ends. The whole structure was held rigidly by several more cross pieces on its underside.

"A strong heavy ladder, Holmes," I said, reiterating his comments.

"Yes, unsophisticated but very robust. There was no need for any precision woodwork here it seems. As long as it was strong and would carry his weight that was all he required. He certainly was not going to be moving it around. Unless he took it off the island there are not many places for it to be used around here."

"Could he be the same man who made the trap in the forest, Holmes, the one with the wedge to hold the tree branches balanced in place?"

"I am sure that he is one and the same, Watson, but lets go and see where it leads to at the top. Perhaps you would stand at the bottom, Doctor, and hold on to it, just in case it slips whilst I am up at the top. If you would kindly leave our oil lamps on the table and adjust them carefully I am sure that they will give us enough light for what we need."

"Of course, Holmes."

After placing the oil lamps on the table as he requested, I stepped forward and after he had climbed up several feet I reached out to hold onto the sides. As he ascended, carefully testing the strength of each rung, some more soil fell down onto my head and I brushed an insect off my shoulder. At that very moment, as I held onto the ladder again, there was a sudden crack. Holmes had nearly reached the top when he gave a loud shout.

"Mind out!" He slipped downwards, his feet swinging just above my head with his hands holding onto the rungs above. For a few moments Holmes's feet flailed around in the air until he had again found a rung below and placed his feet upon it.

"Are you all right, Holmes. That was close?"

"Yes, thank you, Watson, it nearly caught me out just then," he said as he climbed down. Holmes bent down to the floor and picked up a broken piece of wood which until moments ago had formed one of the rungs of the ladder.

Attached to it at one end was one of the small triangular supporting pieces.

"Not quite so well made as we had thought," I said as I looked at the broken fragments now in his hands.

"On the contrary, Watson, it was extremely well made. The criminal had done a most excellent job of making it look solid and firm, then, just when someone had placed their full weight upon the rung, it gave way suddenly, without any warning. It was a most skilful and deliberate trap. I am sure that in most cases at least a bruised leg would result, possibly even worse."

"That would have sent us away from here for a while, Holmes, at least until you had recovered completely."

"Yes it would and by then the criminal would have had enough time to bring about Sir Hugh's demise. With us out of the way he would have a free hand."

"Do you believe that it was set for us, Holmes? Can you be certain?"

"Probably, Doctor. He knew I am sure, that we suspected his trap in the woodlands, even if he had not seen us, then there was the boathouse and the holes in Sir Hugh's boat. He probably thought it likely that we would come over to the island after Duncan Cameron went missing and that we would find his fish catch at least. He set the trap on the ladder just in case we came into here. It was certainly his work making an attempt to be rid of us for a while and it very nearly worked. This man is showing a cunning, which in some ways is quite unique and is proving to be a very worthy opponent. We must really be on our guard now." As Holmes said this I could see his eyes light up as if relishing the challenge and picking up the gauntlet thrown down to him.

"Now we know about the ladder I feel sure that it is worth the risk to go on up and find out where it leads." Moving up to the ladder again Holmes stepped on it, carefully placing his weight upon the bottom rung.

"I am sure that it will be ..." Holmes suddenly stopped.

"What is wrong?" I asked. "Is there a problem?"

"There might be." He paused, looked up at the top of the ladder then down and around him at the floor.

"Can I help, Holmes, what are you looking for?"

"You will recall that as we came along the tunnel leading into here, we stepped over some stones which had fallen from the roof."

"Yes, I do."

"Be kind enough to pass some to me. I believe that even now I may have under-estimated this man."

Leaving Holmes now balanced on the bottom rung of the ladder and taking up an oil lamp, I stepped back and entered the tunnel. After a short distance I located the stones and taking a cluster, returned to the room.

"Thank you, Watson, they are ideal," said Holmes as I walked over to him and passed over what I took to be the most suitable, although I had no idea as to the use he had for them. Knowing Holmes, however, I knew that I would soon find out.

"Now stand back, just in case," he said as he took the stone, leaned back and with a mighty throw, hurled it up at the roof by the top of the ladder. Some soil and small stones fell down, then silence.

"Another one, please," he paused, "perhaps I was wrong," he said as I passed to him a second stone. Again, with another heave he threw the stone upwards with all his force but this time, I was able to see that it went a little closer to the top of the ladder where it rested against the roof. There was but a momentary pause then a crash. I looked upwards. What appeared to be part of the roof by the top of the ladder had moved and I was able to see through to the sky. At that same moment there was a dull thud, and in the now improved light silhouetted in the gap, I could see what looked to be a large pointed axe hanging across the hole. Holmes was jubilant.

"You see, Watson, I was right, look!"

"I can, Holmes, at least I think I can, but what exactly happened?"

"It was a second man-trap, Doctor. Can't you see now, it was fitted across at the top to a folding hatch. As the hatch moved it must have loosened a trigger which in turn allowed this axe head to fall. It is weighted as well."

As he said this Holmes had climbed to the top of the ladder and after carefully negotiating the broken rung, pushed away the axe and eased himself out onto the ground above. He vanished but after a pause he peered back down. "I think that you can come on up now, it's quite safe but be careful of that broken rung."

I in turn, carefully climbed the ladder and with the help of Holmes, scrambled through the hole in the roof. Looking around me I could see that we had emerged amongst the ruins of what must once have been a substantial house. The ground upon which we now stood must have been its floor and the room below, its cellar. Around us the ruined walls were heavily overgrown with trees and thick undergrowth, and I realised that we were in the centre of the island and that on our earlier visit only that morning, we had effectively circled around it.

Holmes spoke, interrupting my thoughts.

"Yes, Watson, we did not have time to explore this island enough earlier and these ruins are well hidden. I can just make out a track going down through the undergrowth which, if my direction is right, should lead to the flat area where we found the fish and cauldrons. However, lets have a closer look at this device. It is most interesting." He turned around and pointed at what was clearly some sort of mechanical contraption. It was partially covered in undergrowth which I realised was meant to conceal it, but Holmes had cleared much of this away when he had climbed through. Lying on the ground, and now pushed to the side of the hole through which we had just emerged, was the head of the axe. I could see that it was attached to a long wooden pole, which in turn pivoted by being fitted to a fulcrum. This was held in place by a wooden frame. Examining it more closely I could see the basic but effective trigger mechanism to which it and the roof door were linked.

"Simple but effective, Watson," said Holmes in my ear. "See here how a counterweight forces down the axe head after it is released. Diabolical."

"Yes, it is, Holmes, and the way in which it works is rather like the mechanism back in the woodlands don't you think. Dislodge one thing in order to release another. But how did you know that it was here?" I asked, pointing to the device. "We could not see it from below."

"I did not, and it nearly caught me out. But if you remember, just as I started to climb the ladder again, I paused and asked you to bring one of the stones."

"Yes, but at the time I did not know why."

"Because it had occurred to me that the broken rung of the ladder was a very simple trap, rather too simple in fact."

"Why?"

"Because its main purpose was to capture my mind."

"Capture your mind, Holmes, what on earth are you talking about. You're sounding like one of those new mental doctors who study the personal problems of their patients. What has that got to do with us and the trap in the roof?" I asked incredulously.

Throwing back his head he laughed out loud, such that it could be heard echoing down the tunnel.

"No, old friend, I meant a different type of capture."

"Please explain, Holmes, I still have no idea as to what you mean."

"It is like this, after the rung of the ladder broke, I fell down and only just saved myself. I examined the rung and found that it was made to look strong but it gave way suddenly when the weight of a person was upon it. Do you agree?"

"Yes, and he did it well."

"Indeed and that was the brilliance of it. The criminal wanted me to think that the breaking rung was the intended trap when it was not, it was a decoy."

"It may have been, Holmes, but decoy or not it nearly worked."

"Yes, and had it done so, he would have achieved part of his aim, to remove us from protecting Sir Hugh. However, as I started to climb back up the ladder again it occurred to me that whilst the breaking rung was effective it lacked sufficient lethality in itself."

"Yes, I see what you mean."

"It seems to me, Doctor, that the broken rung idea was to have the climber pay so much attention to clambering up over it and thinking about what had just happened that he would be paying insufficient attention to the possibility of another danger still being above him. He would probably have been so relieved to get safely out at the top and into the daylight that the thought of anything else would not be uppermost in his mind. That is the time when a potential victim is at his most vulnerable. If I had gone up the ladder and encountered no problems I would have opened the trapdoor with only the greatest caution, expecting the possibility of a trap. As a result it would likely have failed. My mind would have been focused on the issue, not diverted as the result of the previous incident, which I have to admit, Doctor, was still a shock."

"Yes, as it is you're lucky not to have broken a bone."

Holmes ignored my comments and went on.

"The best way I felt able to check if there was another lethal trap was by means of hurling the stones at the trapdoor in the roof whilst I was well clear of it. As it happened I succeeded and it saved me from any further risk. Had it not worked I would of course still had to go to the top but with greater difficulty. It was a risk I felt necessary to take. The more he could divert attention from the danger up here, the more likely he was to succeed."

"Yes, but you had a close call there, Holmes. What a really dastardly fellow he is. What is behind it all I wonder?"

"Yes, he is, but why we do not yet know. Look over here."

Holmes walked over to where a small area of ground nearby had been flattened.

"This is clearly where it was assembled, look there is some sort of rope made from animal skin, unfinished by the look of it. I believe that he probably had something more

124

sophisticated planned but changed his mind as it would take him too long to make, probably when he saw that we had an interest in the island and would likely be here before he could finish it."

"It does look rather like he had in mind making a piece of medieval siege equipment."

Holmes chuckled, "It does Doctor. Our adversary is obviously a man of some learning as well as talent. We must take this as a warning that it is not only Sir Hugh whose life is in danger but ours as well. He has realised that in order to harm Sir Hugh he would do well to remove us, too.

Let's now go down again into this underground room, Doctor. We have found out all we can at this point and I am sure that no more danger exists around here, at least for the while."

With that Holmes and I descended the ladder replacing the trapdoor whilst negotiating the ladder's broken rung.

"Our next move, Watson, is to follow this other tunnel and see where it leads us."

After adjusting the oil lamps, I followed Holmes out along the passageway. It was smaller than the one we had first entered, with bends in places, and I was obliged to walk along behind Holmes. After a short distance I was able to see the light improving and it was clear that we were approaching the exit. Within a few more strides Holmes stopped, then pushing his way through some more bushes, we emerged onto the far side of the island.

In front of us was a narrow sandy beach, which was almost cut off from access to the loch beyond by a large rock. I could see that in order to reach the loch it would be necessary to move out around it to the left and to anyone on the water it would likely be well concealed. I looked up and around me. Behind and above were several huge boulders covered in trees and foliage lying undisturbed for many years. I recalled that only that morning I had passed this spot, but because of the difficulties I was forced to move well above and away from the edge and it had remained hidden from my view. Holmes had been silent for a while now, and I could see that he was looking around and studying the scene. A gentle breeze was blowing in from the loch rustling the trees around us. He looked up.

"There is one of Sir Hugh's eagles, Watson." I followed his gaze and saw high up, circling on the thermals, a magnificent creature.

"All of a ten foot wingspan I should think," I said.

"Yes, I agree, but I think that something may have disturbed it," he replied.

"Possibly us, Holmes."

"Perhaps. Let's see now what can we find down here I wonder? There are some interesting marks on the beach. Be careful where you tread."

We found, cut into the rocks, some grooves forming simple steps leading down. Using these we reached their base and stood looking at some peculiar indentations on the beach.

"Well now, Watson, what do you make of these," said Holmes pointing at a series of grooves cutting into the hard sand.

"All I can think of is some sort of turtle. Perhaps they breed around here, although I can recollect hearing nothing about it."

"If it is, then they are certainly a new species known to man. I am sure that Mr. Darwin would be most interested if that were the case. No, Doctor, a good try though but I believe that the hand of man has more to do with this than the hand of evolution."

I persisted in my argument. "What makes you think that, Holmes? I cannot connect their shape with anything I have seen before. I can see what looks to be rather like the tail marks of three turtles, and surely the other marks against them were made by the scratches of their legs as they propelled themselves over the sand."

"Then why are they so straight and even, Doctor, and why are there marks in between on both sides of the centreline only?"

I would not be beaten and continued to press my case.

"Because the sand is wetter in some parts and will hold the marks more clearly. As it dries they show up more."

"The sand looks to be very even to me, Doctor. I think that its density will be the same anywhere on this small patch of beach. If it were a small amphibian why are the grooves so even. Would not the movement of a flipper make a curved shape and leave a small pile of sand behind each one?"

Holmes now took out his magnifying glass, knelt down on the sand and started to closely examine the marks, much as he had done previously at the boathouse.

"Yes, look here, Doctor, you can see under the lens where the sand has been pushed back clearly enough, a flipper would give a different shape and push up more sand at its outer ends. No, definitely not a turtle."

"What then, Holmes?" I responded.

"Some sort of boat I am sure, but nothing the like of which I have seen before in all my years as a consulting detective."

"Could they not have been made by some other creature, something yet unknown which lives in the loch? It is even possible to see the mark of its body, see the shallow groove it made in the sand," I said pointing.

"There are rumours of such things of course but not here in this loch. They are more likely to be Inspector Lennox's giant pikes," he replied laughing.

As we continued to speculate on their origins, Holmes walked around the tracks in the sand and followed them as they swung around to the right, behind the large rock.

"Look, Watson, as they turn the marks are still evenly spaced. If they had been made by a living creature I doubt that it would be so. See, on the corners, the sand is scuffed up as it was turned around, they now lead directly out onto the water."

I looked again.

"Yes, I have to confess, Holmes, that, as usual, you are right," I acquiesced. "What do you wish to do now? The boat, or whatever it is made those tracks, has been gone some while, probably last night I should imagine."

"H'm, perhaps less than that, old friend. However, we can do no more here for now. No doubt we shall eventually locate it and learn its unique features. Let's now make our way back to our own boat, we still have plenty of oil in our lamps and it will be quicker to go through the tunnel."

We turned and retraced our steps just as a cool breeze swept across the loch setting the island's trees gently swaying as we re-entered the tunnel. It was but only a few minutes before we found ourselves back at the hidden quay, and I could see through the overhanging growth the line of Inspector Lennox's boats as they dragged the loch.

Climbing back into our own vessel I took up the oars, and had just moved out into open water when we heard a sudden shout and commotion. Turning, I looked over my shoulder to see several of the flotilla grouped together pulling at their nets. Nearby the steamboat was being manoeuvred towards them and I could see Inspector Lennox learning over the rails, calling out instructions.

"What do you wish to do now, Holmes," I asked, "join Inspector Lennox, or go back to the beach and wait for him there?"

"Let us go across, Watson, and find out what the Inspector makes of this. It looks to me as if they have just found the body of Duncan Cameron."

Chapter Ten

A Tragedy Unfolds

Pulling hard on the oars I sped us across the loch towards the Inspector's steamboat and an array of smaller vessels now gathered around it. Behind me I could hear much shouting. Holmes was looking anxiously across over my shoulder. He spoke.

"I think, Watson, if they have indeed found Cameron, the sooner we examine the body the better. Merely moving it clumsily may destroy evidence, even small pieces could prove to be of crucial importance, to those who know how to interpret it."

"Yes, Holmes, but from what you have said, are not the police beginning to realise this?"

"In London perhaps. I would like to think that they are up here as well, but I have my doubts."

Holmes's voice trailed off as he said, almost to himself, "It may be the smallest details, Doctor, the smallest details, and with all that water, too!"

"It is lucky that we were nearby, Holmes," I retorted, in between gasps of breath as we neared the Inspector's flotilla.

"Yes, it is, but short of waiting out on the loch with Inspector Lennox, I felt that we had better use for our time by pursuing our own investigations. Meantime, we had to rely on the efforts of the local constabulary, but now I think, it has paid off. Watson, say nothing about the tunnel … just yet."

"Why so, are we not withholding evidence which may be relevant to this case?"

"For the moment, yes, but I think it may be advisable for a while."

"This is not like you, Holmes, you have always been ready to give advice or assist the police when necessary."

"Well, old friend, you may recall the times in London when I have advised Gregson or Lestrade over key issues and they have still interpreted them incorrectly. I am simply concerned that Inspector Lennox will do the same thing, ending up accusing the wrong man and letting the real villain escape. If it happens here I am sure that he will try again later when we may not be around to prevent it."

"I see your point, but won't the Inspector find the fish anyway?"

"Yes, but I also do not want to frighten off the criminal. I have some plans relating to that tunnel and I do not want the Inspector blundering around it. I will let him know all in good time."

"Very well, Holmes, I will do as you wish."

Pausing, I twisted around and saw that crews from the smaller craft were hauling a large net from out of the water and passing it up, over the steamboat's rails. On the deck Inspector Lennox and two constables were trying to unravel its contents.

Holmes said no more as I resumed rowing and a minute later we pulled up alongside. The Inspector, seeing us, came over, and took the bow line from Holmes. I unshipped the oars and we clambered aboard. He was looking grim. "Over here please, gentlemen," he said, moving over to where the net lay over the deck. The two constables stepped away, solemnly. We could see clearly, that lying entangled within its mesh, was a human corpse.

The Inspector knelt down, then, pulling away the remaining piece of netting, stood back. In front of us lay the body of our friend Duncan Cameron. We all stood looking down in silence before Inspector Lennox spoke.

"I have to say, gentlemen, that we have been very lucky. We do not always find people this easily, some not at all. It is a very sad thing, very sad indeed," he said, pausing as if to reflect on the whole tragic situation. "Duncan Cameron was a fine man, Dr. Watson." He turned to me, "As a physician, I am sure that there is no doubt you can confirm death, and that it is indeed the body of our now deceased friend and loyal servant of Sir Hugh."

"Yes, of course I can, Inspector. Perhaps, Holmes, you would kindly assist."

We both knelt down as I started to examine the body of our late friend. Out of the corner of my eye I could see the crews of nearby boats peering at us from between the steamboat's handrails.

The Inspector saw my glance and turned at them. With his look resembling a snarl, it quickly sent them away to find other work.

He resumed watching us, quietly. He had seen it all before.

"I can find no obvious injury, Holmes, perhaps Duncan Cameron just fell into the loch and drowned ... a simple accident. We will need a full *post mortem* to be sure of course."

"Perhaps, Doctor, perhaps. But do you not find it odd that a man with the lifetime of skills he had acquired, should simply fall into the water and drown?"

"Yes, but these things do happen, Holmes, and you have to remember the water is very cold ... the sudden shock you know. Perhaps it stopped his heart ... and he was no longer a young man. But as I said, we will only know for certain later, unless other things show up."

"What sort of things, Doctor?" returned Inspector Lennox.

"Perhaps this sort of thing, gentlemen," said Holmes, pointing to Duncan Cameron's neck. "Although the water has obscured it well, I do not remember seeing a mark or injury on his neck before. If he had one, I would have noticed it."

I peered down, my fingers probing at what appeared to be a small injury on the side of his neck, just below his ear.

"I can't make out what it is, Holmes, but well spotted." Holmes handed me his magnifying glass.

"See what that will have to tell us."

I looked down carefully, the lens showing up remarkable detail.

"Can I see, Doctor?" Inspector Lennox had come forward and leaned across, peering down over to where I held the instrument. Behind me, I could hear steam gently hissing from the boiler as the stoker slowly reduced the excess pressure. I handed the lens to him.

"Yes, I think that Mr. Holmes is right, Doctor. If you look carefully … I can just make out something … like a small round hole on his skin. Could it have been made by a fish perhaps? It is not easy to see as the skin has closed against it."

I took hold of Cameron's head and in turning it around the skin covering the wound opened, revealing a round hole.

"Ah, there you are, just as I thought," said the Inspector, "it is quite obviously a wound caused by something pointed, like a fishing gaff hook, a rowlock, or a spear perhaps. Exactly as I predicted. If you gentlemen will recall I said that Cameron had likely died as a result of a fishing accident. He probably slipped, injured himself in the fall, then fell overboard and drowned. The water has softened the skin, which closed the wound so that we could not easily see it. Mr. Holmes did though, although I am sure that we would have soon anyway."

Holmes ignored the Inspector's somewhat begrudging compliment. "Have you a pair of small tweezers with you, Watson? I know that you sometimes carry a set of medical instruments with you."

I reached into my pocket and passed them to him.

Taking them, Holmes carefully teased open the wound and inserted the instrument. Moments later he withdrew it and I could see that he was now holding what appeared to be a tiny piece of feather. Lifting it up for us all to see Holmes asked, "Now tell me what you think of that? Interesting is it not?"

The Inspector leaned forward again and on his breath I could detect the smell of a single malt whisky, recently consumed.

"Why, Mr. Holmes, it is clearly the piece of a fishing fly. There can be no doubts left at all now. I said all along that it was a fishing accident", repeating his earlier statement, "this finally proves it. You have to accept that I was right," he said, with more than a hint of triumph in his voice. "Perhaps after all, some fresh highland air, much experience on these matters and a little help from a wee dram of whisky, can solve such accidents no matter how tragic. It is not the first time I have had a case like this, and it probably will not be the last," he said, again looking at us both as if to say finally that the whole matter of Duncan Cameron's death was now resolved, but that it was a most unfortunate side issue to that concerning the threats to Sir Hugh's life.

The Inspector's sense of vindication was however not to last.

"Tell me," asked Holmes, "just how did the small piece of feather get into the wound?"

Looking closely at it again, Inspector Lennox replied, "but isn't it obvious? We saw all the fishing flies lying around in the boat Cameron took out last night. One piece clearly became caught in the sharp object which injured him. Indeed it may have been the indirect cause of him falling into the water and drowning. What do you think, Dr. Watson?" He turned to me as if to seek an ally. His tone could not entirely contain the significant hint of frustration in his voice.

"Well Inspector, you may be right of course, but we do not yet know if indeed drowning was the cause of Duncan Cameron's death ... as I first thought."

"Yes, especially if you look here." Whilst the Inspector and I had been talking, Holmes was closely examining the other side of Cameron's neck. He had found another small hole, similar to and opposite the first. "Would that not likely to have been the cause of death, Inspector?"

Inspector Lennox peered down again, looking intently at this new found injury. He sniffed to himself as if to gain a moment to recover his thoughts.

"Well," he said slowly, "you could be right there, Mr. Holmes, but that surely does not mean that my original opinion was wrong. It merely means that the injury to Cameron's neck was more severe than we at first thought. It tells us that it may have killed him, or at least severely injured him and perhaps rendered him unconscious. If he was not dead when he fell into the water he would have died very quickly. Dr. Watson what is your view, now ... in the light of this?"

"I believe it likely, Inspector, that this wound may well have killed him but, as you say, after he fell into the loch he would have drowned and he would also have bled heavily anyway."

The Inspector stood up as if satisfied that he had at least achieved a draw and he would leave it there for the moment, although I heard him say, "just how else could the wound have been caused?" Muttering under his breath, however, was not his usual way and he now asserted his authority by declaring that, "the sooner poor Cameron's body is taken on to the mortuary the better, then the truth will out."

Behind him several police officers were removing the net remaining around the body which they then placed on a stretcher. "I think that we have done all that we can here. I will have the boat sent down the loch from where Cameron's body can be taken on to Glasgow. My deputy will accompany it and deal with the paperwork. Now, Mr. Holmes, I believe that you and Dr. Watson may have found something of interest on the large island. You were gone for quite a while were you not?"

The Inspector was looking at Holmes as if half wanting to gain information, but hoping that anything found would still support his opinions.

"I think that you were right," Holmes returned, "we did find traces of work, by a poacher ... but nothing that tells us about Cameron's disappearance."

"And what was it that you found, Mr. Holmes? Anything may be relevant in a case like this you know." Holmes smiled, as if to put Inspector Lennox at his ease.

"We found some fish. It seems as if they were being prepared for storing for the winter."

"Ah, I knew it! That explains it all," said the Inspector. "Cameron went out last night in his boat. He probably wanted to catch a poacher red handed."

"But why wear Sir Hugh's old clothes?" said Holmes. "He had his own surely, and did not need others."

"Well, yes, I have been wondering about that. But does it really matter? After all, Sir Hugh's clothes were of the best material and probably warmer than his own. Perhaps the thought of wearing them gave him, what ... more of a sense of importance."

"Perhaps, Inspector," replied Holmes. "But he was Sir Hugh's gillie, and I would have thought that he already had enough authority about him to tackle any poacher. Maybe he was impersonating Sir Hugh?" said Holmes, looking across at Inspector Lennox and raising his eyebrows.

"Why on earth would he want to do that, Mr. Holmes? As you have just said yourself, he already had all the authority he needed. Why would he want anyone to believe that he was Sir Hugh? No one would believe that Sir Hugh would go out at night, just in order to catch someone poaching his fish!" He paused momentarily before continuing, "especially in view of recent events. The Laird would never do such a thing ... quite ridiculous, Mr. Holmes, quite ridiculous."

"Yes, Inspector, perhaps you are right," acquiesced Holmes. Knowing him, I knew that he was still maintaining his own counsel on the matter and, like the discovery of the tunnel, would reveal all when ready.

"It seems clear to me, gentlemen, that I need to visit the island as soon as possible."

Just at that moment a call came from the shore. Sir Hugh's coachman had arrived, having been sent down from the house with a large basket of food. Clearly they had not yet been advised of the Inspector finding the body of their much respected gillie.

"I will take care of this," stated Inspector Lennox, with a hint of reluctant authority in his voice. I shall have to go and see them. I have done much of this sort of thing, although I have to say, gentlemen, that it gets no easier."

For a brief moment his face showed the strain, which he had so far concealed.

He turned and moved across to the wheelhouse where his junior colleagues were waiting along with the boat's captain, all talking quietly amongst themselves.

"What shall we do now, Holmes?" I asked. "Something to eat and drink?"

"Yes, then a brisk walk afterwards."

"Have you anywhere special in mind?"

"Yes, I thought that it was about time we visited the waterfall known locally as the Hissing Shaft, or in Gaelic as *Eas Na-Onghail*. You will recall that it was the first event spoken of by Duncan Cameron when he came to consult with us."

"Indeed I do, it is where everything seems to have started."

"In this country perhaps Doctor, but we shall see. I believe that there is more to this business than at first glance appears."

"Why ... do you think that ..."

I stopped. The Inspector returned before I was able to question Holmes further on his intentions.

"I have instructed my officers to take the boat with Cameron's body down the loch. They will leave immediately. Meanwhile, gentlemen, I must now go and see Sir Hugh and Miss Caroline. What do you wish me to do? I can arrange separate transport if you wish. You will presumably now want to go back to London, after you've packed that is. I am sure that you have no desire to stay any longer. We can take over from here. I feel certain that by this time tomorrow we will have apprehended the culprit and the whole matter will have been solved."

Again, I felt that the Inspector was almost willing us to go and leave the crime scene, alone to him, unhindered.

"Thank you, Inspector," replied Holmes, "you are most considerate. Watson and I thought perhaps a bite to eat first, whilst you go and speak to the family. We will wait for you by the side of the loch."

"Very well, gentleman," he replied, "perhaps we can talk again later."

With that the Inspector, Holmes and I leapt down into the rowing boat as the steamboat turned and with smoke streaming from its funnel, left us rocking in its wake.

It was the Inspector who took the oars and we rowed across to the shore in silence. As we ground onto the beach he jumped out, pulling the boat clear of the water. We climbed out and joined him.

"Very well, Mr. Holmes, Dr. Watson, I hope to return here shortly and sum up the case. Perhaps you would be good enough to leave me a little whisk' ... I mean refreshment for when I return. I feel sure that Sir Hugh and Miss Caroline will not feel much like eating today."

"Of course, Inspector, we will see you shortly. Perhaps then we can all formulate a plan of action."

"Plan of action, Mr. Holmes, what plan of action?"

"Well, Inspector," went on Holmes, "as you yourself have agreed we can only be completely certain of Cameron's cause of death after the *post mortem*. As far as the culprit is concerned we have, as yet, no-one in mind ... or have we?"

The Inspector would not be drawn further on the issue. "Very well then, perhaps later we can agree on something, then carry on from there."

Holmes smiled his agreement as the Inspector turned on his heels and made his way rapidly through the woodland towards Inverdaigh House. I felt that he was not only too relieved to move away from Holmes's challenging views but also wanted to impart the bad news to Sir Hugh and Miss Caroline as soon as he could. Life was proving a little uncomfortable for him at the moment, something I felt he was very unused to.

"Let's examine the repast which has been prepared for us," said Holmes, pulling up a camping chair and looking down into the picnic basket.

"Yes, I think we have some curried chicken, Watson, a favourite," he said passing it over to me. "I don't think the Inspector will be too long. Ah, here comes our friend again."

Turning around, I saw Harrison making his way along the beach towards us. He spoke first.

"Why, Mr. Holmes and Dr. Watson, we meet again, what a pleasure."

"Hello, Mr. Harrison, are you carrying out more of your ornithological studies?"

"Yes, indeed I am, Mr. Holmes ... at least that is what I started to do but I have since been watching all the activity on the loch. Is something wrong? With lots of boats and all of the police, it looks to be most sinister."

"Regretfully it is so," replied Holmes. "Duncan Cameron went missing last night and we have been searching for him. We found his body only a short while ago."

"Oh, how dreadful," responded Harrison, looking aghast. "Are you sure it was him?"

"Yes, there is no doubt," said Holmes.

"How absolutely awful," replied Harrison. "An accident, of course."

Possibly, but we cannot be certain yet. Dr. Watson has made an initial examination but his body is now being taken on to Glasgow. We shall know soon enough. Would you like something to eat, Mr. Harrison?" said Holmes, licking his fingers and pointing to the food hamper.

"No, thank you, I really cannot eat at times like this."

"Most understandable," replied Holmes, "but Dr. Watson and myself are not unused to such events."

"Yes, but it will surely be a most awful shock to Sir Hugh and Miss Caroline. I must go up and see them immediately and convey my condolences."

Whilst they were talking my mind wandered as I looked out across the loch. In the distance I was just able to make out what appeared to be a large floating log, still covered in its branches.

"What's that I can see over there, Holmes?" I said pointing and interrupting their discussion.

They both turned to look. Harrison was the first to speak. "Oh, nothing much, Dr. Watson, it's just a tree which has been blown down, probably in our recent storm. It happens from time-to-time, and they end up floating away."

"Are they not a hazard to boats?" I asked.

"They usually soon end up on a beach, blown across out of the way."

"Even if they are moving against the wind," replied Holmes.

"Ah ... yes, I see what you mean, but what you have to remember gentlemen is that around here, by our mountains, the wind can be in a different direction from one side of the loch to the other. It is rather difficult to know from where exactly it is blowing. It can change direction quite rapidly. And then of course there are the water currents. A waterfall plunging down into the loch can create such a local disturbance you know, there is no telling which way the water will go."

"That probably will explain it," replied Holmes.

"Yes, one gets to know the ... oh, look!" Harrison stopped, suddenly pointing skywards, "its *Aquila chrysaetos*," he said, as he fumbled for his binoculars. "How wonderful, what luck."

Holmes and I followed his gaze to see a magnificent creature soaring skywards on a current of air.

"I really must go and follow it. I believe that it may have an eyrie further on ... high up in the forest ... I must find it ... please excuse me, it's been a pleasure."

Without even a backward glance, he hurried away across the beach and quickly disappeared from view, engulfed by the trees.

"What an extraordinary fellow he is, Holmes, but how fine to have such an enthusiasm. A complete devotion to his subject matter. His lecture to the local ornithological group at Inverdaigh House I assume will now be cancelled."

Holmes said nothing in reply, but I could see that he was reflecting on the recent conversation, having entered into that deep state of mind with which I was so familiar at Baker Street.

"Yes," he replied, after a moment in this somewhat distant manner, "but I am sure that he will find another way of occupying his time. Strange though, I had seen the eagle earlier but he made no mention of it."

"Possibly the activity on the loch had diverted his attention for a while. Incidentally, Holmes, I noticed that you gave no details of the injuries we found on Cameron. I suppose that we do not want the whole area to know about it, although it is surprising how quickly people become aware of the sordid minutiae associated with bad news."

"Yes, Doctor, I am sure that you are right. You will have found that from your medical practice in London no doubt. Ah, here comes the Inspector," he said, as we saw him striding towards us from out of the pathway.

"Well, gentlemen," said Inspector Lennox, who upon reaching us pulled up a chair and sank down into it. "I have spoken to Sir Hugh and Miss Caroline. They are most upset, of course, Cameron was almost part of the family. He had been with them for many years and was held in great affection. The news, however, was not unexpected and they were prepared for the worst," he went on as he reached down into the food hamper and removed a chicken piece, which he proceeded to eat with relish. It had been a long trying day and he had probably gone without breakfast.

He sat for a while, eating but saying nothing and was clearly in deep thought. A bead of sweat slowly trickled down his cheek as Holmes and I waited for him to speak again.

His chair creaked, as turning to us he said, "I am sure that you will appreciate I owe it to the Laird and his daughter to quickly arrest not only the criminal who is threatening his life, but to find out how and why Duncan Cameron died." He sat, watching us, clearly waiting for a reaction.

"Do I take it from what you are saying, Inspector," said Holmes, "that you consider you know just who the criminal is, and that you soon plan to arrest him … after pulling together a few loose ends perhaps?"

"Indeed, I do, Mr. Holmes."

"And just who is this man … no let me guess … he is a local man who is likely considered to be a ne'er-do-well, a petty criminal and well known in the area."

Inspector Lennox started to look uncomfortable again as Holmes was clearly ahead of him.

"That is so," returned the Inspector, shuffling a little as he again reached into the food hamper and pulled out a leg of lamb. Taking out a pocket knife, he opened the blade and proceeded to cut off for himself a large slice. Relaxing back into his chair he bit off a piece, started chewing and again waited for Holmes's response.

"I take it then that the man you believe to be the criminal is Brodney McCall."

"Yes, Mr. Holmes, taking all into consideration he fits perfectly. It is quite obvious to me that he is the man we are all looking for. He is known as being a local poacher. Look at what you both found on the island earlier, a hoard of fish. Clearly it was being prepared for winter and stored away. On several occasions he has been caught and brought up in front of Sir Hugh, so there's the motive. Also of course," went on Inspector Lennox making his case, "he lives nearby and knows the area very well ... being raised around here. Finally, Mr. Holmes, there is his clan history ... back from many generations ago, with much bad blood you see, people have long memories you know, especially here, in the glens."

"But you have not yet been to the island and seen the fish we found Inspector."

"No, but I intend to do so shortly, and I have no doubt that I shall find things exactly as you have said, and will draw the obvious conclusions."

"Well if you are content with that," replied Holmes, "although I would counsel against making too hasty a judgement. Sometimes the obvious is not always the truth. One sometimes needs to step back as it were, and ask oneself if the whole matter is just too easy, too convenient perhaps, making apparent facts fit into one's own preconceived ideas."

"Yes, I am sure you are right, but you also have to remember that some things in crime are, indeed, straightforward and do not need so much sleuthing. Leave that for London perhaps. Gregson and Lestrade have told us about some of your deep investigations and remarkable conclusions. No, I have had my suspicions all along and now you have confirmed them, I am most grateful for your help in solving this case."

The Inspector smiled as if to satisfy himself that Holmes did indeed share his conclusions and could happily bring the case to a close. He could probably see a commendation coming his way. Having the great Sherlock Holmes alongside him would do no harm and possibly raise his esteem in the eyes of his colleagues at Scotland Yard.

"Why, thank you, Inspector," replied Holmes, "but I fail to see how I could have been of any help in your arriving at a solution."

"You are too modest, Mr. Holmes. I expect Dr. Watson will confirm that fact," he said, looking across at me.

"Er, yes. Of course," I replied, somewhat embarrassed at suddenly having to agree to the Inspector's views concerning Holmes's abilities. Of all the epithets I would have used to describe my friend, modesty is not the first word that comes to mind.

"There is something else though, which I believe may be of particular interest to you, Mr. Holmes, apart from this case that is," he said somewhat hesitantly.

"And what is that, Inspector?"

"Well, it is rather odd really but I think it would appeal to your sense of the unusual, or even the bizarre may be a better word."

"It sounds most intriguing, please go on. It's beginning to seem like something Dr. Watson writes about in some his accounts of my exploits." As he said this he looked across at me with a sly grin on his face.

"Well," went on Inspector Lennox, "but I must be clear from the start that it is absolutely nothing to do with this case concerning Sir Hugh, or indeed the death of Duncan Cameron."

Holmes now sat back with his eyes half closed and his hands clasped gently together. To those who did not know him it looked as though he was asleep, but in reality I knew that he was at his most intense concentration.

"It seems to have started some months ago, or at least that was when the police were made aware of it. The local constable was told of some most odd goings on in the area."

"What form did these odd goings on take, Inspector?"

"Animal mutilation, Mr. Holmes, animal mutilation."

"What animals and where, Inspector?" enquired Holmes sounding surprised.

"All around this area, but apparently in the hills or on local farms. The animals are deer, which abound around here, and cattle."

"I see, and in what way were they mutilated?"

"In two ways; the deer seem to have had their leg tendons cut away, right up to and around their backs, whilst the cattle have had their horns cut off ... whilst they are still alive that is."

"Would removing their horns cause them much distress, Inspector?"

"The local vet believes that as long as the horns were not cut too close to their skulls then they would cope with it, as any horn amputation would be above the nerve areas."

"But surely, uncomfortable for them at least. They would presumably make some protest in the way cattle do?"

"Yes, I would think so, Mr. Holmes."

"And I assume that the cattle attacks took place whilst they were nearby, and not up in the hills."

"I believe so, the animals were found in the mornings when the farmers went out to attend to them ... as farmers do, of course."

"Did not their owners hear anything during the night?"

"No, most of the cattle mutilation took place whilst they were in the fields away from the buildings, although one did happen in the cattle pen near the farm house. The farmer heard a disturbance and went outside to investigate. He found his prize animal had been dehorned. It was in some distress and would not let anyone come near for quite a while."

"What was special about that animal, Inspector?"

"He used to have a splendid set of horns, Mr. Holmes. Quite outstanding and well known amongst many other longhorn cattle in this area."

"Did the animal's owner see anything at all? Was there any sign of the culprit?"

"No, it seems that he had escaped before the owner came out to investigate. He found nothing. The culprit had obviously left taking the animal's horns with him."

"How long ago was this?"

"It was around the time when this business involving Sir Hugh started, Mr. Holmes. Naturally we gave that a priority and had to leave the animal mutilations for the time, although the local constable is still making enquiries. Our officers did sit up at night on several occasions in the hope of catching the culprit, but to no effect."

"Is it still happening?"

"We occasionally find deer which have been mutilated, but no recent cattle incidents."

"So only the cattle and deer are being targeted, Inspector, but no other animals have been harmed?"

"Yes ... well, not exactly. Sheep have been found, but we put that down to foxes, they can do much damage you know."

"What happened to these sheep, Inspector?"

"Just the sort of thing one would expect, internal organs removed, it happens you know ... it's nature."

"And what did you think was the cause of the deer and cattle mutilations? Not foxes, surely?"

The Inspector looked up at Holmes as he said this. He shuffled in his chair.

"My officers felt that it was witchcraft, Mr. Holmes!"

"Witchcraft, Inspector," I interrupted before Holmes had time to reply, "did I hear you say witchcraft?"

"Yes, Dr. Watson, you did."

"How did you come to that conclusion, Inspector?" asked Holmes.

The Inspector, who was beginning to look most uncomfortable, replied.

"Well, gentlemen," he said, coughing slightly under his breath, "it is difficult I know ... in this day and age ... but despite numerous enquiries, we could make head nor tail of the situation, until that was one of our officers, who had been brought up in the hills, suggested it ... as a possibility that is."

"And what made him suggest that?" asked Holmes again.

Inspector Lennox had now started to regain his composure – he had something more to offer now – something a little more plausible. He went on.

"This officer, as a young boy, had a grandmother for whom he had great affection. She had a reputation as a local healer, wart charming and the like. You must remember that in those days there was little in the way of medical men such as yourself, Dr. Watson. Those we had were ... shall we say, not always the most accomplished, and folk would prefer to go to the local healer. Indeed, I can myself remember as a child having the same problem. My own mother took me to a lady she knew of and, well, it seemed to work for me as my own warts went within days. It is a gift some people have."

He looked across at us both as if to say that it was a fact regardless and to make of it what we will.

We remained silent for a while, absorbing the conversation. It was Holmes who spoke first.

"I have never been asked to investigate a situation like this before," he said turning to me. "This is a new one for us, Watson."

"Yes, Holmes, although I wonder if any investigations you pursue may reveal another cause, something perhaps more mundane," I replied.

"That's settled then," interrupted Inspector Lennox, before Holmes or I could raise any objections to taking on the case. "I will let our local constable know immediately."

Sitting back in his chair, his sense of relief was palpable. It was obvious that he wanted the matter out of his hair, enabling him to concentrate solely on finding Sir Hugh's assailant and having him arrested. I could not help but wonder if he also felt a sense of ridicule – he was not really a witchcraft-solving detective at heart. Leave that to his underlings to play with, after all no one had been really hurt by it – had they? A good murder was more in his line.

Holmes stood up. "As you have now handed us a new case, we will let you carry on with yours," he said, addressing the Inspector again. "I believe that you were going to visit the island."

"Indeed, I am," he replied, turning to look at his boat. "I shall do so immediately. But what of yourselves?"

"Well, Watson and I were planning to see the waterfall known as the Hissing Shaft, or locally in Gaelic *Eas Na-Onghail*, but a change of plan is called for. We shall leave that until tomorrow ... unless, of course, you disagree Doctor?" he asked, looking across at me.

"No, not at all, Holmes. Perhaps it is getting rather too late in the day. What do you propose to do now though?"

"I feel like a visit to the local village. I believe that it is just a mile or two away in the opposite direction," he said, turning to the Inspector for confirmation.

"Yes, it is, Mr. Holmes, by the side of the loch. The people there are most friendly, as they are in these parts," he added. "I will see you later then," he said, as he climbed back into his boat.

Chapter Eleven

Eas Na-Onghail

A sudden cold breeze swept across the loch as, pulling our coats tightly around us, we watched Inspector Lennox rowing away and over towards the island. Standing in silence we saw him reach the trees and disappear towards the hidden beach we had found earlier.

"I don't think that it will take him long to find the fish remains and the metal pot," said Holmes.

"No, but you surely did not believe in that witchcraft idea either, Holmes? Inspector Lennox was trying to pass it over to us and you raised no objections," I said, slightly puzzled.

"Yes, Doctor, you started to question it but I felt it best to relieve him of the matter. I have some ideas of my own. I need to locate their telegraph office. I am sure that they will have one."

"Why do you need the telegraph, Holmes?" I asked.

"Oh, just to keep up with events at Baker Street should anything arise in our absence."

"As you wish, but there is little you can do about it whilst up here in Scotland."

Holmes did not reply but I thought that he had a faint smile on his face as we started on our walk. It did not take us long as we strode out briskly, enjoying the scenery and the views of the loch nearby.

"Have you brought your revolver, Watson?" asked Holmes suddenly after a long silence, as the village came into view.

"Yes, I have Holmes, but I have left it at Inverdaigh House. Why do you ask?"

"I believe that we are getting closer to finding the criminal, or rather that he is probably getting closer to us."

"You think so, Holmes, is it not Sir Hugh who is his target?"

"Yes, initially it was and, indeed, still is, but now that he has certainly removed Duncan Cameron, whether by design or accident, I am sure that he sees us as an even bigger threat to his plans."

As he said this Holmes took out his revolver, checked that it was loaded, then returning it to his pocket said, "A prudent move under the circumstances I believe, Doctor."

"Yes, Holmes, I think that you are right. I will do the same when we return to Inverdaigh House. I should have given it more consideration," I replied, feeling somewhat abashed at my oversight.

We arrived at the village and after a brief enquiry, found the telegraph office. Holmes straightaway went inside. I was not kept waiting long, and I commented to Holmes that there had not been enough time for him to receive a reply.

"You are correct. I simply asked Mrs. Hudson to telegraph me should she consider that something important has arisen, a matter which would require my urgent attention. I will, of course, respect her judgment. All she need do is to contact me at Inverdaigh House, and I will return to London."

"If that is your wish, Holmes, presumably you would want me to stay here and look after Sir Hugh and Caroline."

"Yes, just until I return, but do not forget, Doctor, that you will have the local police around to assist you if necessary … and your revolver," he added as an afterthought, smiling at me as he said it. My omission to bring it along earlier was not lost on me.

As we made our way back, however, I noted that he seemed to be particularly alert, from time-to-time stopping and looking around, particularly as we passed by the denser woodlands.

* * * * *

It was a very subdued meal we all ate that night, with Cameron's absence being most noticeable. Miss Caroline had excused herself that evening, being most upset. She had known Duncan Cameron for all of her life. It was he who had taught her fishing as a young girl and shown her all about the wildlife living around her father's estate. To her he was almost part of the family. Even the servants's depressed mood reflected their feelings over the loss of Sir Hugh's gillie. They had all known and respected him for many years.

During the course of the evening after dining, we retired to the smoking room and Holmes made known his intention of our going to see the waterfall known as the Hissing Shaft, on the following morning. On learning of this Sir Hugh expressed his unease.

"It is the place where all of this business started, Mr. Holmes, and where my life was saved by Duncan Cameron. I would not like to think that you and Dr. Watson were also putting yourselves in danger unnecessarily in view of recent events. The criminal may be watching and follow you there."

"Thank you, Sir Hugh," replied Holmes, "we appreciate your concern but if we are to catch this man there will always be some risk attached, is that not correct Doctor?" he said, turning to me.

"That is so, Sir Hugh, but we are well used to it," I replied, as Holmes sat back and, reaching into his pocket, pulled out his favourite pipe. Filling it with shag he reached down into the fire and, lighting a taper, applied it to his calabash. Drawing deeply, his blue smoke rose up and filled the room. Through the window it was now quite dark. The fire crackled. Sir Hugh sat silently, watching and waiting for Holmes to speak. Outside an owl could be heard. "Tell me, Sir Hugh," asked Holmes breaking the silence, "as we are to visit the waterfall tomorrow it would be helpful if you could give me a few more details ... of the actual event that is."

"Of course, Mr. Holmes, but I do not believe there is any more to tell. Duncan Cameron told you everything, did he not?"

"Well mostly, yes, but as Dr. Watson here will tell you so much can depend on the details."

Sir Hugh looked over at me.

"Holmes has told me this so often, Sir Hugh," I said, replying to his unspoken question.

"What else is it that you wish to know, Mr. Holmes?" responded Sir Hugh.

"Well, first, who was on the leading horse when the rock came down: you or Duncan Cameron?"

"Why, it was Duncan, Mr. Holmes."

"And was it your intention to go right on up to the waterfall itself?"

"Yes, it was."

"Can you go further when you reach the waterfall, or is it a dead end?"

"It is possible to go further, but it is not advisable as it is very dangerous but it can be done with care."

"And I confirm that the rock came down on you before you reached the waterfall, and not when returning from it."

"That is correct."

Holmes nodded his acquiescence to Sir Hugh's answers, as he again put his pipe to his mouth and drew in deeply.

Sir Hugh spoke. "As you are both determined to visit the waterfall may I suggest that I help you? If you wish I will arrange for you to use one of my gigs, it will save you some time. The road through the forest will take you to within a mile, though from there on you must walk the track as no wheeled vehicles can go further. The views are most spectacular, however, and well worth the visit ... as long as the weather holds that is."

"That sounds to be most satisfactory," said Holmes, turning to me, "don't you think so, Watson?"

"Yes ... not quite a London hansom but it will make it much easier."

Sir Hugh smiled and nodded. "Agreed then," he said. "I will make all the necessary arrangements for tomorrow."

* * * * *

We awoke the following morning to a clear day and after a hearty breakfast went out to the stables to where our transport was waiting. Sir Hugh came over to join us.

"I have given you one of my more robust vehicles, gentlemen, as the road can be very rough in places. There are some sharp turns with steep drops close to the sides of the road. You will need to drive with great care, Dr. Watson," he said, as I sat taking hold of the reins. Holmes climbed up alongside me, and after more cautions from Sir Hugh to be on our guard we were soon making our way along a well made road leading up through the forest and around the shoulder of the mountain. Turning to Holmes I asked, "Do you have any special reason for going to see the waterfall today, Holmes, after all events there happened some while ago, and there will be no trace left of any clues by now."

"You are right, old friend, I am sure, but there is more to it than that."

"Which is, I am sure that you will enlighten me again?"

"Yes," he replied chuckling, "there most certainly is. I am sure that by now you know my methods and naturally I shall apply them here. For the moment, however, let us get to the waterfall."

Saying no more I flicked the reins and as our pony responded bravely we lurched up the now precipitous road. In places we could see where the edges dropped away abruptly revealing how in the past, road engineers had found it necessary to cut through and around the head of gullies. It was not long before we passed the trees and reached the road's end where we could see a single track leading away around the edge of the mountain. I pulled us to a halt and whilst Holmes jumped down and looked around him I took the bridle and tied our animal to the stump of a nearby tree.

The day was still fine and we were soon walking briskly along the path towards the waterfall. The views were wonderful, but a stiff breeze told us that we had now reached higher ground. Our host was right, after walking for nearly a mile, we became aware of a haze of spray in front of us, issuing from a gash in the side of the mountain.

"It looks rather like steam boiling from out of a cauldron, Doctor."

"Yes, Holmes, even from here. We will need to take great care, the rocks closer to it will be very slippery."

Reaching our goal we carefully worked our way around a buttress of rock, and were confronted by an awesome sight. A stream of water, like a shaft of glittering silver, came plunging through a cleft in the rocks from high above, down into the chasm below. Holmes and I stood still, taking in its thunderous hissing roar as spray, caught by a sudden gust of wind, swept over us.

"Well, Holmes, I can see how it gets its name and why anyone falling into it might never get out," I said, as I peered down into the depths.

Suddenly he grabbed my arm as, failing to heed my own advice, I slipped on a slab of rock, nearly losing my balance.

"Thank you, Holmes," I said recovering myself. "I remember Duncan Cameron once saying to us how dangerous it was."

"Yes, I recall it too, when he first came to visit us at Baker Street."

"I wonder," he said, looking up at the rocks high above, "do you think that it may have been his original plan?" His voice trailed off as if in deep thought.

"Plan, Holmes? I assume that you are referring to the original attempt on Sir Hugh's life near this waterfall."

"Yes, I am. It certainly was not by chance that he selected this place, but now that I have visited I have managed to obtain a better feel for his thinking. We were not really able to come earlier, events dictated otherwise, but now that we are here it gives me more of an understanding about the man with whom we are dealing."

"Isn't that obvious, Holmes? Surely it was a man determined to kill Sir Hugh. Did I not also hear you say about obtaining a feel for his thinking, not unlike you surely, I thought that you went on facts, and facts alone."

"Indeed, I do, Doctor, however, let us look at these facts," he said as he turned on his heel and walked back a short way along the track. He stopped and looked up again.

"From what Duncan Cameron and Sir Hugh have told us I estimate that the first attempt on Sir Hugh's life took place around here. What do you think my friend?" he asked.

"Yes, I would say so, too, Holmes."

"Excellent, now look up there." As he said this Holmes indicated the rocks above. "That must surely be from where the stone came down."

"Yes, I agree, and it must have hit the track around here," I said, pointing down at the ground.

"This must have been the very place where they were passing."

"Yes, and that small ledge we can just see below us must have been to where Sir Hugh fell before Duncan Cameron was able to reach him," he replied.

"Now, Doctor, would you be kind enough to climb down to it for me. With care I am sure that it can be done."

"If you insist, Holmes. I am sure that it must be important to you," I said, glancing over at him. "Fortunately, I have on my sturdy boots."

Saying no more I slowly worked my way down the steep slope. Twice I nearly slipped but eventually, breathing heavily, I reached the narrow ledge. Turning and looking back up I called out, "Well, Holmes, here I ..." and stopped. He was nowhere to be seen.

"Holmes, where are you?" I called again.

"Up here, Doctor," came the reply, as high up in the rocks above the track, Holmes's head appeared. "There is a deep long gully up here and it seems to run nearly up to the waterfall. It is clear that I cannot be seen from where you are, or on the track itself," he called down. "Give me a minute or so and I will come down to meet you."

Taking my cue from him I climbed back up and sat catching my breath as I watched him leaping down, to join me.

"It is evident, Doctor, that Sir Hugh's assailant could easily hide up there," he said, as he came and sat alongside me. "You look hot, old friend, try this," he said, passing to me a hip flask.

Refreshed, and passing it back, I asked, "What did you find, Holmes, after all this time?"

"Oh, nothing much," he replied casually.

"Come, Holmes, you know that you must share your thoughts if I am to record your exploits accurately for the Strand Magazine."

"Ha," he replied, laughing dismissively. "You and your stories, Doctor. Gross exaggerations of the obvious to the trained mind."

"As you say, Holmes, but I suspect that in your own way you do actually enjoy them, more than you admit?"

He looked across at me with a wry smile. "Very well," he went on, "there are a number of points, some of which I have indicated already, not in any special order, as they are all relevant, each in its own way, but every small piece adds to the picture of our criminal, rather like that of a complex jigsaw puzzle, every clue narrowing the possibilities."

"Yes, Holmes, you have lectured me on this before, but I still wish to know more."

"It is really quite simple, old friend, as the facts speak for themselves."

"How exactly?"

"That this was his first attempt to kill Sir Hugh, and clearly he selected a spot he knew well. This you already know. Second, he knew that Sir Hugh came here from time-to-time. Third he could wait, and was in no hurry. Fourth, it was a site where he could attack him without being seen. Fifth, it is a place where he could get to and from easily. Remember there are no trees around in which to hide. What does all that tell us so far?"

"Well, I suppose that it says that he knew the area quite well I would think, as you have just said."

"And?"

"That he took a lot of trouble to select the best place. Oh, what else can there be, Holmes? You tell me the rest!"

"It tells me that he had been in this area for a while, but not for too long, or else events like this would have happened long ago ... many years back I would think. Therefore, he was likely to have been here for only a year or so, enough to give him time to scout out the area and make his plans accordingly. That is the sixth point."

"Are there any more?"

"Yes, one in particular. He was obviously a very strong and agile man, probably outstandingly so."

"Come now, Holmes, I can accept the first points you have made and also accept their validity, but you now state that he must be something of an athelete. Why do you say that?"

"Because of the rock, Doctor."

"What rock, Holmes?"

"The one which wasn't there."

"Where should it have been ... this rock? If you mean the large one which nearly hit St. Hugh then it obviously rolled away."

"It undoubtedly did so, eventually, having been pushed down into the valley by the criminal."

"Why?"

"Because he needed to remove the evidence. He clearly thought it prudent to remove all traces of it. You will recall that when Cameron first came to see us at Baker Street, he said that the rock which nearly hit them had landed here, on the track."

"I do."

"And when he returned some days later it was gone."

"So how do you make the connection, Holmes?"

"Because when I climbed up to the gully high above us there were none."

"But of course not, as I said, it had been thrown down at Sir Hugh."

"So where were the others?" he replied.

"Why, lying all around there naturally. There must have been some."

"But that is just the point, there were no other rocks. The rock outcrop is solid, there is no loose material up at that point, and no sign of anything having been dug out in order to provide one."

"But we have seen some way off plenty of large rocks which he could have use' ... I see what you mean now, Holmes, that is exactly what he did. He had to bring a large rock from some distance away, and also to climb with it up to the gully."

"Precisely, my friend, and only a very fit strong man could have done that. Do you remember the Battle of Maiwand, when you were with the '66th' and took that shoulder wound."

"Indeed, I do, Holmes," I said, as my right hand went across to where the bullet had struck my shoulder. "It is something I prefer to forget."

"Tell me what happened."

"If I must, Holmes," I said reluctantly.

"We were opposing the Ghazis who were pressing hard against us. We were taking casualties and as I went forward to help bring in another wounded man, I myself was hit by a Jezail bullet."

"Then what happened?"

"I went down and my orderly, Murray, half pulled and half carried me back to the rear and put me on a mule. He told me afterwards that the mule trod on my leg at the time but I was in too much pain to notice it. Without his help I doubt if I would have survived."

"Murray was, no doubt, a very robust man."

"He was so, but helping a wounded man was still not easy for him, and over that terrain as well."

"And that, Doctor, is just what our criminal had to do, the equivalent of carrying an adult male over difficult terrain."

"It could not have been a man like Harrison then, he looks far too frail."

"No you are right it could not, but I see that you have considered him as being a possibility."

"I did wonder about that, trying to apply your methods. He always seemed to be around when at least some events occurred. What about the trees falling in the forest, could he have been involved in that?"

"It is something to consider as our investigation progresses, and we should not yet rule him out just yet."

"If you say so, Holmes, but just now you hinted at there being yet another point of relevance. What is it?'"

"That he is obviously a man who can plan in detail and act accordingly, but at the last minute is still able to change his mind if circumstances dictate. He has the ability to be flexible and not too rigid."

"Is that important?"

"Yes, it is. I think it likely that he intended to try and kill both Sir Hugh and Duncan Cameron at the waterfall itself. You will remember that I found the gully above the track, nearly reaching around to it. I believe his original plan was to throw down a rock at them when they were standing by the waterfall, just as we were when you slipped. A well aimed rock would have accounted for them both. In fact, I wonder if he did not have at least a second one just in case he did not succeed the first time. If so, he must have disposed of them afterwards. For some reason, however, he changed his mind, we shall never know why, and selected instead to try and kill Sir Hugh as he rode along this track behind Duncan Cameron as they were arriving, hence his ability to change his mind at the last moment."

"But why kill both, Holmes?"

"Because of whatever he had in mind, Duncan Cameron would likely have stood in the way. No, it is obvious that at some point the criminal had to remove him one way, or another."

"Yes, I see what you mean, Holmes, most excellent if I may say so."

"Thank you, Doctor," he responded warmly. "Let us make our way back to Inverdaigh House now. We have seen all that we can here. I hope that our pony has not wandered away," he said, looking down along the track as we started on our way back.

Our visit to the waterfall had been most stimulating and as we walked along I fell into a 'brown study'.

"A penny for your thoughts, Doctor," said Holmes, awakening me from my reverie.

"Is it that obvious?" I replied.

"You were very quiet for some while, and from your demeanour it was clear that something was on your mind."

"I was just musing over our situation. We have made quite a few investigations since coming up here to Scotland, but I feel that we are getting no closer to a solution."

"It can seem like that, Doctor, but all of our work has not been in vain as we are forming a picture, a picture of our criminal, what he is like and how he operates. He doesn't know it, but we are closing in."

"What of Inspector Lennox? Do you think that he is making progress on putting his hands on the criminal. From his manner he seems to be confident that he is close to an arrest?"

"Ha!" he exclaimed loudly. "I have no doubt that he thinks so and will probably announce it soon. It will no doubt be the arrest of Brodney McCall, or possibly some other poor local fellow, lowly educated and who will be cowed into submission under interrogation and forced into a false confession. The police will have convinced themselves that they have done their job, found the culprit and await the inevitable guilty verdict at the trial. No, I believe that he is on completely the wrong track. In the meantime the real culprit just sits back and waits, whilst the authorities believe that the criminal crisis is over. He can then resume when everyone is again off their guard, believing that the danger has passed and that all is now safe again. Ah, there is our transport," he said, as our gig came into sight.

Chapter Twelve

Holmes Foils A Trap

"**W**hat are you doing, Holmes?" I asked. We had just returned to our gig, and as I climbed aboard to take up the reins saw that instead of joining me on the passenger seat, he was walking around looking at our vehicle.

"Oh, nothing much," he replied as he slowly made his way around to the side of our pony, carefully examining its bridle and harness.

"Why, is there a problem?"

"I don't know yet, but I just thought it would be prudent to have a look."

"At what exactly?"

"Well, we have been away from here and at the waterfall now for well over an hour, and in all that time we have been out of sight of our transport. Think about it. We know that we are dealing with a fiendish criminal who is very familiar with this area. Does it not occur to you that he may have followed us up here, or had us followed, perhaps with a view to checking on where we go, what we do and be up to no good?"

"Yes, it had crossed my mind a while back, at Inverdaigh House, when we discussed coming here with Sir Hugh, but as we made our way up here through the forest and then out onto the open mountainside, I felt that we would be safe from any possible threat."

"Why should that be?"

"I just thought that being so far out in the open it was most unlikely that the criminal would risk being seen here now, especially as he made the earlier attempt on Sir Hugh's life at the waterfall. He nearly succeeded once but now that he knows we are here, would he take the risk a second time? There must be many other places to try an attempt on our lives?"

"I understand your view, Doctor, but I believe that you have underestimated both his criminal skills and determination. He is a very clever man and will take a calculated risk if necessary. Indeed, I suspect that he obtains something of a thrill in so doing."

Whilst we were talking Holmes continued looking around at our pony and checking the leather straps attaching him to the shafts of our gig.

"No, I can see nothing wrong here," he said, "perhaps you were right and he has not been here after all."

"There is not much left to check, Holmes. All the leatherwork seems sound and you have looked at the metal fittings. Are you not being over-cautious?"

Not replying he moved over to the wheel on my side of the gig.

"What is it, what can you see?" I asked. He was now bent over looking closely at the wheel itself. "There was nothing wrong with the other one I take it?"

"No, there wasn't, it all looked perfectly sound to me."

"So where is the concern Holmes?"

Ignoring my question he went on. "The spokes look to be well fitted I see," he said, "but, aha, I believe that we may have a problem."

I climbed down and stood alongside him.

"What can you see now," he said to me, pointing at the wheel hub.

"Not much, Holmes, it looks fine to me."

"Take a closer look, Doctor, you will not need a magnifying glass, look at the hub cover."

"Oh, yes, clean fresh grease smeared all over it, but surely that is what should be there, it shows that it has been well maintained."

"Indeed, it does, but think now, that would have been done in the workshop at Inverdaigh House, before we left. What has happened since then?"

"Nothing much, we have simply ridden on it to bring us up here."

"So where is all the dust and dirt thrown up from the road? I saw the wheel hub on the other side is covered in it, but on this one we just have fresh grease," he said pointing to it, "most interesting."

"Perhaps the pony licked at it, you know what animals can be like."

Holmes chuckled. "Yes, Watson, but not this time I think, for a start it is too clean and the marks of his tongue would show up. No, this has been handled by someone who has been here since we left. The grease has become smeared over it as it was put back in place. If you look carefully, the cover has not even been screwed on properly, it seems to have been done in haste and has become cross-threaded … most careless. Let me see if I can remove it and look inside."

Taking out his pocket knife he unfolded a curved blade. Wedging it hard against its back edge and after several attempts he succeeded in loosening it. The cover came off suddenly and fell on to the ground.

"Let's have a look at this," he said, pointing at the end of the thread on the axle tree. "Now I can see what he has done. The cotter pin has been removed and the lock nut as well. It is now quite unsafe and will likely allow the wheel to fall off soon. Only the thick grease is securing the main nut now. It is that which is smeared over the cover and did not allow him to grip it properly when he replaced it."

"You are right, Holmes," I said looking closely, "I have indeed underestimated this man. What can we do now? Can we fix it temporarily do you think, otherwise we will have to walk home?"

"I think I know how. It shouldn't be too difficult," he replied. "Let's see what you have in your medical kit, Doctor. If I recall you have a small pointed instrument. We can probably use it to replace the cotter pin. It should hold until we are able to ride back to Inverdaigh House if we drive carefully."

"Yes, of course," I said as I reached down into my pocket. "I should have realised that my medical kit would have other uses. I must remember to add to it that of repairing broken axles!"

It was but the work of a few minutes before we had made a repair of sorts and replaced the cover.

"Right, Holmes, are we ready to return now?"

Holmes stood back.

"Is something else wrong, why do you hesitate now Holmes? Do you have a plan in the light of this?" I said pointing at the wheel hub.

"Yes, I am working out how best to use it to our advantage, but something is not quite right to my mind, Doctor."

"I can see no problem, haven't you just found out how he has damaged our transport and fixed it so as to get us back?"

"I have, but is it just too easy," Holmes replied.

"But if you had not discovered the hidden damage he caused, we would have driven off quite happily, then at some point, probably on a sharp corner, the wheel would have fallen off and we would most certainly have been injured, possibly even killed. Surely we can do so now. Why shouldn't we?"

"Yes, but he knows my methods by now of that I am sure," he went on.

"It is as if he was anticipating the possibility of us finding out about the sabotage he has done and even of our making a temporary repair."

"But what would be the value of that?"

"Because it could lead us into a false sense of security, believing that we had foiled his plans and were then safe to drive back to Inverdaigh House. It therefore suggests to me that he has done some other damage which we have not yet found."

"But what else can he have done? You have checked both wheels now and all around the pony's harness. All that is left is the suspension and that looks to be quite sound, any damage there we would see, it would be so obvious. What is there left?"

At just that moment our pony, seeming now to be rather bored, moved forward with the gig a few paces. From underneath something on the ground, now exposed, was shining in the sun.

"Hello, what is that, Holmes?" I asked.

He had already noticed and moved forward. Kneeling down he looked at it, then licking a finger he placed it onto the glinting material, rubbing it around.

"What is it you have found?" I asked again.

Standing up he lifted his hand in front of my face with the protruding finger just inches away and said, "How long have the Scottish Highlands had metal filings and grease as part of the terrain, Watson? Here have a closer look with this."

Holmes passed to me his magnifying glass, "That should help," he said.

Under its strong magnification I could discern tiny particles of metal clustered onto the tip of his finger.

"Someone has been here cutting metal. What and why I wonder?"

Holmes moved back to the gig and stood alongside the wheel. "Let me look underneath, I think I know. Please hold the gig steady for me."

Saying no more he took off his coat and placed it on the ground beneath the wheel, and then crawling underneath, he lay upon it looking up at the axle.

"Yes, there is something, I can see it now."

"What have you found, Holmes?"

"He has cut into the metal some way and weakened the suspension. I can see a deep groove. Quite a difficult job to do though ... needed the hand of an expert to know what he was

163

doing and cut through just the right amount, not too much or too little."

He crawled back out recovering his coat.

"So he did do two pieces of damage then."

"He did indeed. He wanted to make sure that at least one would fail. The wheel hub was really the most obvious but either way one failing would likely bring down the other. I suspect however that he did not realise that I would anticipate the second piece of sabotage which was less easy to find. I would not have done so had I not considered the wheel hub damage to be so obvious and then find the metal filings underneath. Do you recall the incident of the ladder in the hidden tunnel, Doctor?"

"Yes, I do Holmes, and it was a narrow escape you had."

"Yes, it was, and it is clear that he has tried the same idea again, that of setting a second trap hoping to catch us off guard. It came back to my mind after I saw the wheel hub damage. It will not work twice though. I also believe that he may have hurried too much whilst damaging the wheel hub which is why it was not screwed back on properly."

"Perhaps he saw us returning, Holmes?"

"Yes, but how, Doctor, that is the question. He could see very little from where he was, and remember he was also working on damaging our gig. Perhaps it proved to be more difficult than anticipated," he said thoughtfully. "He probably thought that we would be away for longer than we were though, but my timing was about right."

"Timing, what timing! Are you saying that you expected this? Come to think of it, Holmes, I almost had that impression when we came back here. The first thing you did was to check for any damage to our pony and gig. It's almost uncanny. What are you grinning at, Holmes?"

"Am I, Doctor?"

"You are, you knew all along didn't you? What game are you playing now?"

"Believe me, my old friend, I am not playing a game. But, yes, you are quite right I did expect it, in fact, I would have been disappointed if nothing had happened. You see unlike

164

you who dismissed the idea of any danger in our coming here, I anticipated it and had planned to use it so as to turn the tables on our adversary."

"Are you saying that you are now deliberately setting some sort of trap, Holmes? If so you might have told me," I said rather petulantly.

Holmes looked over at me with a mixture of sadness and surprise on his face and said, "We have known one another for a while now, Doctor, and never once have I had reason to doubt your courage and willingness to face a new challenge. Perhaps though I should have said something earlier, but I wanted to be quite sure that my trick would work."

"Well, yes, I understand, Holmes," I said feeling slightly abashed that I may have let him down. "But you know that you can always count on me, whatever it is."

His face brightened up, "Well done, Watson, I knew that I could rely on you … it will be dangerous … are you ready for another scramble through a forest do you think? I am sure that is where he has now gone."

"Of course, and I have my revolver and spare ammunition today," I said, patting it in my pocket.

"Excellent," he said. "What I want you to do is drive us back slowly and carefully, talking together, as if we were simply out for a drive and enjoying the country as we returned to Inverdaigh House, being quite unaware of the damage he has done to our vehicle. This should, I believe, lead him into a sense of false security, and give us the upper hand."

"And what do you wish to do then?" I said.

"When we get into the forest, keep going carefully down the road as if we had all the time in the world."

"We will have no choice, Holmes, the axle may not hold out otherwise."

"It does to some extent depend on your driving Doctor, but I believe that if you can keep to the smoothest parts it should last a while for our purpose."

"Last until what purpose, you mean your proposed trick?"

"I do indeed, old friend," he replied. "I do not want to disappoint our opponent, I am sure that he will be waiting for us, hiding in the forest and watching for us to have our accident, which he has engineered. What I intend to do is jump off by one of the sharp corners, the one you will recall where the forest is particularly close and dense."

"Yes, I know where you mean, so what shall I do?" I asked quizzically.

"Keep on going to the next corner, and after you have rounded it jump off quickly and run up into the forest, we should catch him in a pincer movement. It is by one of the thickest areas of woodland, and I am sure that it is the place where he will be hiding and watching. He will not expect that. Timing though will be everything."

"But he will surely see that you are no longer on the gig and will realise what you are doing, he will then make his escape before we can catch him."

"Not if I can make him think that I am on the gig."

"And how do you plan to do that?"

"By this method." Saying no more he went around to the valise behind our seats and lifting the lid pulled out a dummy wearing an old coat and held together by two pieces of wood.

"What is that, Holmes?" I said standing back laughing. "You are surely not going to fool him with that," now beginning to be suspicious of what he had in mind. "Where did it come from?"

"Last night I had one of Sir Hugh's servants make it up for me without anyone else knowing."

"Well it certainly worked well then, but what about now?"

"It is quite straightforward, I will pull the gig's hood up over us, looking as if to protect us from the wind and sun. I shall place it in between us and tie it upright, it should hold long enough for our purposes. I will pull over the leg rug and hide under it," he said, as he reached over and raised the hood. "Before we do that however there is some spare rope available, perhaps you would help me to tie it around the weakened piece underneath, it should help ease the strain on it, for our journey back."

It did not take us long to accomplish both tasks, and satisfied that we were now ready I climbed aboard. Whilst I supported the dummy in position Holmes climbed up and settled himself across the seat. After carefully pulling the rug over himself and over the 'legs' of our mannequin, the 'three' of us started off on our journey down towards the forest.

"Are you sure this is going to work, Holmes? I feel quite ridiculous talking to a dummy as if he were human. I am not a ventriloquist you know." I thought I heard him chuckle underneath his cover.

"Remember what actors say, 'You have to believe in the character you are playing and if you do so strongly enough everyone will believe in you'. For the moment let us talk and joke so as to make him believe that we are simply enjoying our ride back. If he sees and hears that he will not look too closely. I can just see out from underneath here."

"Very well, Holmes," I replied, although I have to admit with little real conviction. Despite my earlier expression of bravado and support for my friend, I was feeling increasingly uneasy about his plans and wondered if he was not being over confident. If he had suspected this he did not show it, indeed, if anything, he seemed to relish the situation.

It was not long before our road dropped down and entered the tree line, embracing us in the now familiar fresh woodland fragrance. I tried a few more attempts at conversation, but was more concerned at the integrity of our wheel repairs than any attempt at levity. Try as I would to avoid them our gig seemed to find every rock, bump and groove along the road.

Readers will know, however, particularly those interested in military history that the best laid plans can go wrong no matter how much thought has been given to the operation. On those occasions recovering it often comes down to local initiative. It was thus with us.

We had been driving for only a short while, but not yet at the spot where Holmes had planned to leap off, when we reached a shallow gulley which lay across the road. I remembered it on our way up, and noted it as a place where to take special care on our return. Some large flat slabs of rock had been laid over it forming a bridge of sorts, which, with care, would have been quite safe to drive over. As we did so however and at that very moment, something caused our pony to shy. I could not be certain but out of the corner of my eye, something small seemed to fly out of the forest, hitting him on the flank.

Our animal reared up and now being out of my control, the gig twisted, causing the wheel with the damaged axle to jam into a now opened gap between the slabs. With a sickening crack the weakened suspension gave way as the wheel, now wrenched from its axle, fell off and rolled away a few yards, before stopping against the edge of the road. The gig lurched over, crashing down heavily, depositing Holmes, myself with the mannequin in a sprawling heap, as the hood collapsed over us. The harness had broken away and our pony now finding himself free, went galloping off towards his home, the harness trailing behind him.

For a few moments I lay on the road winded but as I tried to rise found that one of my legs had become entangled between the frame of the hood and the metal arm rest. As I struggled to get free, Holmes found that he was able to push himself clear and although winded himself, quickly got to his feet.

"Are you alright, Watson?" he asked, looking down at me with much concern on his face. I could see a graze on his forehead where he had hit the track surface in his fall.

"Yes, I think so, Holmes," I replied, as I finally dragged my leg free. I could see in front of me where the protruding end of the axle had cut a groove into the surface of the track. Before I could say more Holmes leapt up and turned around. Drawing his revolver he fired three times into the forest in quick succession, the sounds of the shots echoing away through the trees.

"Did you see him, Holmes?" I asked, slowly getting to my feet.

"No, but I have a general idea of where he may be hiding, I saw something hit the pony, too. I want him to know that we are armed and coming after him," he said now reloading his gun.

"Keep low, Doctor, remember your time in Afghanistan," he went on, as he placed his hand on my shoulder pushing me down into a kneeling position.

"But he has no firearm, Holmes, I heard no shots."

"You are right, but a firearm is not my concern right now. Are you ready for the chase?"

"Yes, I think so. I am rather surprised that it has all happened so quickly. It isn't where you anticipated, Holmes," I replied, now drawing my own weapon.

"Not quite, but we must respond quickly, we are not all that far off. Let's try and turn the tables. Can you work your way around up to the left, and I will go up through here," he said pointing to part of the forest into which he had just fired. "Keep down and moving though, and avoid being a stationary target. We do not want to make it so easy for him a second time." As he said this Holmes crouched down and ran crab-like into the edge of the forest looking up into it, eagerly searching for any sign of his prey.

Taking my cue from Holmes, and for the second time during our visit to Scotland, I plunged up into the forest. Over to my right I could hear Holmes scrambling up through the undergrowth followed by two more shots. Ahead of me I thought that I could see movement, so I took aim and fired twice myself. At least our opponent knew that his plan to catch us off guard and possibly kill us, had failed.

Although, since arriving in Scotland I had much exercise and fresh air, it was again not long before I found myself gasping for breath. I seemed to catch up against every low lying branch and thicket, and concluded, not for the first time, that I was not built for much of this activity. I had been eating very well lately and my medical work in London had kept me too sedentary over recent months. Once I thought that something had passed closely nearby, but put it down to disturbing a deer or large bird. I again fired at what I thought was movement, then stopped, hiding against a tree in order to catch my breath and reload my pistol. I remembered from my

Army days to reload as quickly as possible so as not to be caught out with a part empty weapon. As my breathing slowed the forest around me had grown silent as if all the animals were listening and awaiting the next turn of events. I stood there wondering what I should do next as I could no longer hear Holmes, and did not know where he now was. Deciding that I was being of no value waiting behind the tree I dropped down onto my hands and knees and started crawling around to my left hoping that I would not be seen by the criminal, but may close with him if he was nearby.

I had gone only a few yards when in the far distance of the forest I suddenly heard a loud, drawn out, scream. Throwing caution to the wind I stood up and despite now betraying my position, called out to Holmes. In the distance I heard him shout a reply. Waiting no longer, and feeling the comfort of my revolver in my hand, I made my way as quickly as possible in his direction. Fighting my way through the forest, I eventually reached where he was waiting for me. Once again I was out of breath and sweating profusely. I found him standing by the base of a very tall tree looking down at a body. As I arrived he looked up at me and nodded towards the corpse.

"Do you not recognise him, Doctor, take a closer look."

"Good heavens, Holmes," I gasped, "it's the body of Harrison. What is he doing here!" I said as I went over and saw from the angle of his head that he had died as the result of a broken neck. "At least there are no bullet wounds." I looked up. "I thought that we had ruled him out of any involvement in the attempts on Sir Hugh's life," I said returning my gun to its pocket.

"We had my friend, but look about him," replied Holmes, pointing, "these may explain something at least."

I looked around and saw that lying nearby was a pair of broken binoculars, ones which I had seen him carry on both occasions when we had met. Hanging from a small broken branch some way off the ground, was its carrying case with the cover wrenched away. In his hand I could see the remains of a large broken bird's egg and on his clothes the yolk of another, with the shell lying on the ground by his coat. Some broken twigs, clearly from that of a bird's nest, lay scattered around. I looked up trying to see the point high in the tree where it had been. The branches were too dense to see through, but flying around in a seemingly agitated way was a golden eagle, calling with a plaintive cry as if in protest at the recent assault on its fortress home.

"It's not hard to see what happened here, Holmes," I said, looking across at him.

"No, but the question is why was he here at the same time as our visit to the waterfall and subsequent damage to our gig?"

I had momentarily forgotten about the possibility of an assailant nearby and possibly stalking us at that very moment. My hand went back to the butt of my gun.

"I don't think that you will need that now, Doctor. The man we were pursuing has now escaped, for the moment that is."

"We were surely right about Harrison though, but how could he have been involved by being right at the top of a tree."

"That is not entirely clear yet, Doctor, but what is evident is that he climbed up high and was robbing the nest of an eagle. It seems likely that the bird attacked him and that he lost his precarious footing and fell, taking with him his sought after prize."

"There is some poetic justice there at least, Holmes ... what are you doing now?" I said, as I saw him making a start to climb the same tree.

"These particular trees are very easy to climb with many branches conveniently spaced ... did you never do so as a boy?"

"I did, indeed, Holmes."

"Then just help me up to the first branch. I think that Harrison here may have used some nearby log angled against the tree to assist him."

"But why, Holmes, we need to go back to Inverdaigh House and inform the police. They will need to investigate.

Our pony will have returned by now and they will be making haste to find out what has happened to us. I cannot believe that you wish to look at eagles."

"No, but I want to see just how far I can see from the top, it may tell me more about why Harrison climbed up himself."

"You mean that he was not doing any studies of his favourite birds at all?"

"Oh, yes, he probably was, but that may also have been a cover for something else," said Holmes.

"There is also something else up there which I cannot see properly from here. Let's find out."

"Very well, if you insist, we have come this far we may as well see it through," I replied, now pushing him up into the lowest part of the tree. Reaching the first branch he hauled himself up and standing upon it stretched upwards to the one above and commenced to climb steadily up the trunk. As on our first visit to the woodlands he showed a keen sense of balance and agility, so it was not long before I saw him reach close to the top.

"Can you see much from up there, Holmes?" I shouted to him through cupped hands.

"Yes, quite a lot, and something else as well. I'll bring it down."

It only took him a few minutes to climb back down and drop at my feet, sweating slightly.

"What do you think that is?" he said, handing to me a large piece of coloured cloth."

"Some sort of shirt or tablecloth," I replied, "but it does not seem to be like either. Where was it exactly?"

"Caught up in the tree, Doctor, it is clear that it was being used by Harrison," he said, pointing to his body.

"What use would he have for it, Holmes, to protect himself from attacks by the eagle?" I suggested.

"No, using it as a signal. When I reached near to the top I had a very distant view of the track leading towards the waterfall and where we had left the gig. I believe that he was using it to tell the criminal that we were returning so as to give him time to make his way back here into the forest.

Something went wrong, however; you remember that I said he had not screwed the hub cover on properly and that it had become cross-threaded."

"I do."

"Well, I believe that he was given the warning only when we were well on our way back to the gig and was forced to hurry. That also explains why there was no attempt to hide the signs of the metal filings on the ground; he had to rush away before having time to finish the job properly."

"Why did that happen do you think? It was surely most careless of him?"

"Because the signaller had his attention diverted."

"How?"

"Because he had become so engrossed in his egg collecting that he lost concentration on what he was supposed to be doing and saw us returning only just in time when the criminal was not far ahead of us."

"How could he have seen Harrison's signal, Holmes? Our gig was a long way from here."

"My dear fellow, clearly he needed to have a telescope or binoculars, enabling him to see this cloth being waved from high up in this tree. He would have had to keep checking for any signals from Harrison. I saw several very small indentations by our gig near to where we were standing. I did not know what they were at the time but I do now. They were made by the tripod holding a telescope. The criminal must have been very annoyed when he realised that Harrison had let him down. In my view it was a weak part of his plan. Perhaps it is a very good example of the old saying, 'Not to mix business with pleasure'. He did make it rather easy for me though," said Holmes smiling. "But you are right, Doctor, we must return now, they will soon be here to find out what happened to us. For the moment there is nothing else we can do here."

Saying no more we turned and made our way back through the forest. It did not take us long to regain the road and we had not been walking long when we heard in the distance the sound of galloping horses, rumbling carts and men's voices calling. Rounding a corner they came into view in full cry and upon seeing us a shout went up to confirm that we had been found. Inspector Lennox was in the first vehicle, which pulled up sharply upon reaching us.

"Mr. Holmes, Dr. Watson, there you are, thank goodness. I was at Inverdaigh House with Sir Hugh when your pony arrived. We saw the broken harness and knew that something had gone badly wrong, are you both all right?"

"Yes, thank you Inspector we are both well, but if you go back up the road a short distance you will find our gig minus a wheel."

"What exactly happened, Mr. Holmes? Sir Hugh keeps his carriages in the best of condition I know."

"Shall we say that not everyone wishes to keep them like that, eh, Watson," said Holmes turning to me.

"That is true Inspector," I replied, "if you look underneath at the suspension structure as well as the wheel axle and hub, I am sure that you will see exactly what we mean. Holmes and I narrowly escaped serious injury. Our gig was sabotaged whilst we were at the waterfall. We believe the perpetrator came here," I said, pointing up into the trees.

"Yes, and when you do get to our gig, Inspector," went on Holmes, "perhaps you and your men would then make your way back up into the forest. Look for a very tall tree and by its base you will find a dead body. Do you recall a gentleman called Harrison, a friend of Sir Hugh's, who also has an interest in golden eagles and was due to give a lecture at Inverdaigh House?"

"Yes, I do know of him," replied the Inspector.

"Well, he was in the forest and fell from the top of a tree whilst stealing their eggs ... amongst other things that is. You should have no difficulty in finding him, together with all the evidence."

"Thank you, gentlemen," said Inspector Lennox, "we will do so immediately, but I must say that I did not believe that Harrison was a man such as that," he said somewhat surprised. "So it was he who was the culprit, eh, who would have thought it, he just did not look the type ... too studious and not over robust either."

I was about to reply when I saw Holmes turn and give me a sharp look. I realised that he did not want any comment made about the fact that the death of Harrison was only part of the puzzle, and that the real criminal was still at large, but went on to say, "Well, Inspector, if you really believe he was indeed the true culprit it would seem that the matter is now solved. We must leave it to you, after all you are a man of much experience in criminal matters are you not?"

"As you say, Mr. Holmes, I have had much experience, for now, however, we must go on up ahead and find your gig and then locate the body. A larger cart is coming along just behind us, we thought it might be needed so we can use it for Harrison's body as well," he said as he informed his men of the new task in hand. As he said this I thought I detected momentarily a slight frown of puzzlement cross his face as if he suspected a hint in Holmes's comment, a hint perhaps that everything was not completely settled and that there may be more yet to come. If so it did not seem to concern him at the time, but I felt sure that later on that evening, probably over a glass of whisky, he would reflect upon it. He was an Inspector after all, and did not achieve his position without having some ability in understanding his fellow man.

Leaving him to arrange collection of our broken gig and the subsequent removal of Harrison's body, Holmes and I started on our return. The larger cart shortly came along and as soon as it was out of earshot I turned to Holmes, finding it hard to keep a slight irritation out of my voice.

"Why did you want nothing else said concerning Harrison just being an associate of the criminal Holmes? The Inspector will go away believing that the case is now solved and that the danger to Sir Hugh no longer exists."

"Because he would likely make it worse."

"In what way?"

"It's quite simple, he had a number of his men with him did he not?"

"Yes, in total around a dozen."

"So given that if I had told him that Harrison was only the assistant and that the real criminal had escaped us, away up through the forest, what do you think he would have done?"

"Why, he would immediately organise a hue and cry, searching through all these woodlands."

"And that, Watson, is what I did not want to happen, at least just yet. If the Inspector had acted as you correctly surmised, I have no doubt that the criminal would have gone to ground and taken no further action for some time, perhaps many weeks. We would have been right back to where we started, making it much more difficult for ourselves. No, I want him to believe that he has evaded us all again so he will soon formulate another plan, but I intend to make it his last."

"Very well, Holmes, I expect that as usual, you will tell me when you are ready."

"Indeed, I will, old friend, indeed I will," he said smiling to himself as we made our way back to Inverdaigh House.

Later that afternoon a sorrowful procession arrived, the gig was sent on to the blacksmiths for repair whilst the police transferred the body to Glasgow for the usual *post mortem* procedure. Inspector Lennox said very little but we learnt that the previous day, after leaving us to visit the island and finding the containers of fish remains, he arrested the poacher Brodney McCall, charging him with the murder of Duncan Campbell. Later on that evening Brodney McCall was quietly released.

Chapter Thirteen

Death Of An Engineer

"**M**r. Sherlock Holmes, a telegram for Mr. Sherlock Holmes."

Despite the close escape with our damaged gig the previous day I had awoken early that following morning. I was attending to my toilet when I heard a servant calling for Holmes outside of his room. I went across to my door and opening it saw, along the corridor, Holmes reading a newly received telegram. He looked up.

"Ah, Watson, it looks as if I shall have to return to London. I shall go immediately after breakfast."

"But, Holmes," I said, "why do you need to go back now? After yesterday's adventure a day's rest would do us both no harm, you took quite a blow to your head when the gig went over and I have some bruising myself. I was counting on a more relaxing day and remember we still have the criminal to catch."

"Of course, old friend, but this is urgent, I'll see you down at breakfast in a few minutes."

"Very well," I replied, "it must be very important," I mumbled to myself as I went back into my room. I dressed hurriedly, but by the time I arrived down for breakfast found that Holmes was well through his and preparing to leave.

"Can you not tell me why you have to return to London so urgently?" I asked with a puzzled frown. "What about Sir Hugh and Miss McFarlane, don't you owe it to them to stay and finish what we came for? We must surely be closing with the criminal, you said so yourself did you not?"

"Indeed, Watson, but I plan to return here as soon as possible."

"How long do you think that will be?"

"Within a week I estimate."

"A week, Holmes, but much could happen here in that time! Are you not being irresponsible? It is not like you to go off part way through an investigation like this, knowing that the criminal is still at large. Sir Hugh is still at serious risk and I am sure that his daughter will not be impressed."

"Yes, it is regrettable I know, and I would not do so if it was not so important. Mrs. Hudson has contacted me as I asked her to but only if my attention was required urgently in London and I accept her judgment on the matter. Anyway, I have every confidence in you, Watson, and do not forget that you still have Inspector Lennox and the local police to assist you if necessary."

"Yes, I had forgotten about that, Holmes, they have been a great help so far," I said rather disparagingly.

Holmes laughed, "do not be too concerned, Doctor, I believe that the criminal had something of an unpleasant surprise yesterday, and is currently nursing his own wounds. I am sure that at this very moment he is planning his next step but there will be a lull before he takes any further action, as has happened on each occasion so far."

"If you say so, Holmes," I replied, but I confess with little sense of enthusiasm. The servants came in with my breakfast as Holmes was finishing his. He then got up and went to his room to finish packing.

I was pouring myself a second cup of tea when Sir Hugh came into the room. "Ah, Dr. Watson, there you are, you will have heard by now that Mr. Holmes will be leaving us for a few days."

"Yes, Sir Hugh, I am to stay here and look after you and Caroline. He feels that we are close to catching the criminal, and I am certain that he will do so on his return."

"I have every confidence in you both, Dr. Watson," replied Sir Hugh, "and look forward to his return. In the meantime I have had my best carriage made available for him. There is no steamboat due for a while so my new coachman will take him to the nearest station, where he can take a train to Glasgow and then on to London. He should be there by tomorrow at the latest."

"Your new coachman?" I asked quizzically.

"Yes, MacGavern, my usual coachman has been taken ill it seems, so one of my other staff will drive instead. Ah, there you are, Mr. Holmes, all ready to go I see."

Holmes had appeared at the door as we were talking. "Yes, Sir Hugh, I will return as soon as I can, in the meantime I have every confidence in Watson, but please take my advice gentlemen and stay close to the house until I return. We will soon have this whole nefarious business finished." Saying no more he turned, went out of the house to his awaiting carriage and was driven swiftly away.

"Do you have any plans until Mr. Holmes returns, Dr. Watson?" asked Sir Hugh.

"There is not a great deal I can do at the moment, Sir Hugh," I replied, "but will just stay around the area. Between the local constable and myself I am sure that the criminal will realise it is in his interest to keep away from here for a while."

"Very well, I will leave you to your own devices. It is rather strange that Mr. Holmes had to leave so suddenly, especially after yesterday's incident with the gig and your forest adventure," said Sir Hugh, seemingly puzzled. "Please let us know if you require anything, in the meantime I have some papers to attend to. Lunch will be at the usual time," he went on as he left the room.

With Holmes now absent I saw no need to hurry, so after finishing my own breakfast I made my way back to my room. I sat down looking out of my window wondering how best to most effectively spend my time until Holmes's return. I felt that it would be useful to keep up to date notes on events so far, to try and clarify the case in my own mind, so that when we were back in Baker Street I would be able to write a more comprehensive text. Indeed I even played with the idea that, at some time in the future, they could form a basis of study for anyone interested in the science of deduction, and possibly even leading to improved policing methods.

Lunchtime came and went, and again I noticed that Caroline was absent. I later saw her briefly around the house and once we exchanged a short conversation in which she expressed the view of hoping that Mr. Holmes would soon return. She seemed to be rather distracted though and politely made an excuse to leave and go to deal with other matters.

For the rest of that day I wandered around the grounds of Inverdaigh House, but not really expecting to find anything of use to Holmes for when he returned. I had several conversations with the local constable, who had by now become rather bored, but felt that his presence and that of his colleague would likely deter any further activity against Sir Hugh. Instructions had been given to ensure that he was well fed and apart from visits by Inspector Lennox there were no real demands being made upon him. He had even put on a little weight. One matter I did note to pass on to Holmes, however, was that he informed me that the animal mutilations had ceased with nothing new being reported. He could not speculate as to why that might be, but being a local man dismissed it as being just something 'that country folk get up to now and again'. Nevertheless I felt somehow that it could be important, and if so, then Holmes ought to know of it.

The following day brought no changes and I continued to spend my time walking around the grounds and woodlands familiarising myself with the tracks and footpaths. In particular I made note of some of the areas that I felt could be used by someone who wished to come unseen and watch the house, then slipping quietly away again after noting all our movements. I too was becoming very bored.

It was therefore on the third day after Holmes's departure that I took my now regular route, taking care to move around as quietly as possible. I harboured the idea that, in Holmes's absence, I might even now catch the criminal and at last put an end to Sir Hugh's ordeal. I had walked through into a particularly dense area of shrubbery when I thought I heard a noise. I could not be sure whether or not it was someone talking very quietly and moving around. I stopped, hiding against the trunk of a bushy tree. There it was again, and I was now certain that I could hear someone or something shuffling around.

Putting my hand in my pocket I drew out my revolver and with a sudden shout so as to startle whoever it was, I leapt out. There I stood, brandishing my revolver, only to be faced with Caroline in a passionate embrace with a young man. The two lovers, startled, sprang apart. The young man I recognised immediately as being the same one whom Holmes and I had seen and pursued in the woodlands on the day following our arrival. For a brief moment we all stood, looking at one another, not knowing what to say, then, like a gazelle, he suddenly turned and ran off into the nearby forest, leaving Caroline and I facing one another, my revolver in hand. On her face was a look of anxiety and pleading.

"Oh, please do not say anything, Dr. Watson. Father does not know about us yet, he may not understand."

"Why … er …yes, of course," I spluttered, embarrassed at so inadvertently barging into a moment of intimacy. "Of course not, I hadn't realised, please accept my apologies. It really is nothing to do with me anyway," I said returning my gun to my pocket.

Her face relaxed and she gave an anxious smile of relief. "Thank you, Dr. Watson. We know that at some time our relationship will become known, but we feel that now is not the time, not with all the attempts on father's life."

"But isn't he the young man that Holmes and I saw …" Caroline raised her hand to stop me.

"Yes, Dr. Watson, Hamish had told me all about what happened in the forest when you and Mr. Holmes saw him after you found the fallen tree. He saw you both follow him but thought he had evaded you. He then saw you both and pretended that he had not when you returned here."

I smiled in spite of myself, so this man, Hamish, had seen us follow him after all, and knew that Holmes and I had located the site of the second attempt on her father's life. This Hamish was no fool, and I wondered what else was it that he knew.

"Just who is Hamish, Caroline?" I asked. "Why do you need to keep it so secret?" I felt that in view of events I ought to know so as to keep Holmes fully informed. "Would not your father be pleased?" I continued.

"Have you not realised, Dr. Watson, Hamish is the eldest son of Brodney McCall, the man whom Inspector Lennox charged with the attempted murder of my father, but has just been released from custody."

For the second time I stood still, saying nothing, absorbing its implications.

"Er, no, I did not ... yes, I can see just how it complicates matters."

"So you see, Dr. Watson," replied Caroline, "we do not wish this to be common knowledge just yet, I am sure that you will keep your promise ... but you may share it with Mr. Holmes when he returns.

"Thank you," I replied, "Mr. Holmes is, of course, a man of absolute discretion."

"Yes, Doctor. Father and I have every faith in him, and you naturally. We feel sure that he has everything in hand and that all will soon be resolved. I must go now or I will be missed, perhaps I will see you at dinner tonight." With that she turned and quickly made her way back to the house.

Here was a complication indeed, and the sooner Holmes was made aware of it, so much the better. Completing my route through the grounds I was in such deep thought that had I walked past the criminal himself I doubt if I would have noticed him. I felt a desperate need for Holmes's wisdom and wondered just where he was right now.

Dinner that night passed uneventfully, with little being said and Sir Hugh trying unsuccessfully to encourage conversation, putting our subdued manner down to Holmes's absence and wondering what new event may arise. From time to time, Caroline glanced across at me, knowing the secret we now shared and clearly uneasy at having to keep it away from her father. I suspected that this was the first time in her life she felt so distant from him.

After dinner I went out for a walk, checking again with the constable that he had seen nothing amiss. He had not, and after I bade him goodnight, I returned to my room.

I cleaned and reloaded my revolver, then laid it alongside my bed before settling down for the night. At first I slept fitfully, with dreams of chasing opponents whom I could just not catch no matter how hard I tried.

It must have been just after midnight when I awoke suddenly. Something had disturbed me. I could not be sure what exactly but I thought I heard a noise not of the night. I lay there listening, being uncertain that it had not been a dream caused by my earlier meal. No, I heard it again and I was sure now that it came from downstairs. Could it be that Sir Hugh's potential assassin had decided that he would succeed only by breaking into Inverdaigh House itself. If so he was taking a big risk. It was not his style to date, but perhaps he deemed it necessary to take a more direct approach.

I rose and quickly dressed, then, holding my revolver, quietly opened my door and stood, listening. I heard the sound again and now was certain that it came from the entrance hall. Creeping along the corridor, as quietly as I could, I reached the top of the stairs and paused. All was now silent so I made my way slowly downstairs.

Try as I might, every step I made seemed to echo around the house and twice I stopped, listening again. I could hear nothing now, the house was silent and I fervently hoped that any intruder may have quietly slipped away. I was, however, determined to follow up on my quest, as not to do so would seem like cowardice on my part, and perhaps lose me the best chance I had of apprehending the criminal himself. I reached the bottom of the stairs.

Still hearing nothing I started to creep along the hall when my foot trod on what could only have been a piece of broken glass. It gave a loud crunch and moments later I was certain that I heard movement ahead of me. Whoever it was had now moved into the large drawing room. Again I stood listening but could only hear my own heartbeat. Try as I could I was unable to reduce my breathing to that of a hunter stalking his prey.

I passed through the door and had taken but two steps when I sensed something behind me. My heart nearly stopped as I felt a strong hand grasp over my mouth, stifling any sound, as a familiar voice whispered in my ear, "Quietly now, Watson, or you'll awaken the whole household."

Loosening his hand from around my mouth, I spun around. "Holmes," I gasped, "it's you, what are you doing here? We all thought that you were in London. I thought that you were the criminal we are all pursuing and that he had broken in."

"Regretfully, not, Doctor, but I know where he is," he replied, "but as for my arrival I have been back here for a while now."

"But how, Holmes? You could surely not have gone to London, dealt with the issue Mrs. Hudson spoke of then returned back here by this time."

"No, for the simple reason, Doctor, that I never went to London."

"But why? You had a telegram from Baker Street did you not?"

"Indeed, I did."

"Then what happened?"

"The reason, my good friend, was that I had indeed sent a telegram to Baker Street, and it was to Mrs. Hudson. It was intended, however, as a ploy. Mrs. Hudson did exactly as I asked her … to send a telegram asking me to return urgently. She knew though it was sent just to let people believe that I was required elsewhere. I, of course, went through all the motions of leaving, even as far as going to the station to catch a train on to London."

"So what happened then?"

"As soon as my coachman left the station to return here, I took steps of my own to do so, by another means."

"But as you are back here again why leave in the first place? Did you not trust me to go along with your deception?"

"I do, Watson, absolutely, and I believe that you have played your part splendidly. It had become clear to me, however, that we had more chance of apprehending this man if he thought that I was not here. I wanted to let him believe that he had been presented with the opportunity he had been waiting for."

"I see, Holmes. So where have you been all of this time if I may ask?" I said, with a slight disapproval in the sound of my voice.

He smiled as he replied, "You will recall that by the edge of the loch, by our canoe, there is a houseboat. With a little adjustment it makes quite a comfortable hideaway for a few days. It also allowed me to move around the estate discreetly and observe activities. Indeed, I saw you checking around on one occasion."

"Why, thank you, Holmes, I am pleased that you approved of my work in what I thought was your absence, I need not have bothered it seems."

"But, my dear fellow, you played a key role. It was crucial that everyone, including you, believed that I had gone away, and it worked!"

"So where is he now? You said that you knew."

"I watched him go across to the island. The game's afoot, my friend, so are you ready? I see that you have your revolver with you. I have mine, too. Before the night is out we may need them both."

As I looked at him, despite the poor light, I could see his eyes glinting. I had seen this previously, just before setting off on another adventure, it was as if he had become alive in a new way.

"Of course, Holmes, as always you know that you can count on me. What do you want to do now?" I said with an edge of excitement in my voice.

"I see that you are dressed so we must leave the house quietly and work our way back down to the loch side. We will need to take the canoe and make our way across to the island. Try not to tread on the broken glass again. I'll explain it all to you later. I came in through the window by the way, but we can use the main door now," he grinned.

He turned and together we crept out of Inverdaigh House.

Once we were clear of the house I felt able to relax but kept my voice down. It was a quiet night and sounds carry a long way, particularly over water. In the distance a night bird called, probably a heron, and further off a stag was roaring, his call echoing through the hills. Reaching the water's edge we found the canoe drawn up on the beach by the houseboat. We climbed in carefully and pushed off into the silence.

The surface was flat calm as we eased our way across the sheltered inlet out onto the open loch and with firm, but quiet strokes, slid through the water. As we touched upon the beach amongst the trees our canoe made barely a sound, and with hardly a splash we climbed out.

"Where to now, Holmes," I whispered, "where is he do you think?"

"I believe that he will be in the tunnel, the enlarged section where we found the table. He is using it for a workshop."

"Why? When we found it the other day all that was in there was the table but no tools. I assumed that he may be using it just as a hideaway."

"Yes he is, but more than that, amongst other things he is using it to build a crossbow."

"A crossbow, Holmes, did you say crossbow, why would he want to make one of those? So medieval a weapon, why go to all that trouble?" I said almost laughing at the very idea. "If you wanted to shoot anything what is wrong with a rifle? We had plenty of them in the army you know, good ones, too."

"Indeed, that is so, Watson, but what you have to remember is that they do have a number of drawbacks as well as advantages … the latter are of course obvious."

"And the former?"

"Five primarily; the need to have a good industrial base from which to manufacture them; an efficient logistics organisation to supply them with ammunition and spare parts; they are very subject to moisture; they make a lot of noise and a great deal of smoke, but does that not tell you something?"

"Well, yes, of course, it does, but I fail to see how a crossbow could be viable for him, more of a plaything really, not a serious weapon in this modern world … far to short a range for a start."

"Not so, old friend, not so, but we can discuss that later, for the moment we have to catch him whatever he is doing. Are you still ready for the chase, crossbow or not, even if they are just playthings?" he grinned again.

"Of course I am, Holmes, let's get on with it."

"Splendid," he replied smiling, placing his hand on my shoulder. "We will need to go in and flush him out of his lair. It will be dangerous work but fortunately he does not yet know we are here."

"But it has three entrances, Holmes, if we include the one in the roof."

"Yes, that makes it more difficult so the plan is this, you make your way to the other side of the island, to the far end where we saw the tracks in the sand and wait just above there, in the trees. I will move in from this end, with the overgrown entrance. Fortunately we have a clear night and a good moon. But take great care, Watson, if he hears us coming he will try and slip away."

"Won't he see your light as you move towards him along the tunnel?"

"No, for the simple reason that I shall not use a light, I will feel my way along. I know it now, and as I approach his workshop area I will see the lights he must be using. I will surprise him there, but see yourself as a wicket keeper just in case he escapes away down the tunnel. If he does manage to slip away out of the roof he will still need to make his way to his boat, where you will be waiting to catch him."

"Very well, Holmes, but what boat do you mean, we did not see any boat earlier."

"Yes, we did, a very unusual one, he has designed and made. We saw its tracks. We will see it tonight I am sure, but for the moment though, let us move into position. I will give you ten minutes, that should be enough time I think."

"It's at times like this that I wish we had the Inspector along, as well as his constables," I said, almost to myself.

"They will be here in a while, I have already sent for him," Holmes replied. "They should now be racing up here in a steamboat. The problem is that it can be seen and heard from several miles away. It will give our opponent plenty of warning and a chance to escape before they arrive, which is why we have to catch him first. He is quite ruthless as you know, so we shall have to move without delay. Here, take a light for yourself, in case you need it but use it sparingly," he said passing one to me.

Taking the light from him, and moving as silently as possible, I started to make my way back across the island following the route I had taken on our previous visit. Fortunately the moonlight allowed me to see the trees and ruined walls I had skirted around. Looking about me I could see no sign of Holmes, so I realised that he was already moving across into position by the other tunnel entrance, and I knew that I must now move on as quickly as I could. Glancing up I looked back along the loch and was surprised to see in the far distance the faint glow of a light and recognised it as being that of a steamboat. Inspector Lennox had obviously received the information from Holmes and responded immediately. Across the loch whispers of mist were beginning to form.

Moving quickly now I stepped over some old stonework, remembering that it was around here that I nearly fell into a hole amongst the ruins. The last thing I wanted now was a broken ankle.

Suddenly, out of the corner of my eye over to my right, I saw a shadow move. I froze. Surely it could not be the man we were trying to catch. As I reached into my pocket for my revolver a breeze swept through the trees causing the moonlight to cast dancing shadows all around. This is ridiculous I told myself, how could he know that we were here. What would Holmes say, allowing myself imagining our opponent behind every tree. I laughed inwardly and took a deep breath as the breeze died and all was still once more. I moved on again.

Possibly it was the sharp relief of the shadows cast in the moonlight and my reluctance to use the lantern but a short way on, as I reached around the trunk of a small tree, I placed my foot down – and stepped – into nothing. Fortunately as I reached around I had taken the precaution of grasping a small branch and this I clung to as I swung around struggling to hold on and pull myself back up again. My foot flailed around trying to find something solid, but in the process kicked against the edge of the hole. As it did so I heard a loosened rock crash down followed by a showering of earth and smaller stones. Regaining my balance, I recovered myself, thankful that I had not fallen in. I realised however that the noise I had created would now have alerted anyone nearby, and that I was also falling behind the time Holmes had allowed for me. Throwing caution to the wind I lit my lantern and it was not long before I found myself overlooking the hidden cove from which we had earlier seen the mysterious tracks.

The moonlight showed everything clearly and there was sign of no one. I relaxed, extinguished my lantern and sat down against a large rock, feeling its coldness through my coat. Some branches from a nearby tree brushed against my face. The loch, spread out in front of me, looked beautiful, and I pondered on how any nefarious activity could happen around here and wondered just how long it would take Holmes to flush out our quarry – if he had not been caught by Holmes already he must be here soon. I sat in silence listening for footsteps but could hear nothing except the occasional rustle of leaves as the breeze again swept over the island. I became aware of a toad crawling over my leg as he made his way into the moist leaves by my feet.

I was now beginning to feel distinctly uneasy. Surely I should have heard or seen something by now. A conviction was growing in my mind that for some reason our quarry had become aware of us and had managed to evade Holmes. If so he could be here by now, possibly even suspecting a trap for him at this end of the island. Was he perhaps just a few yards away, creeping through the trees I thought to myself, as my imagination went wild. Little did I know, however, just how true this was.

As my sense of unease grew stronger it seemed to me that, in the event of a sudden attack, I would be better placed if I changed my position. Therefore moving as quietly as possible, I started easing my way across to a selected spot nearby.

Suddenly I heard a twig snap. For the second time that night I froze, listening intently as I heard the sound of small stones rolling down the high bank above the beach. I realised that the criminal was indeed here, and that I would need to move quickly if I was to catch him. I stood up and through the overhanging branches I could make out a dark figure standing on the ground below me holding something I could not see clearly. Pulling out my revolver I called out to him a challenge. On hearing my shout he turned to look up at me, pointing the object he was carrying.

"Look out, Dr. Watson!" A voice shouted out as a dark human form hit me, throwing me down, my weapon falling from my hand, as a projectile hurled inches past my head with a hissing noise. "Are you alright, Doctor," said the same voice, "that was close, he only just missed you."

I struggled to rise, but was held down by my saviour.

"Stay down, he is nearby and reloading," the voice spoke softly into my ear. I twisted and looked upwards – straight into the face of Hamish McCall.

"What happened?" I asked, "where did you come from, what are you doing here?"

"The same as you and Mr. Holmes, Dr. Watson, trying to catch a dangerous criminal."

Rolling over onto my knees and feeling around the ground, I located my gun and stood up. "Where is he now?" I asked, peering through the trees and down at the beach below me. In the moonlight I could make out a figure pushing a boat of sorts towards the water. Seeing a movement from him I instinctively ducked as my assailant, now realising my position, loosed another crossbow bolt in my direction. I heard it again fly past, making its distinctive hissing sound as the shaft cut through the air. Seconds later I heard it strike a tree far behind me. Aiming quickly I fired twice at the now retreating shape as he disappeared between the large boulders forming the entrance. My shots ricocheted, echoing through the night across the water, as I became aware in the distance of the now fast approaching steamboat.

"I think he has escaped us, Doctor," said Hamish, looking over my shoulder as at the same time I heard three more shots, fired from across to my left.

"Are you alright, Watson," I heard Holmes calling, his voice clear in the night, "I think that I may have winged him, what about you?"

"No," I don't think so, but he nearly got me with his crossbow," I shouted back as a cloud passed across the face of the moon changing the waters of the loch into an inky blackness. "The crew of the steamboat will never see him now."

"We can still catch him," replied Holmes. "Can you get back here quickly, we may be able to chase him across in the canoe?"

"I'm on my way, Holmes," I called, then turned to Hamish but he, anticipating my question, said, "I'll use my own boat, Dr. Watson, if you don't mind." He then turned away, quickly making his way across to where he had left it on the far side of the island.

Re-lighting my lantern I hurriedly made my way over to where I heard Holmes's last call and found him waiting, standing upon the high point of a small promontory.

"Ah, there you are, Watson, he came your way then after all, but he won't get far, he knows the net is closing."

"Yes, but he nearly escaped me. Hamish saw him just in time."

"Ah, yes, Hamish, I knew that he was around somewhere, a useful man to have about you in a scrap."

"How did he escape you, Holmes?"

"As I was making my way along the tunnel something must have happened which alerted him," he said looking over at me.

"Do you know what it was?" I asked, saying nothing about my near fall into the hole, and suspecting that to be the cause.

"No, he escaped by using the roof exit just before I reached him. When I realised what had happened I came back out and started making my way around towards you. However, just after you shot at him I saw him in his boat as he went out into the loch I was able to get three rounds at him just before the moonlight faded."

"You hit him then?"

"I believe so, just enough to slow him down, but he is out there somewhere," he said, pointing out into the darkness, "but look, perhaps the Inspector will catch him if he is quick."

We could see the Inspector's vessel fast approaching, lit up by the light of its firebox, reflected in the fog rapidly forming over the surface of the water. As we watched the drama unfolding the cloud covering the moon passed by and the light now freed of its curtain, unfolded its full brightness upon the loch.

"See there, Watson," said Holmes again, "that's where he is."

In the moonlight we could just make out a small figure, barely rising out of the mist, with the steamboat pulsating at full speed, sparks leaping from the funnel, charging along through it.

"I don't think they have seen him, Holmes, he is in their direct path," I said as at that moment shouts from the crew could be heard as the vessel's whistle blew shrill across the night.

"They have now," replied Holmes as it became clear that the criminal in his small boat would be unable to evade the steamboat bearing down on him only yards away. Seconds later there came the sound of a heavy impact followed by a loud scream stopping abruptly, and much shouting from the steamer. Above all we could hear the voice of Inspector Lennox calling out instructions to its helmsman who, putting it into full reverse, brought it quickly to a halt. The steamer now lay stationary, throwing over the mist a glowing sheen of light as the crew, peering down into the murk, sought to locate their victim.

"Let's get to the canoe, Doctor, I don't know if we can help. It may be too late."

"Yes, but at least we should try, if they do find him and get him out of the water he may be in need of immediate medical assistance."

Saying no more, we ran as quickly as we could down to the beach where we had left our canoe.

Climbing in we pushed off and moved out across the flat calm water, immediately finding ourselves enveloped in the mist now covering the entire surface. It was an eerie feeling paddling towards the muffled calls emanating from the vessel ahead, with every sound echoing all around us. Approaching the steamboat now looming out of the mist we showed our lantern and pulled up alongside. Inspector Lennox saw us and came over.

"There you are, Mr. Holmes, we came as soon as I received your message. I had realised from our earlier conversations that I was wrong about Harrison, that he was not the key criminal we were after, but his assistant. You were of course quite right, I had jumped too hastily to the wrong conclusion. I had been expecting your call but was unable to get here in time. The mist was just too dense for us to see him otherwise I am sure he would have been caught. When we hit his boat I know that he went under our hull ... we felt something hit the propeller. There was nothing we could do. I am certain that he has drowned."

"Yes, Inspector," replied Holmes, "I am sure that it is so and with the mist covering the loch like this, it is something we could not foresee. I believe that he tried to take advantage of it to escape us both as he knew the local weather. He nearly succeeded, too, but it would have been only for a while."

"Indeed, Mr. Holmes, I did as you advised and have already placed my men nearby, even if he had got ashore he would have been arrested. But we do not even know who this man was, or even his name, do you have any idea?" he asked looking at us both.

"I simply refer to him as 'The Engineer'," Holmes replied, "but I am sure that your investigations will eventually lead to finding out more, Inspector. After all your department has many resources for that does it not?"

"Yes, we will have to start work on that tomorrow, gentlemen." He paused looking around him. "There is nothing much more we can do here, the mist is just too thick, we can hardly see the water to recover his body now, we have no choice but to wait until daylight … after the weather has cleared. What do you both intend to do now?"

"Dr. Watson and myself will make our way back to Inverdaigh House and catch up on some sleep, then we will see what the morning brings. I am sure, however, that Sir Hugh and Caroline will be very relieved to hear that their ordeal is now over."

Chapter Fourteen

Return Home

I awoke late the following morning somewhat annoyed with myself as I had intended to be up earlier after the previous night's events. On arriving downstairs for breakfast I met up with Sir Hugh.

"Good morning to you, Dr. Watson," he said cheerily, "I hear that you, and Mr. Holmes, have had quite an adventurous night."

"We have indeed, Sir Hugh. One I shall never forget," I replied, as a servant came in with my food. "Where is Holmes now?" I asked looking around me.

"He was up some hours ago, Doctor, and is now I believe out on the loch with Inspector Lennox. They are all searching for the body of the criminal mastermind who has been blighting my life for so long. I have to say, Dr. Watson, that I am most grateful indeed to you, and Mr. Holmes, for your most devoted efforts, I understand that you were in great danger yourself and were almost killed. Now that the criminal has met his just desserts I hope that you both will stay on here with us awhile, you can relax and enjoy the Highland scenery and fresh air."

"That is most kind of you, Sir Hugh, but I suspect that Holmes will want to return to London as soon as he has finished here, and as for the danger it reminded me of some of my Army experiences," I said grinning. "It sometimes puts some spice into life don't you think?"

"I can understand that, Doctor, but you are too modest. We will not underestimate the work and risk to which you both have been exposed on my behalf. Caroline is also enormously relieved. It is really thanks to her that you are both here. She was quickly aware of the danger I was in, which I have to admit, I too easily dismissed."

"Yes, when she first contacted us in Baker Street it was obvious to Holmes that something nefarious was happening. Where is Caroline by the way, I have not seen her this morning?"

"She has had to go out early again, between you and me, Dr. Watson, I am beginning to suspect that she may have a secret assignation," he replied with a knowing wink.

"I see, Sir Hugh, you will no doubt find out soon enough I feel sure," I said pouring out for myself another cup of tea. "As soon as I have eaten I will take myself down to the loch if you don't mind?" I went on now trying to change the subject. "Will you be coming along, too, Sir Hugh?"

"Yes, I will, Doctor, but there is something I must do first," he said as he went out.

I quickly finished breakfast and a brisk walk took me once again to the side of the loch. With the dawn the fog had dispersed and the air over the water was now crystal clear.

Across the loch I could see a line of boats obviously searching for a body. Nearby stood a police vehicle, the constable standing by it walked over to me.

"Dr. Watson, sir, I have been asked by Mr. Holmes to let you know that he and the Inspector had to leave the search for the deceased as they have been called away."

"Do you know why, constable?" I asked.

"Yes, sir, apparently there was a fire in a property not far away, and it is believed to be connected with events of last night. A man has been arrested, a foreign looking gentleman, and they have both gone to interview him. They may be away for the rest of the day, Doctor."

"Is there no more you can tell me?"

"Not much, sir, but I heard someone speak of a servant who had been brought over from India. The house in which he lived was not far from that of, Mr. Harrison, the gentleman in the forest, sir. I was one of the police officers who came up with the Inspector and collected his body.

"Ah, yes, I remember you now. Tell me, I see that there are some more boats and a floating platform as well, further over, what are they doing?"

"Searching, for Sir Hugh's boat which sank a while back and in which he nearly drowned. I understand that you, and Mr. Holmes, located it earlier on, Doctor."

"Yes, but it was further over, please tell your colleagues, they are not all that far off. They should try closer to the island."

"Thank you, Doctor. If they can find it soon we may be able to raise it before the day is out."

"That would be splendid, we would then be able to find out if Holmes was correct in his deduction on how it came to sink in the way it did. I can do nothing of any use here now. I shall return to Inverdaigh House, constable. Please see that I am kept informed of events."

"Indeed, I will, Dr. Watson," he replied as he called and signalled across to his colleagues.

Later that afternoon I was sitting comfortably in the library, reading of events written just after the Great Indian Mutiny in 1857, when a servant came in.

"Dr. Watson, sir, a police officer has just arrived to say that Sir Hugh's boat has been found and brought to the surface. It is now being drawn up onto the beach. I believe that you wanted to know ... Sir Hugh has been informed, and he will be here presently."

"Dr. Watson," said Sir Hugh as he came through the door, "you have just heard the news ... shall we go and have a look, I may be lucky enough to find some of my fishing tackle."

It did not take us long to return to the loch, and as we approached Sir Hugh's boat the police officers stood back to allow us a closer look.

"We have found much of your fishing equipment, Sir Hugh," said the sergeant. "We have placed it all over here."

He turned and with Sir Hugh went over to examine the recovered items.

"Wonderful, sergeant, most of it is here, good news, eh, Dr. Watson?"

"Indeed, Sir Hugh, but I would like to have the boat turned over if I may. I would like to check underneath to see if I can find the deliberate damage which Holmes deduced was the cause of its sinking and you nearly drowning."

Summoning over several police officers it took but a moment for the boat to be overturned, and I went over to examine its underside. Leaning across the upturned hull I started to scrape away the encrusted mud by the keel at the place where it butted against the garboard plank. As my fingers gradually exposed the wood, on the left-hand side eight neatly drilled holes emerged, exactly as Holmes had predicted.

"See, Holmes was right, Sir Hugh," I said as he came over to examine my findings, "his deductions were perfect," I went on, as my fingers pointed to the holes.

"Indeed, they were, Dr. Watson, it is most gratifying to know that we have a man available to us of such unique talents as Mr. Holmes. Indeed his outstanding abilities must be seen as a great asset to those of his friends in Scotland Yard."

"Yes, I expect so, Sir Hugh," I replied, smiling inwardly to myself as I thought back to Holmes's encounters with Gregson and Lestrade.

"I'll have my boat sent for repair now, Doctor, I am so glad to be able to recover nearly all of my fishing equipment as well. What are your plans now, we were still hoping that you will change your minds and stay on with us, for a few more days at least?"

"That is most kind of you," I replied as we started walking back.

"Tell me, Sir Hugh, are you still certain that this whole nefarious business has nothing to do with your late brother out in India?"

"Why do you ask, Dr. Watson?"

"Before we came down to the loch a short while ago I was, as you know, in the library. I had taken out a book which was protruding from the others, and it was obvious to me that it had recently been read and hastily returned, as if the reader intended to continue his study of it. Was it you by any chance, as its subject matter covered the aftermath of the 1857 mutiny?"

Sir Hugh went silent for a moment before continuing.

"Yes, it was me, Doctor," he replied, "I should have known by now that between you and Mr. Holmes little of significance escapes your attention. I have for a while been considering the possibility that there may have been some connection, and when I heard that an Indian servant had been caught by the police and questioned I felt that it was just too much of a coincidence. I was hoping that by re-reading the letters of events that something in it may have sprung out at me, afresh, after all this time."

"And did it?"

"No, not yet, but I shall finish it and there are several others to peruse as well."

"What is Caroline's opinion?"

"We have had a few discussions, but she takes a very feminine view that we should leave matters in the past and plan our lives for the future. What is your opinion, Dr. Watson?"

"I believe that she is right, Sir Hugh. I can understand that you wish to try and find the truth, as he was after all your brother and a man of much influence, even though it was so malign. But Caroline never knew him and she does, after all, have her own life to live."

"Yes, I am sure that is a most common sense approach," he replied, although I sensed with not wholehearted conviction.

"You may rest assured, Sir Hugh, that after we return to London tomorrow we will still be available should you require us further."

"Thank you again, Dr. Watson, we shall be sad to see you both leave us but we do understand. I expect that when you return Mr. Holmes will find much work to do, with many people needing his help. He is after all such an important man. Do you know when he will be returning here today?"

"No, Sir Hugh, but knowing Holmes I expect that it may be very late. He will need to examine the remains of the burnt house. I am sure that it will have a great deal to tell him even though much evidence will have been destroyed by the fire. He will also want to learn all that he can from the Indian servant and so will Inspector Lennox. I am sure that you will also," I said, turning and smiling at him reassuringly. It was becoming clear to me he was now convinced that, somehow or other, recent events were all linked into his past. Indeed, whilst I had said nothing, I, too, had arrived at a similar conclusion.

We walked back to the house in silence knowing that there was nothing more for us to do now until Holmes returned. I went to my room and tidied my things ready for our journey back to Baker Street, hoping that Holmes would not be too long delayed. Sir Hugh decided to make repairs to his fishing rods, but later on he retired to his library in order to continue with his researches. Holmes did indeed arrive back very late that night, but I had by then retired and was asleep. I saw no sense in waiting up as I knew that he would give me all the details the following day as we returned home.

The following morning found Holmes and me making our way along side of the loch towards the ferry, our luggage having been sent on ahead. We had earlier bid a tearful and fond farewell to Caroline and Sir Hugh, who again pressed us to stay with them a little longer. Holmes had been up early again that morning and discussed matters with Sir Hugh, giving him as many details as he could concerning recent events. It had, however, now fallen to Inspector Lennox to continue with his own investigations. He would ensure that the family were kept informed as more information emerged.

"Well, Holmes," I asked, breaking the silence, as we walked along, "what did you find yesterday at the burnt house?"

"The fire had been well set, Watson. The Indian servant had instructions to ensure that everything should be destroyed in the event of his master's demise."

"And was it?"

"Mostly, yes, he had done a very good job. When he found out about events at the loch he immediately went to work. There was an arrangement you see. The criminal was due to return and when he failed to do so his servant investigated and discovered that his master was now dead. He then knew just what he had to do and set about it without delay."

"Was there nothing of value you could find, Holmes?"

"There were the burnt out remains of what must have been an engineer's office, like Mr. Brunel would have, with drawings and many papers. Unfortunately nothing which could be read to throw more light on events leading up to the attempts on the life of Sir Hugh."

"So that's it then, we are little further forward."

"Not quite, old friend, there is still the other workshop."

"Which other workshop, do you mean the one on the island?"

"Yes, the one we discovered lying under the ruins of the old house. You will recall I said to you that he was using it to build a crossbow and that I would talk more about it later. We were rather busy at the time."

"But as it was some way from his house it is not clear just how they are linked? I had assumed that it was originally used by a poacher, what with all those fish skins and cauldron nearby. The criminal found it later and set a trap for us, perhaps they were one and the same."

"Close, but not quite," he said smiling.

"Please explain, Holmes."

"You recall that we found in the cellar a strong wooden table."

"Yes, I do."

"And what else did we find?"

"Some string-like material and pieces thought to be from broken fishing equipment."

"Anything else?"

"Not much, we found some recessed holes cut into the wall at one end, and at the opposite three metal rings firmly embedded, and then there was the other tunnel, also the ladder and hatch up into the roof."

"Yes, good, we know about the last, but what about the first two you spoke of … what were they for do you think?"

"If I recall correctly I suggested that it looked as if someone had started to cut a recess and that the rings were for a hoist of some sort. As we now know that he was building a crossbow in there, I assumed they were connected to his need to have some heavy items, such as a blacksmith's forge, to be lowered down. Perhaps the axe trap on the ground above might have been part of the mechanism as well. Am I right, Holmes?"

"Again not entirely, but a good try."

"So where am I wrong?"

"Where was the evidence of a blacksmith's forge, and why would he need one?"

"I assumed that for some reason he had needed to remove it later, but would he have not needed it anyway in order to make a steel crossbow? The one perhaps he used against me."

"He did not need heavy blacksmith equipment."

"Why not?"

"Because it was not made from steel."

"But what else could it have been made from, what little knowledge I have is based on all European crossbows, from Mediaeval times, having steel bows. Really, Holmes, you will be telling me next that it was made of rubber!"

"That may not be as far fetched as you may think, Watson. Some years ago a gentleman called R. E. Hodges did some interesting work on that, although it is not well known."

"So what was the bow made from then?"

"Do you recall, old friend, that several unusual things have happened which the police could not understand."

"You mean the animal mutilations and dehorning of cattle."

"I do indeed."

"So where do they fit into this puzzle, Holmes?"

"As a consulting detective I realised that in order to aid my work it would be very useful to gain better ideas as to the wide range of weapons used by various peoples throughout the world. I spent much time investigating museums and, as I am sure that you know, their exhibits cover large spans of time."

"Yes, I know that, you sometimes disappeared for whole days. I had assumed that you were pursing some research or other related to your cases."

"I was. One of the features which I found to be of much interest was that of Oriental archery equipment."

"What was so special about it?"

"That they had found a way of making bows which had a great deal of power and flexibility. They were usually made primarily from animal sinew and animal horn glued to a shaped piece of wood in the centre. The animal mutilations were nothing to do with witchcraft as the Inspector believed. The string was of course made from the animals' sinew. Also required was wood in order to make a stock with which to hold the bow and trigger mechanism. Any pieces of metal he needed were only small and could be fashioned from any small items. He did not need a forge for that, just a strong table. "

"But not steel for a bow?"

"No, it was not needed. Their technology dated back well over two thousand years and far exceeded the performance of steel equipment ... for bows at least. It was a question of 'needs must', the people had to develop equipment based on the materials which were available to them and they succeeded well."

"What was it then that first led you to consider a crossbow was used, Holmes?"

"Please just think back, Watson, do you remember the fatal wound we found in the neck of Duncan Cameron, the one which Inspector Lennox was convinced was caused by him having a fishing accident. The Inspector believed that it was the result of him falling on to, if I remember correctly, a fishing gaff hook, a rowlock or spear, presumably the one he borrowed from Sir Hugh's collection."

"Yes I do, but you did not seem convinced, especially after you found the tiny piece of feather in the wound."

"You were correct, Watson, I was totally unconvinced even though the Inspector had concluded that it was just a fishing fly which had been found floating around in the bottom of the boat. He tried to interpret the facts so as to fit into his preconceived ideas, and that will never do. Whatever goes on to my epitaph, Doctor, never let it say 'that he did not follow the true evidence'."

"But surely, Holmes, one must form some idea as to the events or how could you solve the crime?"

"Indeed, but be quick to reject that which the evidence does not support."

"So what did the small feather tell you, Holmes?"

"Two things. Ask yourself from where did it come and why was it so small and shaped. It was quite obvious to me that the wound could have only been caused by Cameron being hit by a projectile of sorts. There are only two I know of which are capable of that, a rifle or a crossbow. Had it been a rifle someone would have heard it and possibly even seen the smoke from the discharge. To my knowledge though a rifle wound would have been different, no, it was quite clear from the start that some sort of dart-like projective was used. The small piece of feather we found was therefore one of its small flights used to keep it stable as it flew through the air, it then became dislodged."

"That certainly explains its shape and size, but where did it originally come from?"

"It was an eagle's feather, Watson, that is part of the reason I was in Inverdaigh House the other night. I had broken in so that I could compare it with those of the feathers on the trophy specimen in the hall. You will no doubt recall the one I mean, but unfortunately I was careless and knocked into a nearby glass case. It was that which awoke you, but at least it brought you down and saved me going upstairs to awaken you."

"Yes, it was something of a shock meeting you like that, when we all thought that you were still in London. But I am not clear as to how everything fits together. Did we not find the hidden cellar on the island just before we found Cameron's body?"

"We did and I was not entirely sure at the time as to what it was being used for. Making something, yes, but what exactly? I had my suspicions but finding the wound and feather confirmed it. When I heard about the sinew and horn animal mutilations it simply completed the picture. The rings fitted into the wall of the cellar were for holding the crossbow when it was loaded and the recesses in the wall were the impact points of the projectiles he was testing. It needed to be a very powerful device."

"I can vouch for that, Holmes, but why go to the trouble of using the island, why not by his home?"

"Because he could not risk being seen, and also the strong smell of the glue he was using."

"Which glue?"

"The fish glue in the cauldron with the fish skins. They were what he developed and are required for that type of bow manufacture."

"So they were nothing to do with a poacher's hoard then?"

"No, but if they were found people may draw that conclusion and not realise what he was really using it for. He needed to be able to work unhindered and the island was obviously ideal. He probably found the tunnel by accident whilst looking for somewhere remote to work. Any genuine poacher going there would say nothing of anything he saw, it would not be in his best interests."

"I suppose the lights people saw there would help, with all the local superstitions."

"Yes, a nice idea that, he probably took steps to ensure that the stories of the haunted island were true, and so discourage local people investigating for themselves."

"What was it then that hit our pony in the flank as we returned from the waterfall. It was surely not the same as that which hit Cameron?"

"No, he had adapted it to shoot smaller round projectiles as were sometimes used to shoot small game. I believe that it was his intention to try and hit us with a proper crossbow bolt as we were driving back. However, when he saw that we had a cover over the gig and could not see us clearly, he had to find some way of stopping us. As you saw he was able to use it to frighten our pony and overturn the gig. Fortunately I was ready for him and after we recovered from our fall I leapt up and shot at him deep in the woods where I knew he would be. I think it was quite a surprise, and one, which he was most certainly not expecting. Realising we had turned the tables on him, he needed to escape."

"But he knew Harrison was also there?"

"Yes, as you know Harrison was the second member of his small gang. I believe, however, that he was probably less than pleased with Harrison at that moment by letting him down with insufficient warning. Whether they had a moments time to agree on another plan we shall never know, but either way Harrison, whether by design or accident, diverted our attention giving the criminal enough time to slip away. Harrison's subsequent falling from the tree was fortuitous, don't you think so, Watson?"

"I do, Holmes, but surely even if we had caught him he could simply say that he was only egg collecting ... nothing more than that. He would claim that his being there was only coincidence, no jury would convict on that alone."

"Yes, you are right, Doctor, he was very well known for his ornithological enthusiasm. It does not matter now of course."

"You have said nothing yet about the special boat the criminal used. It must have been quite unique."

"It was indeed. I have never seen one like it. As I am sure you realise, he needed one to move across the loch as discreetly as possible. You remember when we were waiting for the Inspector, sitting by the loch after finding Cameron's body, Harrison suddenly arrived."

"Yes, you and he were amiably talking when I asked about the large tree floating across the far side of the loch. He explained that it happened from time-to-time, then saw the eagle and hurried away."

"He did indeed, Harrison wanted to quickly change the subject. He knew what it was, our opponent took something of a risk there so Harrison needed to divert our attention elsewhere. I think that the criminal felt he would be caught if he did not quickly move out away from the area."

"In what way was his boat special, Holmes? When we first saw signs of it by the beach on the island I thought they were made by a turtle or similar."

"Anyone could be forgiven for so thinking, but as you know, after pretending to go to London, I hid in the houseboat and crossed over to the island so as to keep watch on his movements. It was there that I saw his boat fitted with outriggers and propelled by pedals driving a continuous belt. He was able to lie low in it and by putting branches over make it look like a floating tree. It was very well done."

"I get the impression, Holmes, that the criminal, the man you call 'the engineer', was a very talented man."

"He was undoubtedly, I knew from finding the collapsed trees, then the sabotaged boat of Sir Hugh's that we had an opponent worthy of our metal. A man of exceptional abilities … inventive and practical. Such men are rare. Remember, Watson, it is engineering in all its forms, from the most primitive onwards, which sets us apart from the animals. It is important to understand that success, particularly in human conflict, involves two things," he went on. I looked over at him, listening.

"First, the quality of engineering resources available, whatever form they may take and, second, the ability to use those resources most effectively. I believe that this applies throughout history, and, no doubt, always will."

"I have never thought about it in that way before, Holmes, but I feel sure that Mr. Darwin and Mr. Brunel would agree."

"Yes, and I am certain that during this man's wanderings around the Orient he would have found such well-made equipment as that crossbow. As a man of such engineering interests he would have taken time to study them, probably having made some for himself. When his earlier attempts on Sir Hugh's life failed he knew that would be his best remaining option, although it is ironic that it was Cameron who fell victim to it, probably certain that he was Sir Hugh."

"I believe that your analysis is right, Holmes, but where exactly did MacGavern fit into these events, you have not said? It was surely not coincidence that he was taken ill and then disappeared, just when you announced that you were going to London."

"No, I simply wanted him to believe that I would be away for a while. After the engineer had lost his associate Harrison, he realised that he had to act quickly as matters were coming to a head. MacGavern of course was the third member of his gang, the man on the inside whose job it was to keep him informed of events at Inverdaigh House and Sir Hugh's movements. As soon as MacGavern heard that morning that I was to leave for London, or so he thought, he knew that he had to let his criminal boss know immediately. He fell for my trap and slipped away claiming illness, which then gave me the chance I needed. He has now disappeared. We will leave that to Inspector Lennox."

"I see but has not the Indian servant given us any more information yet, he must surely know how all this awful business came about."

"Yes, but like all good servants, especially those from India, they are reluctant to divulge even the most trivial detail about their masters. It is a point of honour with them to maintain absolute discretion."

"So what then happened, Holmes?"

"When it was explained to him that his master was now dead and he would in no way be held to blame and that eventually he will be allowed to return to his own country, he started to talk and gave us the whole story as far as he knew it."

"Would I be correct in thinking that it was indeed linked to Sir Hugh's older brother after all?"

"You would, indeed, Watson, you would, indeed. It was a long and convoluted story and this man knew only the outline of key aspects but sufficient to complete the picture for our investigations."

"I am much intrigued," I replied, "I would like to know at least something of the man who shot at me and who killed Duncan Cameron."

"It was like this Watson, after Sir Hugh's older brother went out to India, his real name was Robert by the way, although his servant simply referred to him as the Sahib, his talent for gathering around him a group of unsavoury associates continued undiminished."

"Sir Hugh never told us of his real name," I replied, interrupting Holmes, "I have wondered why not."

"No he did not, although I am sure that because of the scandals that went on before his leaving, Sir Hugh was unwilling to even give his brother's name, such was the shame and distress he brought upon the family at the time. Had he lived of course he would have inherited the family estate and been known as Sir Robert McFarlane.

"It seems that at some point he produced an illegitimate son. The servant was only able to supply us with the vague details that had been passed down to him by his own father, who at that time was Robert McFarlane's previous servant. You will of course realise, Watson, that around the time of the Great Mutiny matters were very chaotic with much fighting still taking place. The boy's mother was unknown but she was thought to have been an Englishwoman who was killed. The boy was brought up by servants and also called Robert, after the man who was known to be his father ... Sir Hugh's brother."

"Then he was the nephew of Sir Hugh, and Caroline's cousin."

"Yes, but as the illegitimate heir he had no claim to the estate even if he could have proved his birth-right. What is clear, however, is that he inherited his father's considerable abilities. You will recall Sir Hugh saying that his brother was a very talented man but lacked the perseverance to use his talents to good effect."

209

"I do, indeed, Holmes, a prime example of an ability ill-used."

"From what the servant has told us, the boy was brought up into believing that he had been tricked out of his inheritance and that his uncle was responsible. He and his father's remaining friends, (his father had died by now, caught up in some local skirmish apparently) took an oath to the effect of returning and regaining the estate for him or at least revenge for losing it to Sir Hugh. As time went on, however, they died or were killed. You will be aware Doctor, will you not, that this also happened to many a fine Englishman who went seeking their fortunes?"

"I do, Holmes, I know of many who either expired of disease, heat stroke or in one of the frequent conflicts. As you know, I nearly did so myself. But just how did Robert McFarlane meet up with Harrison, do we know? Was it in India?"

"No, I do not believe so. Whilst his servant said that Harrison had spent some years in India working on the railways, they had never met. You will no doubt recall me saying, that I believed he had been in tropical climes, after we had first met him."

"Yes, I do, Holmes, so what happened?"

"After Robert McFarlane returned from the East bringing his servant with him, he moved into this area in secret. His plan was to find just how he could regain the estate he felt to be rightfully his. He may also have hoped to court Caroline, who was of course his first cousin but what he did not know was that she already had a paramour.

At some point he met up with Harrison who came here in order to recover his health. He was probably also drawn here because of the railway developments. Harrison also had a passion for ornithology and that is how he met Sir Hugh. Just how he became involved in Robert McFarlane's scheme we may never know but a financial inducement probably helped with promise of more. Remember his fine binoculars, Watson. Harrison seems to have been a morally weak man but there is no telling as to what poor health and weak finances will do to someone."

"I see, and what of McGavin?"

"He had worked for Sir Hugh for some years, the family clan went back to the Jacobite rebellion but secretly like many, old grievances died hard. I believe that Sir Hugh felt he had to assist the poorer families and gave him a job, but under the strong influence of Robert and no doubt future promises of better times it did not take much to have him become their inside man.

However, one thing is sure, Watson, Sir Hugh's illegitimate nephew and his nefarious friends are all dead and he and Caroline can now get on with their lives. No doubt the Inspector will eventually obtain more details but it need not involve us further. As far as we are concerned the matter is now closed, don't you agree old friend?"

"I do, Holmes, it has though been a most interesting case," I replied as we walked on admiring the passing scenery. "I must make some further notes on it as soon as possible. I do not want to forget any of the details."

Holmes did not reply but out of the corner of my eye I thought I saw him smile, then pointing said, "Look, you can see in the distance the steamboat approaching. The landing stage is just ahead of us, too, and the coach is there waiting with our luggage. If we step up our stride we should all arrive together. By this time tomorrow, Watson, we should be back in Baker Street having enjoyed one of Mrs. Hudson's most wonderful breakfasts."

Without replying I looked up and above me, soaring on the wind was a golden eagle, its plaintive cry calling as if bidding us farewell.

Epilogue

On our return to Baker Street Holmes was immediately thrown into a frenzy of work. During our absence a number of events had occurred, which required his urgent attention. This is not the time to recount these happenings but as a result, our 'Little Scottish Adventure' as Holmes later referred to it, very quickly receded into the background of our busy lives.

It was therefore around eighteen months later that I found myself seated at my desk, overlooking Baker Street, updating my notes. Spring had arrived and the sun was shining across London as I saw our post being delivered. Minutes later Mrs. Hudson came up the stairs and entered our rooms.

Letter for you and Mr. Holmes, Dr. Watson," she said passing me the envelope.

"Thank you, Mrs. Hudson," I replied, noting immediately that it had a postmark indicating a Scottish origin.

She quietly retired as I examined our letter, noting that it almost certainly originated from Inverdaigh House, and was written in Caroline's handwriting.

I was naturally intrigued as to what had caused her to contact us again, and I confess it did cross my mind that yet more events had occurred which required Holmes' attention. I need not have worried.

Opening the letter I saw that it was indeed from Inverdaigh House and sent by Miss Caroline.

It read:

213

My dear Dr. Watson and Mr. Holmes,

It seems to be such a long time ago since you were here with us and the dreadful events which occurred at the time. So much has happened since then that I feel I must write and tell you both about them.

As you know Dr. Watson, Hamish and I were very much in love and it was not long after you left us that we had to tell Father of our secret affair, and that we intended to marry. Strangely it seemed of no great surprise to him, except for the fact that my husband to be was the eldest son of the man once arrested on suspicion of being his criminal assailant and a renowned poacher as well. By then, however, father knew that Hamish was an able young man who had saved your life on the island when the criminal shot at you with his crossbow. We were married soon afterwards and only a few months ago I gave birth to a son. I have not seen Father so happy in a long while. He was almost dancing with joy at having a grandchild.

As you will know since we lost dear Duncan Cameron we have had nobody to help run the estate. Father has now retired and given the job of estate manager to Hamish and guess what, he has an assistant, his own father! A classic case of poacher turned gamekeeper. They are both doing very well and the estate is thriving.

Recently a local widow lady, younger than Father, has been taken on to help him with the paperwork and also assist his researches into past events in India.

They seem to be becoming very close and often go out for long walks together, to look around the estate according to Father. The other day he took her to see the spot where the trees fell down upon him, and where Mr. Holmes so accurately deduced events.

I really must tell you of an event recently involving the police. As part of the policy of sharing information on major crimes with colleagues in other parts of the country, Inspector Lennox invited two of your London friends, Inspector Lestrade and Gregson, to come up to Scotland. As part of what they called a conference, it was arranged that they come here to Inverdaigh House to have a look at the sites of the actual events. Personally, I think that it was also an excuse for them to escape London for a while. Naturally Father was pleased to see them and later entertained them where they could discuss issues and share ideas. As time went on, however, they indulged themselves quite freely with alcohol, Inspector Lennox's whisky in particular, and when it was time for them to go they could hardly stand up.

It took several constables to assist them back to their coach transport, two each for Inspectors Lestrade and Gregson. As you know Inspector Lennox is a very large man and it took three officers to help him, one on each side with one pushing and guiding him from behind. He almost fell into the coach. As it started to move away the door came open and his leg fell out.

They had to stop the coach again as a constable came forward and lifted his leg back in. I was able to look inside and could see them piled up in a heap, sprawled all across the seats and floor. I have never laughed so much in all my life, Dr. Watson, it was the funniest sight I had seen in a long time. What Inspector Lennox's wife said to him when he got home I really don't know, but I am sure that she must have had some very fine words. As for Inspectors Gregson and Lestrade, they were returning home to London the following day and must have gone back with frightful headaches.

I must finish now as I can hear my baby crying and in need of attention, and my husband has just come in, but in my quiet moments I often think back to the time when you both came up here and saved Father's life and probably mine also.

Will you no' come back again.

Yours, with greatest affection,

Caroline

I re-read the letter, and as I did so my mind went back to those most dangerous adventures when Holmes bested the vile criminal who threatened the life of Sir Hugh and his daughter as well. Reaching down I pulled open a lower drawer of my writing desk and took out a cardboard box. Opening the lid I saw inside the items which Holmes and I found when we first discovered the underground cellar in which the criminal, whom Holmes later called 'the Engineer', had as his workshop. In addition was another length of sinew string which we later recovered wrapped around the propeller shaft of the steamboat. Tipping them out onto my desk I picked them up one at a time, twirling them around my fingers, remembering how Holmes's sharp observations had found them in the underground room and subsequently realised they were part of the mechanism for a deadly crossbow.

Pushing them aside, I pulled over some sheets of paper and a pen. It had been my practice for a while to make extensive notes on events involving Holmes's criminal cases and write them up when I found time. I had not done much recently as my medical work had kept me very busy but, nevertheless, I felt it my duty to keep the public informed and now was as good a time as any. I was about to put pen to paper, hesitating over the title, when I heard the door behind me open. It was Holmes.

"There you are, Watson. I have not seen you recently," he said coming across to where I was sitting. "I assume that you have had patients needing your attention."

"Yes, Holmes, but there is something of a lull at the moment, so I thought that I would try and catch up with my writing.

"You are about to tell of our adventures in Scotland are you not?" he replied, looking over my shoulder. "Have you thought of a proper name for it yet, one that reflects the true events?"

"Indeed, I am Holmes but cannot think of a suitable title. Something or other in Scotland suggests itself but does not seem quite right."

"How about *The Case of the Hissing Shaft*, after all there were two of them were there not, your readers would have a choice?"

"You mean the first being the waterfall known in Celtic as Es na-onghail."

"Yes, I do, where our criminal friend first tried to kill Sir Hugh and where you yourself nearly slipped in," he added, reminding me.

"The other presumably being the crossbow bolts shot at me when we were on the island ... they did make a distinct hissing sound as they hurled close by. I shall always be grateful to Hamish for saving me by his quick reactions, it was a very near miss though," I replied recalling the incident.

"Yes, Holmes, that seems to be a most excellent title. Oh, by the way, I am sure that you would like to see this as well, I said, passing Miss Caroline's letter over to him.

"Thank you, Watson. I saw it as we were talking."

Taking it from me he read it through carefully.

"How nice to see that all is going so well for them, a little babe as well, most charming. Perhaps some time in the future we ought to go there again."

"That would be something we could plan for," I said, "but you know just how much your criminal work makes such sudden demands on you, it is difficult to plan for anything."

"Yes, and that is why I am here, Watson. You probably realise that I came in the back way. There is a most difficult and trying case underway. I would like your help if you don't mind, if you feel ready for it of course. You can leave your writing until later."

"Of course, I am, Holmes, just tell me what you require."

"Splendid, old friend, I knew that I could rely on you. I have just come in for a bite to eat, then I will go out again until dark. I will return to collect you with a hansom, come dressed for action, oh, and bring your revolver I shall have mine too, it's going to be dangerous. The game's afoot, Watson, the game's afoot."

Postscript

I hope, dear reader, that you have very much enjoyed hearing about Mr. Sherlock Holmes and his latest adventure in Scotland. As you will know from reading the preface, I was able to recover this new story by means of deciphering the obscure script found at my aunt's home after her death. It was not easy but was I am sure, worthwhile.

There are several points which may be of special interest to readers, particularly those with an interest in engineering.

First, the design of the boat, which the criminal used for discreet movement around the loch, we now refer to as a trimaran (in this case basically a canoe with two outriggers). This, you will note, has been spoken of by Holmes when he and Watson were starting on their return to London.

Readers in engineering will no doubt have noted that its propulsion by means of the continuous track principle was first designed in 1770 by R. L. Edgeworth, and underwent subsequent development by various inventors (Polish, British and Russian) up to the Crimean War, 1850, and beyond.

It is well known today for its use as tank track propulsion and for snowmobiles. Indeed, the author has often wondered over the years, if such a system could be used to propel certain types of hovercraft and boats needing to be used in very shallow draught waterways where conventional marine propellers risk danger or damage.

The second point of interest is the high performance crossbow used by the criminal. Crossbows were known to the Chinese at least as far back as 1050 B.C., and were well established by the time of the Han dynasty. In addition crossbows were developed by the Greeks at Syracuse, circa 399 B.C., with evidence of them having been used by the Romans as well.

Bows themselves are referred to in mechanical engineering terms as 'leaf springs', albeit very sophisticated ones, and many thousands of years ago represented humanity's successful attempt to improve food gathering (hunting) and self-defence capabilities. They were only surpassed by the invention of gunpowder in China by around 800 A.D.

For readers who find this branch of mechanical engineering to be of special interest (or archery generally) they could do no better than make contact with an organisation called The Society of Archer-Antiquaries. Formed in 1956 it is classed as a learned society and its remit is to study the history and development of archery and related spring-powered projectile launchers, in all their forms, from the very earliest known up until the present day and from all over the world.

Finally readers may also wish to consult the book *Man Powered Bullets* by Richard Middleton, which also gives a wide insight into much of the above, with great detailed knowledge and expertise.

Lightning Source UK Ltd.
Milton Keynes UK
UKHW021115070920
369491UK00018B/1435

9 781901 091755